Kendall Talbot is a thrill seeker, hopeless romantic, virtual killer, and award-winning author of stories that'll have your heart thumping from action-packed suspense and steamy bedroom scenes.

Kendall has sought thrills in all 42 countries she's visited. She's abseiled down freezing waterfalls, catapulted out of a white-water raft, jumped off a mountain with a man who spoke little English, and got way too close to a sixteen-foot shark. When she isn't writing heart-thumping suspense in exotic locations, she's watching action-packed movies, enjoying wine and cheese with her crazy friends, and planning her next thrilling international escape.

She lives in Brisbane, Australia with her very own hero and a fluffy little dog who specializes in hijacking her writing time. Meanwhile, Kendall's two sons are off making their own adventures – look out world.

Kendall's book, *Lost in Kakadu* won the acclaimed title of Romantic Book of the Year 2014, and her books have also been finalists for Best Romantic Suspense, Best Crime Novel, Best Continuing Series, and Best New Author.

Drop into Kendall's website sometime: www.kendalltalbot.com.au

Or check out her crazy life on her facebook page:
https://www.facebook.com/KendallTalbotBooks

Also, by Kendall Talbot

Deadly Twist

Extreme Limit

Zero Escape

Treasured Secrets

Treasured Lies

Treasured Dreams

Double Take

Lost in Kakadu

First Fate

Feral Fate

Final Fate

Extreme Limit

KENDALL TALBOT

A Maximum Exposure Novel

This is a work of fiction. Names, characters, places, and incidents are either the product of the author's imagination or are used fictitiously, and any resemblance to actual persons, living or dead, business establishments, events, or locales is entirely coincidental.

As always to my wonderful husband, Dean, who allows me to live my dream, and to my amazing sons, Jordan and Alex – may there be adventure in your lives forever.

CHAPTER ONE

From the moment Holly climbed into the helicopter, an ugly sense of foreboding plagued every thought. Three times in her life she'd had premonitions about death. Each time it'd come true. But she wouldn't say anything. Not when Milton, her new fiancé, had paid so much money for this exclusive trip. And especially not when he'd looked like an excited teenager when he'd first spied the chopper at the ski resort. Holly forced her brain to focus on the mountain scenery around her, rather than the tendrils of dread inching up her spine.

This once-in-a-lifetime opportunity was supposed to be fun. But the buffering wind and shuddering windows made it so far from fun she could barely breathe. According to the pilot, a private picnic on the west summit of one of Canada's highest peaks had never been done before. But Milton had charmed the man with both his expert persuasion skills and fists full of money. So much so that the pilot simply couldn't refuse.

Twelve thousand dollars had been his tipping point. For that, not only did they get a private helicopter, but the pilot also provided expensive champagne, a gourmet feast, and a folding table and three chairs, ready to be set up wherever they wanted.

Milton was capable of convincing anyone to do anything. Her being on Whiskey Mountain was a testament to that. She never did anything that even hinted at danger.

Death had a way of following her. Her brother died as a three-week old baby. Her father went to work one day and never came home. Her best friend died in a freak accident that'd perplexed all the authorities. Even her one and only pet didn't make it past puppy stage. And Holly was only twenty-four years old. Based on that average, one death every five or so years, she was due again. She smacked the disturbing statistic away and wiped her sweating palms on her ski pants.

Shielding her eyes from the sun, she looked up at the mountain peak. The snowcapped granite wall jutted skyward like an enormous shark fin. It was an interesting color, like the rocks were gilded in copper. Maybe that's why it'd been named Whiskey Mountain. With each foot they rose, it appeared to grow wider and higher, and the very tip glistened like a diamond.

The helicopter shot over the ski resort's highest cable car station, leaving behind the last signs of civilization. The lump of dread, deep in the pit of her stomach, hit a whole new level. The white terrain stretched as far as she could see. Even the trees had given up trying to live here.

When Holly had suggested to Milton that they take a vacation, she'd envisaged lying in hammocks on a deserted beach, sipping fancy drinks out of coconuts. Not this. Not high in the mountains where snow and ice blanketed every surface. Cold weather seeped into her bones. Her mother said it was because she didn't eat enough. Her fiancé said it was because she didn't eat meat. Ever since their first date, two years ago, Milton had been trying to coax her off her strict vegetarian diet.

"Having fun?" Milton beamed at her. His eyes were hidden behind mirrored glasses, but she could picture the dazzle of excitement in his brown irises that she'd come to love.

Swallowing a bitter taste in her mouth, she decided to dodge his question. "It's magnificent." The last thing she'd do was voice her fear, not when he looked to be enjoying it so much. And especially not in front of Milton's son, who'd commandeered the front seat next to the pilot. Kane had visited more countries in his seventeen years than Holly had dreamed of.

He hated Holly. . . and had made it his mission to tell her so at every opportunity. He blamed her for breaking up his parents' marriage. She hadn't. Their marriage was fractured long before Milton strolled into the coffee shop where she worked.

Holly had suggested to Milton that a vacation would be the perfect opportunity for Kane to get to know her better. She was desperate to prove to Milton's son that she was worthy of his father's love. At least, that'd been her plan.

The helicopter crested another peak, and other than the occasional jagged rock, snow covered every surface. The pure white was almost blinding. Whiskey mountain loomed in the near distance, and instead of marveling over its majestic grandeur, Holly felt its ominous presence like it were a demon. She clutched her knees, desperate to stop them trembling.

The first three days of their vacation had been a mixture of heaven and hell—Milton being the heaven and Kane being the latter. The kid was driven to steal Milton's attention at every opportunity and voiced his anger at Holly frequently. Kane liked to remind her that he was grown now, and not just in age either. He was taller than her, which wasn't hard given that she was only five foot three. He was heavier too, and could almost outweigh her twofold.

This helicopter ride and proposed mountaintop picnic was Milton's idea. His grand plan of alpine seclusion meant they'd have no distractions and would be practically forced to talk to each other. Maybe that's what was driving Holly's fear. So far, her attempts at conversation with the cantankerous teenager had resulted in either insults or silence.

The helicopter banked sharply to the left and Holly clutched Milton's wrist. Either he didn't notice her grasp or he was too engrossed in the scenery out his window. Whichever it was, he didn't look her way. Kane whooped from the front seat, obviously feeling none of her apprehension. The pilot maneuvered the chopper through a couple of twin peaks that skyrocketed into the air like dueling monoliths.

The second they crossed the threshold, wind slammed into the windshield like buckshot. Vibrations rattled every bone in her body, and with fear twisting her gut she clutched Milton's wrist harder. The padded headphones were no match for the thunderous roar and her seat shuddered—as did everything else.

Terror dug its claws into her throat as she watched the pilot's white-knuckled wrestle with the gear stick. His lips were drawn into a thin line, his eyes bulging.

Her heart exploded and she dug her nails into her knees.

They plummeted. She screamed.

And in that instant, Holly knew her premonition was about to be realized.

The chopper ricocheted off the icy surface, and one of the helicopter's skids snagged on something, pitching the aircraft sideways like it'd been punched in the gut. Her head whipped back, slamming into the window. Spears of pain shot up her neck, blinding her with dazzling stars.

They hit the snow nose-first. Glass shattered. Metal twisted. Everyone screamed and the spinning rotors sliced at the snow, splintering into hundreds of missiles.

Kane shrieked. As did the pilot.

Blind panic had her clawing at the seat, desperate to hang on.

With a thunderous roar a giant chunk of ice fell away, opening an enormous crevice. The dark gash cut a swath through the white surface and the chopper plunged into it.

Kane shrieked as he hurled through the shattered windshield and disappeared into the dark hole.

"Kane! No!" Milton lunged forward; fingers outstretched. Desperate. But it was too late.

The chopper kicked into a violent spin and Holly smashed against the side of the cabin. Her door sprung open, spitting her from safety, and she released a bloodcurdling squeal as she fell.

Ice walls whizzed by in a blur.

She slammed onto something solid, punching the wind out of her. Every bone crunched upon impact. Her face hit the wall and an explosion of pain ripped through her brain.

She fought agony.

She fought blackness.

A squeal in her ears pierced her conscience. It was a couple of thundering heartbeats before she remembered what'd happened.

The crash.

The gaping hole in the snow.

Falling from the helicopter.

The pain. All the excruciating pain.

She forced herself to focus through the torture. Her tongue seemed foreign, as did her lips, and she swallowed back the metallic taste of blood.

Agonizing shrieks lured her from her own horror.

For a couple of panic-stricken heartbeats, she thought she was blind. But it was blood in her eyes causing the darkness. She tried to reach up to wipe it away, but her left arm was a useless lump at her side.

Screams echoed from every angle.

Milton!

Alert now, she forced her body to move. Gasping at the pain and fighting dizziness, she dragged herself upright. With her right-hand glove she wiped blood from her eyes. "Milton." She tried to speak, but either no words came out or she couldn't hear.

"Milton!"

Blinking away blood, she deciphered shapes and shadows. Pain and terror flooded every thought. About fifteen feet above to her right, the helicopter loomed. The craft was jammed into the crevice, trapped by walls of ice. It was tilted sideways, with the nose wedged against one side and the tail on the other. Inside, the pilot's face was blazoned with agony. It was his screams that echoed in the frozen chasm.

"Milton." Her voice was a brittle croak and she swallowed back another mouthful of blood.

As her eyes took in her situation, her brain struggled to comprehend it. Holly had fallen into the crevice. The ledge she'd landed on was barely two feet wide. Milton and Kane had fallen from the helicopter too. But she couldn't see either of them.

Gripping with her gloved fingers, she dragged herself forward and peered into the void below.

"Milton!" His crumpled body was a bloody blemish on a lower ledge of the opposite side of the chasm. His legs were bent at shocking angles. He was only fifteen feet away, yet it might as well have been a thousand.

"Milton."

He didn't move.

"Milton!" Despite the pain in her jaw she yelled his name.

The pilot's shrieks made it impossible to hear anything else.

Holly panted against her pain, rolled onto her stomach, and wailed at the agony slicing through her. Gasping for breath, she stared at Milton's body, begging for a sign of life. Dark blood stained the ice around him. He was facedown, but his head was turned her way. He looked peaceful. Like he was sleeping.

"Milton."

The pilot's screams changed...more shrill, more desperate.

Holly looked up at the chopper and her heart leapt to her throat. Flames licked the inside of the cabin. The pilot fought the blaze with his bare hands. His shrieks cut to her core and she tore her eyes away. Shielding her ears with her gloves, she rolled away from the edge and squeezed her eyes shut, blocking out the horror.

An explosion ripped the helicopter apart.

Metal and giant chunks of ice rained down on her. Forcing past the agony, she curled into a ball, covered her ears, and prepared to die.

Thousands of missiles pelted her already battered body. Searing pain burned her face. Her hip and back suffered the brunt of it. But it was over as quickly as it started. The ensuing silence was deafening. It took Holly a few heartbeats to convince herself she was still alive. Ice and snow weighed her down and she wrestled herself free.

With the chopper gone, sunlight permeated the crevice. Blinking against the glare, she crawled to the edge again and looked down. A sob caught in her throat.

Milton was gone.

The plummeting chopper carcass had swiped the opposite side, taking Milton and his narrow ice ledge with it. She burst into tears. Great racking sobs shuddered through her, hurting like hell.

It was an eternity before the tears stopped and the enormity of her situation hit her.

She pushed back from the edge and glanced to her left.

What she saw made a scream tear through her like rusty razor blades.

Her world tilted, darkness crept in, she fell sideways.

Everything went black.

KENDALL TALBOT

CHAPTER TWO

Blip. Blip. Blip.

Holly couldn't move. Her arms were lead weights. Her body was pinned down as if covered in a concrete blanket. She searched her memory, trawling for something… anything to help piece things together.

Blip. Blip. Blip.

Her tongue was leather, hard and dry, and rolling it around produced no moisture. A broken body flashed into her mind; legs bent at hideous angles. She groaned at the gruesome sight.

"Hey, it's okay."

A woman's voice floated to her; it sounded miles away.

"Doctor, I think she's waking up."

Holly pried her eyes open, but the bright lights pierced her brain. A hand on her arm was warm, yet she felt chilled to her bones. A frozen body appeared in her vision again, then another. Ice clung to their eyelashes. Their lips were blue. She groaned at the images, desperate to shake them free.

"It's okay, Holly. You're in the hospital."

Hospital.

"Do you know where you are?"

Holly tried to see the man who was talking. But the images kept coming… flashing across her brain like an old 8mm film. Shattered glass. A broken body. Blood stained snow. A golden heart-shaped locket. Two frozen bodies. A fiery explosion. Falling… falling.

Groaning again, she blinked against the glare, searching for clarity, but at the same time wanting to hide from reality.

Blip. Blip. Blip.

Images of her fiancé swirled through her mind… smiling… laughing… bleeding… lifeless. "Milton."

The soft touch of a hand had her believing it was him. Milton's hands were soft, his touch always gentle, delicate, like he cherished every inch of her body.

She rolled her tongue and smacked her lips together. "Milton?" All she

9

heard was blipping. Nonstop *blip, blip, blip*. She squinted against the blazing lights. The pounding at her temple shot painful spears through her brain. But a sharp light pierced the dark fog, and her mind flashed to a memory filled with piercing lights. She'd been on a trolley. It was surrounded by people and they were moving her, fast, running alongside as they pushed her forward. Bright lights had flashed overhead. Disinfectant had filled the air. The taste of metal had coated her tongue.

Victoria had been there. Milton's ex-wife had never looked so shabby. Holly could remember her squeezing her arm. Fear and anger had blazed across the blonde's bloodshot eyes. And as Victoria had dug her long nails in, she'd yelled at Holly, "Where's Kane and Milton? You killed them, you fucking bitch!"

Victoria's mouth had twisted with fury as she'd continued her rant. "She wanted his money. She killed them!" Spittle had landed on her chin. "She killed my son!"

Holly tried to think now. Think of Milton and Kane. They'd fallen into the crevice. Just like she had. Kane had vanished into the black hole. Swallowed by the never-ending void.

Milton hadn't, though. He'd landed on a ledge. She pictured his face. His beautiful chocolate eyes and the faint laugh lines at the sides that crinkled when he smiled. His long dark lashes that fluttered when they kissed. His lips, the color of red wine. But the last time she saw him, his lips were blue and flurries of snow had landed on his cheek, piling up and covering him in a fluffy white blanket. She'd wanted to swipe it off but she couldn't. She was too far away.

Tears spilled down her cheeks.

"Hey, don't cry." A hand touched her shoulder.

She squinted against the glare. The harsh light burned into her brain. "Milton, Kane, are they okay?" Her voice was brittle, foreign.

The ensuing silence made her wonder if she'd spoken aloud.

"Is anyone there?" Holly followed a movement to her side and a woman in a white nurse's uniform touched her arm.

"Yes, Holly, I'm here."

"Then tell me where Milton is, and Kane."

The woman shook her head. "I'm sorry, Holly. They both passed away."

Holly couldn't wipe her tears away. She was pinned down, trapped by her own body. Broken bones, broken heart.

"Milton." Rivers of tears tumbled down her cheeks.

"Hey, don't cry."

The nurse's words were futile, because she did cry. She cried for the one and only man she'd ever loved. She cried for their love, which was just beginning to blossom. She cried for the promises they'd made to each other that would never be fulfilled. She cried for herself, knowing she'd never be the same again.

Her body was broken in so many ways, but it was her heartache that'd ultimately break her.

Holly closed her eyes and let the weight of the world lure her back to sleep.

But she couldn't sleep. Her mind flashed to the icy cavern and the other frozen bodies. Two of them. Two frozen bodies that'd mocked her with their loving embrace. They were already dead. Long dead.

A cloth glided up her arm. It was soothing, therapeutic, tempting her to believe that everything was going to be okay. But it wasn't okay. She was all alone. Scared and alone. Cold, scared, and alone. Agony gripped every part of her body, inside and out.

Darkness as black as molasses was swallowing her whole. She tried to scream. But the burn in her throat made it nothing more than an agonized croak. Her eyes flickered and she saw black and white. Black and white. A blinding explosion danced behind her eyes. As did frozen bodies. Dripping blood. A gold necklace. And a brown suitcase. The images were real. Vivid. Tangible. She reached out, trying to touch them and a hand touched her arm.

Holly snapped her eyes open.

"Hey there, sleepy head."

Holly blinked and tried to sit up but couldn't move.

"It's okay. You're okay." The woman's voice was a soothing balm to the violent images crashing across her brain. She moaned and blinked her eyes open. The nurse's pretty smile was out of place with the torment battering Holly's mind and body.

"Hello, I'm Alison. One of the nurses here. How're you feeling?" Alison pressed a button and a bell sounded in the distance.

The back of the bed eased upright and Holly's body seemed to groan with the movement. A lanky man of Indian descent, with gray streaks peppering his coal black hair, walked through the door.

"She's waking up again, Doctor," the nurse said as she held a straw to Holly's lips.

Holly sucked the cool liquid. Swallowing hurt.

"Hello, Holly. I'm Dr. Mirami."

She wallowed in a numb fog as the doctor tested her with one gadget after another.

Blinking at her surroundings, she spied a sign to the left of a door. It was blurry at first but as the words formed, she frowned. "Where am I?"

The nurse squeezed her arm. "You're in a hospital."

"Hospital. Which hospital?"

"The University of Washington Medical Center."

The last thing Holly remembered was being on a mountain in the Canadian Rockies. Confused, she cleared her throat. "How did I get here?"

The nurse held the straw to Holly's lips again and she took another sip.

"You were medevacked out after the accident." The woman adjusted Holly's pillows.

"How long have I been here?"

The nurse's eyes lowered briefly before she met Holly's gaze. "It's been eight months since the accident, Holly."

Eight months. Her mind raced and she shook her head.

How could I have lost eight months?

"Is my mother here?"

The nurse shot a glance at the doctor and he nodded. "We'll get the Social Worker."

Bolts of fear shot through her chest. "I don't need a Social Worker. I need my mother." She clutched the nurse's wrist. "Where is she?"

The nurse placed her other hand over Holly's and when she saw the sorrow in the woman's eyes, a chunk of her already broken heart slipped away. "No! No. No... no... no."

"I'm sorry, Holly. Your mother died last month."

A wracking sob burst from her throat.

"Hey sweetie, don't cry." The nurses hand touched her shoulder. "You'll be okay."

But she wasn't okay. Nothing was ever going to be okay.

CHAPTER THREE

Reginald sensed the quiet from downstairs. It wasn't just the loud music that'd vanished. It was all the other sounds that'd gone too. Either his mother had passed out on the sofa, or she'd taken her boyfriend to her room. He hoped it was the latter. Thomas was as much a sleaze as all the other dipshits his mother brought home. The last thing Regi needed was to see the pair smooching on the sofa.

Regi could go to sleep and pretend none of it happened. Not the yelling and screaming. Not the smashing of glass. And not the loud music they'd pumped up in an attempt to drown out their fight. He'd heard it all before. Thomas could be great for his mother… he was in a decent job, appeared to have decent money. Trouble was, as her drug supplier, Thomas was also his mother's worst enemy. Regi was pretty certain their relationship was meant to be secret, given that Thomas was his mother's boss. They never went anywhere, as far as he knew anyway, and all their partying was done here, in his mother's home. His home.

Deciding to get it over with, Regi left the sanctuary of his bedroom and headed down the stairs. His mother looked to be dozing in the overstuffed sofa. Regi knew otherwise. She was most likely in a drug-induced stupor. The fix she'd taken hours ago would've worn off by now and her mind and body had settled into some kind of zombie state.

A cigarette dangled in her bony fingers, dangerously close to tumbling onto the cheap shag pile rug his mother had bought to cover her previous cigarette incidents. It was a wonder the house was still standing. Regi plucked the cigarette from trouble and clamped it between his lips. He inhaled slowly, allowing the smoke to seep into his cells, and his lungs welcomed the toxic cloud. Smoking was his one and only love, and it didn't disappoint.

Inhaling again, he let the smoke out in a long lazy stream that wafted upward like a drunken ghost. While enjoying the noxious reprieve, his eyes fell on his mother.

Considering the self-torture she crammed into her body, she was still striking. A classic beauty with flawless china skin, ruby lips that barely needed enhancing, and a strong jawline that she liked to clamp when forcing back anger. Her pale blue eyes were the only telltale signs that something was amiss; they'd lost their glimmer some time ago and the whites were closer to pale yellow.

Regi hated these bouts of self-loathing that had his mother tumbling into depths of despair. She'd had them on and off for as long as he could remember, but in the last nine months she'd hit the drugs heavily. He had no idea what had instigated the latest bout of depression.

Whatever it was, if she didn't snap out of it, it was likely to kill her.

She'd only just hit forty, and had marked that significant milestone with a week in bed. Sometimes Regi felt sorry for her. She'd been just eighteen years old when she'd had him. Now that he was twenty-two, he could nearly appreciate what she'd gone through. Nearly. But she hadn't just survived; the two of them had thrived.

They lived in a three-bedroom home in a decent area of Seattle, and she never seemed short of money. Regi had everything he needed and more. And she could afford her drug habit, which must cost a fortune. As far as Regi was concerned, despite the drugs, she did alright as a single mom.

He never knew his father; his mother refused to discuss the "sperm donor." Whenever Regi pushed the issue, his mother's consistent reply was that his father was the best worst mistake she'd ever made.

Regi stubbed the cigarette out and shoved the ashtray aside. He leaned over and shook his mother's shoulder. "Come on, Mom, I'll take you to your—"

Thomas groaned and his eyes snapped open. He blinked at Regi several times before he cleared his throat and scratched his stubbled chin. "Hey, Regi. What're you doing?" Thomas's gravelly voice sounded like he'd eaten from the overflowing ashtray.

"I'm taking Mom to her room." Regi nodded at his mother.

"Oh, it's okay, let me." Thomas rolled to his feet and staggered sideways before he caught himself. Then he shook his head like a dog shaking himself awake and smiled at Regi.

The man's grin bordered on creepy, and Regi was torn between letting him escort his mom to her room and punching the sleaze bucket in the nose.

"Hey babe, come on. We fell asleep." Thomas's tender touch on her arm was the only thing stopping Regi from the roundhouse punch.

His mother blinked awake. A lopsided grin formed on her face and her eyes rolled around before they seemed to focus. "Regi, hi. Are you hungry? I can make—"

"I'm okay, Mom. Thomas's taking you to your room."

As if confirming his plan, Thomas curled his arm around her waist and pulled her upright. With their arms around each other, they giggled like drunken teenagers as they bounced off the hallway walls and headed to her bedroom.

They shut the door, yet Regi could still hear his mother's laughter. As long as that was all he heard, he was happy. He reached for the crumpled packet of smokes on the coffee table and flipped the lid. Annoyed that it was empty, he pegged it across the room.

It was only half past ten, too early for bed, so he grabbed the remote, clicked on the television, and plonked onto the sofa. Flicking from one station to the next, he pushed back on the cushion and something wedged in the sofa's pillows caught his attention. He plucked it out. Two seconds later, a grin crept across his lips.

It was Thomas's wallet. After glancing over his shoulder to ensure he was alone, he flipped open the leather billfold. A cursory glance at the driver's license confirmed it was Thomas's wallet. Given that his mother had at least three frequent male friends, it hadn't been a certainty. The driver's license stated Thomas was fifty-one, much younger than he looked. Regi plucked the cash out and counted it. Three hundred and sixty-six dollars.

It was his lucky night.

Figuring Thomas wouldn't miss fifty, he shoved the note into his pocket and reluctantly put the rest back in the wallet before shoving it down the sofa again. The taste of nicotine was still fresh on his tongue, and with the cash burning a hole in his pocket, he decided to walk up to the shops and satisfy his craving.

He stood, and that's when he noticed the car keys on the coffee table. Turning off the television, he listened for sounds coming from his mom's bedroom. They were loud and unmistakable; his mom and Mr. Sleaze were snoring their heads off.

Regi's luck just got a whole lot better.

Without even a second thought, he plucked the keys off the glass and headed for the door. He'd have the car back before Thomas even knew it was gone. He tossed the keys up and down once, then strode out the front door. As usual, Thomas had parked the car in their driveway as if he owned the place.

Regi approached the beast with the respect it deserved. He'd give anything to have a sweet ride like this. As far as he was concerned, the 1978 Pontiac Trans-Am Firebird was about as good as it got. He considered himself a bit of an expert on the subject, given he'd held a casual job at Sparkle Car Wash for a little over a year.

The door was unlocked, and it pulled open without the signature creak that so often plagued cars of this vintage. Regi slipped into the driver's seat. The inside was in pristine condition. Everything looked original: the racy-looking gauges, the steering wheel, even the gear stick. Regi was impressed that Thomas had chosen the four-speed manual over the lame automatic alternative.

Maybe Thomas was worth getting to know after all.

He keyed the ignition and turned it on. The car roared to life and then settled in like a purring lion. Regi adjusted the mirror, wound down his window, and put the car into reverse. He cruised down the street with one hand on the wheel and his elbow out the side. It was a smooth ride, and it had everything he wanted in a car. Not that he could afford one. On his wage, Regi could barely afford to buy his own cigarettes.

The IGA was less than a mile away, and the Pontiac hadn't even opened her throat yet. Deciding to cruise right on past, he headed for the King Street wharfs. He'd done a bit of street racing with his friends down there a year or so ago, and with a bit of luck the place would be empty.

Twenty minutes later he turned onto Jackson Street and cruised down the warehouse-lined street like he owned the joint. Only three things could improve this moment: one was a cigarette, the second was a hot chick in denim shorts and a string bikini in the passenger seat, and the third was if someone he knew actually saw him.

But none of them came to fruition. He did, however, get the opportunity to open the throttle and hit seventy miles per hour along the deserted wharf. The eight-inch wheels handled the pavement perfectly and angled the corners like a sleek panther chasing dinner. Regi was literally having the ride of his life. It was nearly midnight when he aimed the car toward that packet of cigarettes that'd motivated him initially.

He pulled into the first IGA he came across and parked the car right next to the shop's front door. Regi climbed out and paused to admire the Firebird emblem painted on the car's hood before he strolled inside.

In addition to the cigarettes, he bought a pie and a cola and sat outside, admiring the Firebird as he consumed them. The paint job was so well buffed he could see his reflection in the blue paint. He liked what he saw.

His mind flicked to Thomas. It was hard to imagine him behind the wheel of this beast. Thomas was needle thin, sported a cheesy fake tan, and had a mustache that he should've shaved off two decades ago. In spite of all that, Thomas's choice of car rocketed him up into the interesting ranks, and Regi wondered if he should get to know him after all.

Once he finished his pie and cigarette, he tossed the trash into a trash can, then climbed back into the driver's seat and settled the car into its signature purr. He adjusted the side mirror so he could see his own reflection, put the car into reverse, and pressed the gas pedal.

A violent crunch of metal on metal shattered his reverie. He slammed on the brake and looked in the mirror. His heart set to explode at what he saw. Barely able to breathe, he pushed open his door and stepped from the Firebird.

From that moment on, everything seemed to go in slow motion.

Behind his car was the most expensive car he'd ever seen in real life. A Corvette Stingray. Price tag approximately three-quarters of a million bucks. It was as sleek as a panther; it sat low to the ground and sported fat wheels for stability. It wasn't the type of car that could be found at a local dealer. This one was special.

And that meant Regi was in deep shit.

But when a man climbed out of the driver's seat of the Stingray, and Regi saw the calm indifference on his face, he had a gut feeling the shit pile was about to get a whole lot bigger. The man wore an expensive navy suite, a crisp white shirt trimmed with gray, and leather shoes that were polished so highly they reflected the IGA's lights.

Regi expected him to yell, or launch at him with a clenched fist, but instead the man smirked. Or sneered. Whatever it was, it was the polar opposite of what Regi expected, given the situation. Regi's feet were rooted to the asphalt as he stared at the damage to the Stingray. Its sleek lines were no match for his forty-year-old muscle car, and the side fender had crumpled like a paper bag. On a car like that, it was about fifty grand's worth of damage. At least.

With every step the man took toward him, Regi debated making a run for it.

"Seems like we have a situation, Mr.—" The man held his hand forward and Regi stared at it like it contained a loaded grenade.

He swallowed so hard he was certain the man could hear it. Regi offered his hand and the man squeezed it, letting the hold linger too long for Regi's liking.

"What's your name, son?"

He cleared his throat. "Reginald."

"Reginald what?"

"Reginald Tate."

"Well, Mr. Tate, that's a fancy car you've got there. Is it yours?"

Regi gulped. That shit pile just stacked on another layer. "It belongs to my mother's boyfriend."

"Hmmm. And he knows you have it?"

Regi glanced to his left, assessing the distance to the shop corner, and tried to calculate if he could make a run for it.

The man stepped sideways, blocking Regi's intended escape route.

"You don't want to do that, Mr. Tate." The man's voice was calm. Too calm.

"What?"

"Run."

"I wasn't."

The slap came from nowhere, fast and hard, right across Regi's left cheek.

"Shit." Regi rubbed the sting from his flesh. "What the fuck was that for?"

"For lying. I don't tolerate liars."

"I wasn't—" Regi saw the second swipe coming and ducked beneath the blow. But when he saw the fury in the man's eyes, he instantly wished he'd taken the hit. "Look, Mr...."

"Carson."

"Mr. Carson, I'm really sorry about your car."

"I know you are. Just hand me your insurance details and—"

"I, um—I don't have insurance." Regi's gut churned like acid in a blender.

"Give me your license."

Regi fished his wallet from his back pocket and withdrew his license. Carson snatched it from his fingers and studied it. "Looks like you live in a decent neighborhood. We'll set up a payment plan."

"I don't have any money."

"Who said anything about money?" Carson folded his hand around Regi's license and turned on his heel. "My men will be in touch, Mr. Tate."

Daggers of fear burrowed into Regi's skin as Carson eased into the Stingray, and without even a glance in his direction he drove away. Regi wasn't fooled. Despite his fancy clothes and even fancier car, Carson was a thug. He'd just as likely break his fingers as offer him a hundred-dollar martini.

Regi had collided with the devil.

CHAPTER FOUR

Three years later

Holly did a double take at the name written on the front of her mail. Amber Hope. It'd taken her a full month to decide on her new name. Even though she'd changed her name legally a year ago, she still couldn't accept it as her own. Amber had been her great-grandmother's name and Hope was her mother's maiden name. Holly liked to think they'd both be proud of her decision to use their names to create her new identity.

But that wasn't all Holly had changed. When she'd woken up from that coma three years ago, she was a different woman from the one that had fallen from the helicopter.

She'd lost Milton, the love of her life, and had been labeled his gold-digging murderer on social media.

She'd lost her mother, thanks to an aggressive form of cancer that she hadn't had when Holly had last seen her.

She'd recovered from so many injuries that her doctors had hailed her survival as a medical miracle.

She was now riddled with scars, including a hideous burn scar that dominated her right cheek.

And if all of those changes weren't enough, Holly was also $1.7 million richer.

Two years of treatment, both physically and mentally, had fixed some of her problems. Not the unbearable heartache or the profound sense of loss— they were ingrained in her being now. A dark stain smothered her heart from the moment she woke till she drifted to sleep at night. Sometimes it even attacked her in dreams, and she'd taken to trying to remain awake as long as possible, fearing her nightmares more than the sheer exhaustion.

Leaving the envelope unopened, she went to her kitchen, opened the fridge, and stared at the relatively empty shelves for a full minute before she plucked a Tupperware dish from the middle shelf.

Holly wished she'd died on that ledge. And not just fleetingly either. She truly, truly meant it. Especially when people blamed her for Milton and Kane's deaths. Milton's ex-wife had made it her personal vendetta to continue Holly's suffering. The fact that Milton willed Holly a fair chunk of his money, while Victoria got nothing, probably had something to do with that.

It was Holly's therapist who'd convinced her to move to another city and start over. One benefit was that changing her name would hide her from the never-ending lineup of complete strangers asking for money. And a new home would supposedly allow her to move forward rather than dwell on her past.

She'd been reluctant at first, because other than that horrendous trip to the Canadian Rockies, she'd only been out of Seattle twice. Holly had stewed on the idea for months, but when her therapist put her in touch with a legal practitioner who'd handle her name change and everything else, the whole transaction had taken just nine weeks.

Holly shoved the leftover mushroom curry and rice into the microwave and set it to cook for two minutes. Then she peeled open the envelope and unfolded the lawyer's letter. The litigation over Milton's will was still pending. Not one cent of his money had been allocated. Because his ex-wife had been willed nothing, she'd made it her mission to ensure nobody else got a dime either.

Not that Holly cared. She had no desire for his money. It was the $1.7 million inheritance from her mother that Holly had used to buy her small apartment in Brambleton. She could hardly believe her mother had that much to offer. Apparently, she'd invested the insurance payout from her father's death wisely, and the value of their family home had skyrocketed in recent years.

With her mother's inheritance, Holly had purchased a fancy computer and other equipment she needed to set up her home business. The job wasn't lucrative—it wasn't interesting either—but it allowed her to live a reclusive life, and it gave her something to do.

Boredom was a soul-crusher, though, and every second she wasn't busy, her mind would drift to that day and night she'd spent injured and alone on the icy ledge. The memory was so vivid she could recall every second. Pain was at the top of that recollection. As was the cold.

But it was the bodies in the ice that played across her mind in endless loops.

Nobody believed her story. Not one person. Not one of her so-called friends had considered her recollection true, especially since none of her rescuers had mentioned the frozen couple. Their disbelief had hurt as much as some of her deepest wounds. Holly often wondered if she'd imagined the whole thing. On the odd occasion she did speak of it, people looked at her strangely, as if the accident had left her possessed. She was obsessed, she'd admit that.

Obsessed to find out who those people were.

If it was a figment of her imagination, then she truly was crazy.

She could recall every inch of their frozen bodies. They were a man and a woman. A married couple or lovers, she was sure. The man was positioned seated behind the woman, his legs splayed, and she was in his arms, her knees tucked up to her chest, no doubt trying to keep warm. They looked peaceful, like they were sharing a loving embrace rather than the final seconds of their life. The ice preserved their bodies so perfectly Holly could see her eyelashes and his stubble. Their clothing and the battered brown suitcase at the man's feet were also frozen in time.

They were so perfect, it was like they'd been positioned there, like a forgotten scene from a movie set. The way they were dressed gave Holly the impression they'd been wealthy.

A heart-shaped locket on a golden chain had been threaded through the woman's slender fingers, and if Holly had to guess she'd say the woman had been fondling it when she'd drawn her final breath.

Holly had been spooked by them at first—spooked was an understatement. Their sudden appearance after the giant chunk of ice sheered away from the helicopter explosion had scared the shit out of her. Holly truly thought she'd gone mad.

But as the minutes had ticked away, then the hours, she was able to examine their bodies. The man's left shoe had been within reach, and it'd taken some serious mental debating before Holly had convinced herself to touch it.

Once she did, though, she was relived, because it confirmed that not only were they real, but also that she wasn't crazy.

Not that it helped. Her handful of friends had visited in the months following her waking up in the hospital, and each time she told the story of the bodies, she instantly wished she hadn't. Their looks of pity hurt as much as their unwillingness to believe her.

She plucked a bottle of Riesling from the fridge and a wineglass from the cupboard. She'd taken to drinking one or two glasses of wine every night to help her relax, and she found she usually slept better. Usually.

Holly still had no memory of being rescued. One minute she was sharing an ice crevice with two frozen bodies, then she woke up eight months later in a Seattle hospital. There was nothing connecting the two points.

Not one damn thing.

Trauma-induced memory loss was what her therapist had called it. Holly called it her sanity. Her body had shut out the pain she would've suffered with all her injuries. Ironically, she remembered everything before the crash and after. She remembered the whiskey-colored mountain glistening in the sun and the twin peaks that rose skyward like ancient stone sentries. She remembered every second of the crash as if it'd happened in slow motion. She remembered the excruciating pain after she fell onto the icy ledge. She remembered Milton's final moments too, and the helicopter explosion. But her therapist couldn't explain why she remembered all of that, yet nothing to do with her rescue.

The microwave dinged and she removed the meal, grabbed a fork, and set it down on the coffee table next to her wine. She sat on her sofa, plonked her heels up on the table, settled the Tupperware dish on her lap, and turned up the volume.

On the television, the camera panned from a snowcapped mountain to the tail of a plane that protruded from the snow like a blade. A shaggy-haired man with a giant camera around his neck smiled at the screen. The writing across the bottom introduced the man as Carter Logan, National Geographic Photographer.

Holly turned up the volume and ate a spoonful of dinner.

The picture on the television switched to an elderly woman whose red-rimmed eyes glistened with tears. When the woman held a photo up to the camera, Holly gasped, and her dinner went flying as she launched at the remote. She hit rewind, then pressed play. Her jaw dropped and she blinked in shock as she listened to the elderly woman's sad story.

Holly watched the news report six times before she sat back, her heart pounding.

She gulped back the last of her wine and stared at the still image of the photograph on the television.

Finally, she had a clue.

For the first time in three years, Holly had a reason to live.

CHAPTER FIVE

The squeal of tires had Regi running before he even turned to see what it was. He'd been expecting this. Yet he wouldn't give in without a fight. Couldn't. Flight or fight was in his blood. Flight first, then, once they got him, he'd put up one hell of a fight. Pounding feet sounded behind him. Adrenaline shot through his veins. He forced his brain to concentrate on planting one foot in front of the other and not the beating that was coming.

The chain mesh fence ahead wasn't a problem. Regi threw himself at it and launched over in one swift move. On the other side he shot a glance at his pursuers. Only three this time. *Maybe Carson is getting soft.* Pumping his arms and legs again, his feet sloshed through one puddle after another as he bolted up the narrow alley.

Regi cursed himself for taking this route. After each beating, he'd try to learn from his mistakes. Constant beatings were a sharp motivator. Yet this dark alley was another stupid mistake. A squeal of tires echoed ahead of him. He snapped his eyes up and his heart launched to his throat at the sight. A black van blocked the alley.

Regi was surrounded.

He looked back. The three thugs weren't gaining on him, they were simply herding him into their trap. Regi looked upward, searching the red brick buildings lining the alley for an escape route. But it was pointless. These weren't residential buildings with ladders that could be conveniently plucked from the air. These were the walls of warehouses. Most of them empty. He wanted to slap himself for his stupidity.

Pretending defeat, he put his hands in the air. "Hey now, fellas. Let's be reasonable." Despite his pleas, he knew negotiation wasn't an option. This wolf pack was out for blood—his blood.

The beefed-up chumps barreled right at him. The fastest of the three lunged in a full body tackle. Regi used his boxing training to dodge the attack, sending the thug sprawling onto the wet asphalt. Light on his feet, he managed to get off a quick jab and thumped the second brute square in the nose. Bone and gristle shattered beneath his closed fist.

But his success was brief.

A fourth man approached from behind, and Regi didn't see him till it was too late. He spun on his heel, but the blow to his temple knocked him flying.

Regi hit the asphalt face-first, tearing flesh from his cheek.

Thick hands launched him to his feet. His arm was yanked up behind his back and Regi howled at the agony.

"Shut the fuck up." The fastest man, the one who'd gone sprawling, punched Regi in the jaw. Stars blazed across his eyelids.

They shoved him forward, manhandling him toward the van's open door. Each step had his mind stricken and his heart exploding.

He'd expected the beating. He'd expected blood and pain.

But he hadn't expected this.

Never before had they taken him.

CHAPTER SIX

Holly had never thought of herself as pretty. Now, though, with the brutal scar on her cheek, she thought of herself as hideous.

After the coma, once she'd learnt to walk again and was able to leave the rehab clinic, she'd spent months searching for a plastic surgeon willing to offer a miracle. But it wasn't to be. Not when the burn had damaged all layers of her dermis. There was nothing left for them to work with.

"You'll have to learn to live with it." That's what they'd said. All of them.

Live with it.

She did, of course.

Her daily battle was trying not to look at the damn scar on her cheek. But she did. Every single day. Holly told herself that becoming reclusive was so people wouldn't recognize her, but the real reason was way more obvious… her embarrassing scars.

Hiding from the world made it easier. She didn't need to see the stares from complete strangers. Some were blatant in their viewing; others would quickly glance away, clearly repulsed by her disfigurement.

Before the accident she'd worked in a coffee shop, and the best part was getting to know all the regulars. And not just their coffee choices either. Most of them she only saw for about five minutes each day, yet she felt like she knew every single one of them.

But after she'd emerged from the hospital, she'd found it harder and harder to cope. Her therapy sessions became her haven, which meant they also became the crux of her problem. The only places she felt safe were her own home and Dr. Andrews's office. Holly was certain her therapist had thought long and hard before she'd advised Holly to move to another town and start again. Not only did Dr. Andrews lose a client, she lost a bucketload of income too.

When they'd discussed what Holly would do in the new town, Dr. Andrews had offered to hire her as a medical transcriptionist. Every day the therapist dictated her findings onto a device that was subsequently forwarded to Holly via email. It was the perfect job—flexible, consistent, and the best part was she could do it from home. In just over a year, Holly had increased her transcription service to nine doctors.

Holly sat down at her computer, nudged her chair forward, and put her feet on the footstool. Shuffling the mouse, she woke the monitor and opened the document she'd been working on all day. The number of words at the bottom indicated she was just shy of two thousand. She sighed. She normally did that in an hour; she'd already been at it for seven.

Determined to complete the report before four o'clock, she clicked the play button on the audio file and began typing. The doctor's voice sprang from her computer speaker at a snappy clip and his English was thick with his Japanese accent, requiring her to concentrate.

It was usually the perfect distraction. That's what her life had become, an endless search for distractions. Anything to stop her mind from drifting to her previous life. A life that'd been filled with loving family and friends. A life where she was giddy with love for the most amazing man in the world. A life where she was free from pain and disfigurement.

Not anymore, though.

But now, with her new mission, she'd have to emerge from her sanctuary. It was impossible to do what she was planning without it. Ever since she'd seen that National Geographic report she'd been working on a plan. It required lots of little steps. Just like when she'd learned to walk again. But these steps forced her out of seclusion and way beyond her comfort zone.

Home was her comfort zone, even though it was a small apartment with just one bedroom, a combined kitchen and lounge room, bathroom, and a laundry. It wasn't homey either. She didn't care for trinkets and knickknacks, and it showed.

Since she'd moved to Brambleton she'd met a couple of her neighbors, but had made zero attempts to get to know them.

And that's exactly how she liked it.

But that was about to change.

The prospect of being in close proximity to a stranger was nauseating enough, but her plan required more—a lot more. Just the thought of physical exercise had her stomach twisting into knots. She had no idea if her body could handle it. Other than years of grueling physiotherapy, she hadn't done any exercise since the accident.

In her early twenties, Holly had held a gym membership for years and had been proud of the muscle definition she'd once had. Now, though, on the odd occasion when she looked at the rest of her body in the mirror, she saw a physique that appeared to be eating itself.

She glanced at the clock and noted she had twenty minutes before her self-imposed four o'clock deadline. Not that the doctor would care, but it was how she liked to operate. The time on the audio recording indicated there were about fifteen minutes remaining. She picked up her pace, determined to meet her target. With one minute to spare, she finished the file with her usual disclaimer and emailed it back to Dr. Makinoma.

Before her mind began playing procrastination games, she opened her internet and typed "Upper Limits" into the browser.

She'd already reviewed the website over a dozen times, yet she studied the opening page again. Moving to such a small town had seemed like a good idea at the time, but she hadn't realized the implications until now. Brambleton had just one gymnasium. And it wasn't like any gym she'd frequented in her life.

Upper Limits was a rock-climbing facility.

At first she'd been horrified, but after hours of scouring the website and analyzing the accompanying photographs, she'd realized that Upper Limits was exactly what she needed. It'd been over a week since she'd first looked up fitness facilities in Brambleton, and every day since then, she'd conjured up another excuse why she wouldn't go.

Today, though, she was determined to force herself out her front door to have a look at the gym firsthand. She fooled herself with the notion that she was just looking… she had absolutely no intention of going inside. Not today.

She pulled out her notebook and reread her notes.

At the very top she'd written: "Remember you are Amber Hope."

It was an incredible thing to change identity at twenty-eight years old. The paperwork to change her name had been relatively easy in comparison to the mental change that was required. She still thought of herself as Holly. If someone called out Holly on the street, she'd turn around in a heartbeat. If they called out Amber, however, she'd likely keep on walking.

"Hi, I'm Amber Hope." Even saying her name aloud sounded false.

She stood and moved to the mirror. Angling her head so she couldn't see her scar she said. "Hi, I'm Amber Hope."

Shaking her head at how ridiculous she sounded, she squared her shoulders and repeated it. After four attempts, she plonked back down at her workstation and scanned the next point in her plan: Secrecy was paramount.

Ironically, her coma had been some kind of blessing. Not only did it allow her body to heal, but it also kept her oblivious to the storm of accusations that'd abounded after the crash. The story had been front page news for longer than it warranted. And Holly hadn't realized the implication of that until she'd left the hospital.

The scar on her cheek was like a six-foot billboard announcing who she was, and there was no hiding from it.

It seemed that everybody recognized her. And every one of them had an opinion.

A whirlwind of newspaper headlines flashed across her mind: *Murder on the Mountain. Medical Miracle or Cunning Cover-up? Gold-digger to inherit a fortune.* A lump formed in her throat as she grabbed a red pen and underlined the words: Secrecy was paramount.

Shoving the emotional landside from her brain, she tugged on her shoes, grabbed her handbag, and strode out the front door before she found another procrastination technique. The instant she left her apartment her hands began sweating and her stomach twisted into knots. Downstairs, her mother's old car was in the garage. She barely used it, though, and she wouldn't need it now. According to Google, Upper Limits was an eleven-minute walk from her apartment.

Every step had her mind flipping from one daunting thought to another. Her feet were dead weights that took effort to drag forward.

Holly could barely breathe by the time she arrived at the rock-climbing warehouse.

There was a garden bed between the road where the cars were angle parked into the curb and the front windows of the gym. Holly slinked in behind the hedge and watched the activity inside the brightly lit facility.

There were about two dozen people working out. Several were at the far back corner and looked to be doing some kind of martial arts training. The remaining people were up the walls; each one was tethered by a rope to a partner who watched them from beneath.

She spied the owner of the gym immediately. Oliver Nelson. He looked exactly like he did on his website. His thick and wavy hair was an interesting sandy blond color, intermingled with hints of ginger. Oliver stood out from the crowd, not just because he was about six foot five, but because he seemed to have a commanding aura about him, like he'd earned respect from every person in that building.

He appeared to be genuinely concerned for the woman climbing above him. His eyes didn't falter and occasionally Holly heard his words of encouragement. They were assertive yet kind. It reminded her of the dozens of doctors who'd assisted in her recovery. Yet every one of them had maintained a clinical distance... like getting too close would be trouble should she not achieve her goals.

Oliver, however, had an intense gaze that showed he was more than just casually invested in the climber's success. He genuinely wanted her to succeed.

His physique was also a world apart from all the doctors who'd helped her. Oliver had broad shoulders and narrow hips, and she was mesmerized by the bulge of his biceps beneath the fabric of his black uniform each time he braced against the rope.

The music stopped, casting a pleasant silence over the gym. She heard laughter and watched the people at the rear of the gym gather their things from the back wall.

The climber above Oliver must've said something to him, because he changed his stance and adjusted the rope at his front, then gazed up at the climber again.

People began walking toward the exit, and with towels flung over their shoulders and faces flushed red they all looked exhausted. But despite their appearance, it was their smiles and lighthearted banter that captured Holly's interest the most. Every one of them seemed happy. It had been years, but Holly understood that sense of euphoria that only a workout could provide.

Now, though, her heart was thundering for all the wrong reasons.

CHAPTER SEVEN

Oliver pulled on the rope, maintaining tension for the climber above, who stretched out with her right hand. Her fingers twitched as she attempted to lengthen her reach, but she was still an inch away. Oliver increased his tension, ready for the moment she leapt. But she didn't. She gave up and pulled back. "You can do it, Larissa."

"I can't." She yelled her fury.

"Yes, you can. Center your balance on your right foot. Engage your core and go for that pinch hold."

"I can't!"

They'd been neighbors most of their lives, so Oliver had seen the depth of Larissa's hotheadedness many times. She was a fiery one. Which wasn't surprising; he knew her parents well and it was a wonder she had a nice bone in her body. But she did, lots of lovely nice bones. And although she'd given him plenty of opportunities to jump those bones, he wouldn't. Larissa was more like a sister than a love interest, and that's the way it was going to stay. She was also a paying customer, and he'd never jeopardize that.

"Take a deep breath and get your butt up there."

"Stop looking at my ass." Larissa wriggled her hips for emphasis, but he ignored it.

"Stop talking and start concentrating." Once, at a party, when he and Larissa had consumed a little too much alcohol, Oliver had made the mistake of kissing her. Thankfully he'd managed to pull up before it went too far. That kiss was a mistake he'd like to erase from his memory.

Larissa, however, had never let it go.

Oliver glanced at the other instructor to his right, who was belaying another rock climber. Robert was a good man. A little unreliable at times, but when he *was* at work, he gave it one hundred percent. Oliver learned the hard way that he couldn't run this business on his own, and it'd been with reluctance that he admitted he had to share his measly profits with an employee. That was seven months ago, and the extra clients he'd been able to take on because of the additional pair of hands around the gym had made the investment worthwhile. So much so that he'd hired another two staff members since then.

The music that'd been pumping from the back of the gym cut off abruptly, casting a strange quiet over the converted warehouse. Moments later, the clients who'd finished the cycle class began strolling past. Oliver made a point of saying goodbye to each and every one of them. His clients were as important to him as their dollars, and he was determined not to lose either.

"Climbing," Larissa called from thirty feet above.

She finally made the leap and Oliver readjusted the tension on the rope. "Good one. I told you you'd do it. Two more and you can smack that bell."

Larissa squealed as she fell and Oliver squeezed the rope, halting her fall.

"Shit," she bellowed as she dangled in wild circles above him.

As Oliver lowered her down to the padded mat, he prepared an encouragement speech in his mind. Once down, he touched her shoulder and she glanced up at him. The disappointment in her eyes was unmistakable.

"You did great. The highest you've ever been."

"It's not good enough, Olly. I should've made it to the top by now." She clamped her teeth, bulging the muscle along her jaw.

"You'll get there."

Shaking her head, she unhooked the rope from her belay loop and stepped back. Larissa was already tough on herself, so Oliver didn't need to say any more. The championships were four months away and she'd set her mind on winning this time. If there was one thing he knew about her, when Larissa set her mind to something, there was no changing it.

"Hey, Olly, you coming to Baxter's after?" Patrick wiped sweat off his forehead as he strolled toward Oliver.

"Nah, man, I'm coaching Kurt's baseball straight after this."

Patrick tapped Oliver on the shoulder. "We'll probably still be there when you're done. Come by."

"Maybe. We'll see."

"Your loss."

Oliver rolled his eyes. "Tell me about it. You coming on Friday?"

"Of course, man. See you then." As Patrick approached the exit, Oliver spied a woman standing to the side of the doorway. He hadn't seen or heard her come in and waved in her direction. She inclined her head slightly as if acknowledging his attention, but didn't move from her spot.

Larissa huffed as she stepped out of her leg loops and kicked them away. "I'm outta here." She stormed off, scooping up her bag without pausing, and headed for the door.

"See you Friday."

"Maybe," she called over her shoulder, then she disappeared out the door.

The woman followed Larissa's exit, then she turned and aimed her eyes back at Oliver. He'd never seen her before, and he prided himself on getting to know everyone, which in a town like Brambleton wasn't hard.

He turned to Robert. "Hey, Rob, do you know who that is?"

"Who?"

Oliver nodded his head toward the door and Robert glanced that way, then shook his head. "Nope."

Oliver finished looping Larissa's belay rope and secured it to its designated hook on the wall. He unclipped his harness, hung it up, planted a smile on his face, and walked toward the woman.

She stepped back and lowered her eyes as he approached. Her chest rose and fell with a deep breath, then she straightened her shoulders before looking up at him.

"Hi, I'm Oliver. How can I help you?"

"I need to learn how to do that." Her eyes indicated the rock-climbing wall.

Her assertive words were diminished by the quiver in her voice. Oliver's gaze fell to the nasty scar on her cheek. He'd only seen a burn scar once before, and from what he'd heard they were painful. This one must've been agony. She blinked at him and loosened her dark hair from her ear so that it fell over her cheek. Oliver instantly hated that she'd noticed him looking.

He rubbed his hands together. "Well, you've come to the right place. We have classes six days a week."

"I'd like private lessons."

"Well, we don't really—"

She cut him off. "I'm hoping you can make an exception."

Her eyes were that of a wolf. Incredibly blue, and laced with something… determination, fearlessness, mistrust? Unable to pinpoint what he saw, he cast the curiosity aside and held his hand forward. "Like I said, Miss…"

She hesitated for the briefest of moments before she offered her hand. "Hol— Amber, my name's Amber."

He tried to catch her gaze but her eyes were aimed at the gym behind him. "It's lovely to meet you, Amber. Like I said, we offer classes—"

"You don't seem to understand. I want private lessons." Her voice was level, assertive, yet laced with a quiver.

"Well, Amber, what we want and what we get aren't always the same."

"I'll pay."

Amber's shifty eyes had him wondering what she was on. One of his oldest friends had fought drug demons a few years ago and Oliver had seen every one of its debilitating side effects.

"It's not a case of—"

"One hundred dollars."

He had no idea what she thought one hundred would buy her. His casual lesson rate was twenty-two dollars; equipment hire was an additional eleven dollars. It'd be cheaper again if she signed up for a monthly package. She seemed keen, though, and not being one to knock back money he decided on a different approach. "Would you like to come into my office?"

"Do we have a deal?" She pursed her lips and Oliver was certain the woman was a few screws short of a toolbox.

Deciding she'd be more trouble than she was worth, he shook his head. "No, as a matter of fact, we don't have a deal. What exactly do you think one hundred dollars will buy you?"

Her eyes darted from him to behind him and back again. She looked confused. "A lesson," she finally said.

His jaw dropped. "One lesson?"

"One private lesson," she clarified with a nod.

"Hey, Olly, you coming to Baxter's?" Neil eased next to Oliver and he turned to his customer.

"Not tonight. I'm coaching Kurt's baseball."

"Shit, man, it's going to be a good one."

Oliver rolled his eyes at his longest paying customer. "So I've heard."

"Alright, buddy. See you tomorrow."

"Sure thing." Neil cast his eyes over Amber before he spun on his heel and headed out the door.

Oliver returned his gaze to her. She was clutching the shoulder strap on her bag like she feared it was about to be snatched. Her already small frame seemed to have shrunk even further and he had a terrible feeling the woman was petrified.

"Look." He softened his stance. "I think we got off on a bad foot. How about you come into my office and we go over our packages."

The knuckles on her right hand bulged as she squeezed her strap tighter. After a moment's pause, she nodded.

"Okay, it's right this way." Oliver pointed toward the small room about a third of the way down the side of the warehouse and indicated for her to go first. When she didn't move, he decided to lead the way. He could only assume she'd stepped in behind him.

When he'd bought this old warehouse three years ago, he'd transformed it into a customized indoor rock-climbing facility and fitness gym. Other than the outside walls, his tiny office was the only structure that was original. He'd spent nearly every penny he had on this establishment and had taken a gamble on its success. He had no competition, though, and this concept of exercise was new to Brambleton. Fortunately, he'd kept in touch with nearly every person he'd met in his thirty-one years and word spread fast. Neil was the first to pay for a lesson, and others quickly followed. Oliver considered himself a lucky man almost every single day.

"Hey, boss, you need me to stay and lock up?" Robert was at the back of the warehouse, walking toward the office.

"No, I've got it." Oliver shook his head. "See you in the morning."

"Great. See ya then." Robert stepped into the office and three seconds later came out with a pack slung over one shoulder.

"Hi." Oliver assumed Robert was talking to the woman he hoped was still behind him.

Amber spoke her first words since he'd tempted her away from the front door. "Hello."

Oliver stepped through the office door, went around the other side of his desk, and remained standing. "Please, take a seat."

She fiddled her hair over her cheek before she eased onto the chair and pulled her bag onto her lap. Every person that'd visited this office had been practically bursting with energy, except his brother. Dane was what Oliver called a sloth; he moved with methodical precision that drove Oliver crazy, and the most exercise he got was brushing his teeth. They were complete opposites, which was probably why they got along so well.

Amber looked around Oliver's office, and although he liked to think of it as organized chaos, it was probably closer to chaos. He made a mental note to put some effort into cleaning it out. Truth was, the one and only other job he'd had kept him inside four walls. It was the last place he wanted to be.

Oliver plucked a brochure and a waiver from the rack on the wall. "So, Amber, what's brought you to Upper Limits?"

"I already told you. I need to learn how to climb walls."

He was a heartbeat off chuckling when he stopped himself. Her steely expression indicated she wasn't joking, and the fact that she'd used the word "need" waved a red flag in his brain. Nobody *needed* to know how to rock climb. It was a passion, a desire, born from an urge to get fit and have fun doing it. Not because they needed it.

Shoving his curiosity aside, he unfolded the brochure to the four-page spread showing a panoramic photograph of his rock walls. "Then you've come to the right place. We have all stages of training, from beginner to expert."

"I need to learn them all."

Again, with the need? He frowned and cocked his head, trying to capture her gaze. "So, what's your ultimate goal?"

Her haunting blue eyes seemed to pierce his brain. "What do you mean?"

"Well, is this for fitness, fun, to get social, or do you want to do competition stuff? What's your motivation for coming in?"

She shifted her gaze, and Oliver had a weird feeling she was about to dart for the door. Sensing her uncertainty, he said, "Most people start it for fitness and take it from there."

"Yes," she said, but didn't elaborate.

"Okay, well, I just need you to fill out this form and sign the waiver, then we can lock you in."

"For private lessons." She said it as a statement rather than a question.

"Look, Amber, I don't—"

She pointed at the brochure. "Your lessons are twenty-two dollars. I'm willing to pay you four times that amount for private lessons."

Her argument was a strong one. "But our lessons are group sessions, so I usually have four to six people in each group, therefore I'm making at least one hundred dollars per session.

Her intense gaze deepened. "Two hundred dollars."

He blinked, hardly able to believe the offer. It was ludicrous, but mighty tempting.

"Three hundred dollars."

"Oh jeez." He held up his palms in a peace gesture. "Okay, sure… private lessons."

"For that price I want the building to myself. No other customers."

"That's a big ask. We're open every night till seven, six days a week."

"Then we'll start at seven."

"Look, Amber. This is my business, and I make the decisions around here."

"If you're not interested in my money, Mr. Nelson, then I'll find someone who is." Her voice was firm, but she strangled her fingers like she was wringing a rag.

Her use of his surname caught him off guard, though. It seemed Amber had done her research. He flicked his gaze from her lupine eyes to the scar on her cheek. He instantly regretted it when she angled her head to hide it.

It wasn't all she was hiding. Amber seemed to have a whole bucket of mystery going on.

Oliver felt he was about to enter into something he'd completely regret, but the money was too good to refuse. Not only that, Amber had captured his interest. It'd been a very long time since anyone had done that. Especially a woman.

In a small town like Brambleton, it was an opportunity he wasn't willing to blow.

"You strike a hard bargain, Amber."

Her pale pink lips drew into a thin line and she simply nodded in response.

"Okay, so when do you want to start?"

"Now."

He burst out laughing. "We're not starting now, and that's not negotiable. I coach my brother's baseball team every Wednesday night." He glanced at the simple round clock hanging over his business certificate. "It starts in thirty minutes."

Her shoulders slumped and she seemed to stew on her response. "Tomorrow night."

"Okay, tomorrow it is."

She folded the brochure and collected the waiver form, shoving both into her bag and then she stood. "Mr. Nelson?"

"Please, call me Oliver."

"Oliver, I need you to keep my patronage a secret."

He frowned, and when her fingers wandered over the brutal scar on her cheek, he thought he saw fear in her eyes.

"Okay, my lips are sealed." He made a twisting motion on his lips as a joke.

But Amber seemed to crumble before him. A powerful desire to protect her fluttered over his heart. He couldn't pinpoint what it was, but Oliver had a strange feeling he'd been destined to meet this troubled woman.

CHAPTER EIGHT

After six hours of trying to finish Dr. Nikanomar's patient report, Holly gave up just before four o'clock and shut down her computer. She wandered to the bathroom and turned the shower faucets on full. All day she'd tried to picture herself climbing that wall at Oliver's gym, and each mental image ended in failure. As she stood under the hot cascade, her mind sparked endless questions and her stomach flipped at her inability to produce answers.

By the time she stepped from the shower, the urge to throw up was so strong that she leaned over the toilet bowl and fought the hideous wave with short sharp breaths. It was a long horrible pause before she swallowed back the bile and stood again. She glanced at the mirror but quickly snapped her eyes away from her ghostly reflection.

After drying off, she dressed in track pants and a long-sleeved t-shirt and put on the brand-new gym shoes she'd bought online months ago but hadn't even removed from the box. When she'd purchased the shoes, she'd had every intention of taking a daily walk, but her fear of being seen had overridden her urge to exercise.

Holly's thoughts tumbled to the last time she'd done any form of voluntary exercise. It was the same day her life had become a living nightmare. She been at the peak of her physical fitness when she'd fallen into that crevice. Maybe that'd been what saved her. It certainly hadn't stopped the pain. She could vividly recall sitting on that ledge and begging the agony to subside. A mental image of the couple she'd shared that crevice with catapulted into her mind. They were the reason why she needed to fight past her fear.

The vision was the jolt she needed. She turned back to the mirror and clutched the sink. Staring into her own eyes, she forced determination into her brain. "You can do this."

She strode to the kitchen, pausing at the bench to pinch two leaves off her gotu kola plant and pop them into her mouth. After she'd given up on the plastic surgeons, she'd turned to alternative medicine. This plant was the result of extensive research. Two leaves each day were meant to be enough to help with scars. Burn scars in particular. She had no idea whether or not it'd helped, but she'd hate to see what her cheek would look like if she hadn't been eating them.

Holly strode to the sofa, grabbed the remote, and settled back to watch the documentary that'd given her a sense of purpose again. She hit play and the footage on the television panned from pristine mountain scenery to the tail of a plane jutting above the white snowy blanket like a blade. Carter Logan, the National Geographic photographer who'd discovered the plane, was a jovial man who described the discovery with delightful animation. Holly had watched the documentary so many times she could recite his monologue word for word.

Like every other time she'd watched it, she paused the footage on the image of Dorothy holding up the photo.

Despite their significant age difference, Holly felt a strange connection to the elderly woman. It was like they'd walked the same life-changing path. She saw the pain in Dorothy's eyes when she talked about the accusations against her one and only child.

It was the same pain she saw in her own reflection each morning. Holly knew how it felt to be falsely blamed for a person's death. Although she may never be able to clear her own name, she was determined to help Dorothy before the light faded out of the old woman's eyes.

By the time she walked out her front door and headed toward Oliver's gym she was ready to give this thing—this quest, or mission, or whatever she wanted to call it—everything she had. Or die trying.

Which was just as likely too.

Nothing in the last three years had made more sense than this.

She was ten minutes ahead of schedule and, slinking into the shadows outside Upper Limits, she watched through the open door. Oliver was holding a rope for a man who was halfway up the wall. His obvious concern for the man he was helping seemed so genuine that Holly was mesmerized by his facial features. She recalled the way he'd looked at her yesterday. His eyes had an intensity about them that she hadn't seen in a very long time. Several times during that first meeting she'd teetered on the urge to run from his office, but he'd seemed so genuine and his gentleness coaxed her through her fierce apprehension. She wouldn't be there otherwise. Of that she was certain.

Occasionally, Oliver's deep voice was loud enough to carry to her outside, presumably also to the man on the other end of the rope. His words were assertive, yet laced with a gentle encouragement.

She wondered what Oliver had thought of all her secrecy. Not that it was important.

She needed her privacy.

Becoming a recluse was much better than risking the same humiliation she'd suffered back in Seattle. Changing her name and moving cities was the only thing that'd kept her sane.

The climber made it look easy. Each movement upward was as smooth as a cat. He shifted lightly on his feet and gave the impression that the tiny lumps he was clinging to were the size of bricks rather than mere finger holds. He scaled at speed, barely pausing from one colorful knob to the next. Based on his swiftness, Holly assumed the man had followed the same route upward dozens of times, and at the top he smashed a bell with his fist and cheered.

She just about yelped when the man fell backwards. But the rope that slithered down the wall caught him, and hand over hand, Oliver lowered him to the padded blue mat. Oliver and the climber high-fived each other and seemed to share a joke.

The last time she'd laughed with Milton flashed into her mind. The two of them and Kane had spent the morning skiing and were on their final run before they planned to stop for lunch. As usual, Kane had been showing off his expert skiing skills and after a moment of egging, challenged his father to a race. She'd never known Milton to back down from a challenge and this was no exception. When Milton had leaned in to kiss her cheek, he'd whispered, "See you in a sec."

Father and son took off in a flurry of powdered snow and colorful jackets, and when they disappeared around a tree-lined corner she pushed off the ledge and skied down behind them. But when she next saw him, Milton was face down in a mound of snow. Her heart had been in her throat as she'd dashed to his side. But it'd all been a ploy. Kane had raced on ahead, which meant Milton and Holly could finish the ski run on their own.

They'd laughed together as she'd flicked the snow from his beard stubble and straightened his beanie. Little did they know that less than four hours later, he'd be dead.

Holly cast the ill-timed memory aside and watched Oliver and the man finish with the climbing apparatus. The man grabbed a pack and the two of them strolled toward the front door. Oliver said goodbye and the man left. If Oliver saw her in the shadows he didn't indicate. Instead, he ambled toward the back of the gym.

She waited a few more minutes, making sure everyone had left, and when Oliver disappeared into his office, she sucked in a huge calming breath and walked out of the shadows.

As if he'd known she was there, Oliver stepped from the room and smiled. "Oh. Hey, Amber."

She still couldn't get used to being called that, but returned his smile all the same.

"Head into my office, I'll just shut the front door." He walked past her and she was surprised at how tall he was. She hadn't realized that yesterday.

41

Or maybe it was because she had on her new gym shoes rather than the three-inch wedges she'd worn when they'd first met.

She settled into a seat in his office and looked around. The side wall was cork-lined, and every inch was covered in photos. Most were of people climbing walls and working out. Beaming smiles were the theme.

"Okay, how did you manage with those forms?" He strolled in and pulled out the chair opposite her.

Holly plucked the paperwork from her pack, unfolded the pages, and pushed them across the table. Oliver scanned his eyes over her responses, his forehead corrugated into a frown as he paused about a third of the way down the page. She had an inkling he'd paused at the previous injuries and ailments section. Holly had answered nil to every one of those questions.

"Looks like you're fit and healthy."

She scrunched up her nose. "Hmmm, I wouldn't say fit."

A grin transformed his face and his eyes twinkled in the florescent light. "That's why you're here, right?"

"Correct."

He signed the bottom of the form, stood, and placed the signature page on the top of the photocopier glass. "Okay, so how do you want to pay?"

Holly cleared her throat. "About that."

He groaned and met her gaze.

"I noticed you have a monthly rate of two hundred dollars for unlimited lessons."

"Group lessons," he clarified.

"Right. Well, what would you consider a fair price if I chose to take the monthly option?"

He blinked at her, maybe trying to understand her worth, or maybe seeing a business side to her he hadn't expected. He finished at the copier, sat back down, and handed the copy to her. "How many nights a week do you anticipate coming?"

"Six."

He burst out laughing. "I love your enthusiasm. But I can't commit to six nights per week."

She huffed out a sigh. "How many nights can you commit to?"

"How about we work on three nights per week to start and reassess in a month's time?"

Holly stewed over his response. But there was really no choice—Brambleton had no other facility like this, and she needed him. "What would your price be for three nights a week?"

"This's fun." He leaned back and folded his arms. "You start."

She frowned. "Start what?"

"The negotiation. You say the first amount."

"Oh, um." She did the math in her head and calculated his casual rate into a monthly figure. It was less than she'd offered yesterday for just one lesson. She felt like a fool, but it was too late to rectify. Getting value for that money was now the priority. She leaned back and copied his move by folding her arms across her chest. "I'm willing to offer five hundred—"

"Done." Oliver slapped his hand on the table and she jumped.

"You're a bit hasty, Mr. Nelson. I haven't stipulated what I *want* for that price."

He offered her a sly grin, and looked to be enjoying this way more than the negotiation warranted. "Okay then, Miss Hope, let's hear your demands."

"I want three nights each week. Monday, Wednesday, and Friday."

"Can't do Wednesday, 'cause I coach my brother's baseball team. Can't do Friday either."

She'd forgotten about his brother's baseball. "What's wrong with Friday night?"

"Friday's drinking night."

She glared at him; he obviously wasn't taking this as seriously. "How about Monday, Tuesday, and Thursday."

"Done." He held his hand forward.

She ignored his hand. "I haven't finished."

"Sorry." He curled back. "Carry on."

She fiddled with her hair, trying to angle it over her burn scar without covering her eye. "I need complete secrecy."

"Interesting… but okay, agreed."

She blinked at him, surprised that he hadn't queried her request. "And I want my equipment included."

He seemed to consider that for a moment. "Okay. But you'll need to buy new shoes."

"These are new shoes." She glanced at her feet.

"I noticed. But they're not good enough."

She cocked her head. "Why not?"

"Believe me, Amber, when you're up that wall, you'll want to feel every inch of those holds. You need as little fabric as possible between the hold you're clinging to and your flesh. If you're as serious as you say you are, then you need proper footwear."

She fought the red flush leaching up her neck and lowered her eyes. "Okay, I understand."

"We sell a range of shoes specifically for rock climbing."

Her heart skipped a beat as the ghastly wounds to her left foot flashed across her mind. It was imperative that he didn't see her feet. Holly's only hope was that her socks would conceal her foot enough to go undetected.

Other than the buzz of the florescent light above, a silence settled over the room. It surprised her that it didn't make her feel awkward. Oliver had a calming quality about him that had her relaxing a little. She met his gaze and had a crazy notion that he knew how important this mission was to her. Which was strange given that they'd known each other for all of ten minutes. "Okay, I'll take a look at your shoes."

"Excellent." He opened his palms as if welcoming her. "Now, I have a few requests."

She raised her eyebrows. "Like what?"

"If you really truly want to learn this, and I think you do, then you need to follow my instructions exactly."

"I will."

"In order to understand how well you're progressing, you need to be honest with me."

"Agreed."

"At all times," he stressed.

"I will."

He trailed his hand across the wooden desk. "Even with the slightest problem."

She looked him square in his hazel eyes. "I said I will."

"Good." He paused, and when he drew his lips into a thin line, she braced for what he was about to say. "You'll also need to tie your hair back."

"What?" she snapped. "Why?"

"Because you don't want it obstructing your view."

She clenched her jaw. The temptation to get up and scurry out was strong. But the image of Dorothy, the elderly woman with the lifetime of sorrow, was stronger. Unclenching her jaw, she held her hand forward. "Do you have a band?"

His bulging eyes indicated he was surprised by her request. Oliver tugged open his top drawer, rummaged through its contents, and pulled out a red rubber band.

She watched his expression as she ran her fingers through her shoulder-length bob, drawing it behind her head. To his credit, he didn't once glance at her cheek.

It felt weird to have her hair up again. Almost every day of the first twenty-four years of her life, Holly had worn her hair in a ponytail. But all that changed when she woke up with the burn scar that spread from her ear to her nose. After months of humiliation, she'd had a hairdresser style her hair in a way that ensured it fell forward, giving her cheek as much coverage as possible.

Oliver clapped his hands together, making her jump again. "Okay, shall we get started?" He stood and waited for her to do the same.

"Do you want my credit card?"

He flicked his hand. "We'll worry about that later. Come on, let me show you the shoes."

Twenty minutes later, she'd succeeded in not removing her socks. She had also committed another hundred and twenty dollars to this crazy venture. But it wasn't crazy. And it wasn't just a venture. It was a mission, and she intended to succeed.

With her new shoes on, Oliver led her to the section of the wall at the back of the building.

"Okay, Amber, this is our beginner wall. It's just ten feet high and, as you can see, we have extra padding at the bottom." He bounced up and down on the mat for emphasis. She looked up the wall and tried to follow the path of the colorful lumps up to the top. There didn't seem to be any kind of pattern.

"These are called holds. Come and have a look at this one, see how your fingers can fit snuggly into here."

She leaned forward to inspect the lump. Sure enough, there was a gap between the fake rock and the wall.

"Go ahead stick your fingers in."

Doing as instructed, she noted how rough the inside of the rock was against her fingertips.

"See how each hold is different? Some are held like this, some like this." Oliver demonstrated how to grip the different colored knobs and then turned to her with a curious gaze that seemed to see right into her mind. "As you climb, you'll learn to use different parts of your feet too."

Again, she glanced up the wall. Her stomach flipped at the idea of hanging off one of those knobs.

"This's your harness. It's your safety device, and it's designed like a chair to help you should you fall." Oliver explained all the aspects of the apparatus. "So step in and I'll show you how it works."

He held the harness open and she had no choice but to hold onto his shoulders and place one leg after the other into the leg loops. Up until this point, Milton was the only man she'd allowed to enter her personal space— except, of course, for the dozens of doctors that'd poked and prodded her body with a clinical approach. The warmth of Oliver's body, so close to hers, sent a flush of heat blazing up her chest and neck.

Yet Oliver was completely at ease as he adjusted the harness on her hips, seemingly unaware of the heatwave bathing between them. "It sits above your hips on your natural waist. See. The harness works both ways, so if you ever flip upside down, it'll catch on your hips."

She gasped. "I can flip upside down?"

"If you want to."

"No. No, I don't want to."

"Okay. Noted." He grinned. "No flipping upside down for Amber."

She frowned at his joke and wondered if she was placing her life in the wrong hands.

"I promise you won't flip upside down." The tenderness in his eyes caught her off guard and she tore her gaze away.

He went on to explain other safety features and spent a significant amount of time explaining and demonstrating the climbers knot.

"Once you show the correct way to tie the knot, you can take your first climb."

"Oh." She tugged her bottom lip into her mouth. He'd demonstrated the knot twice, and although she'd watched, it was technical. Seeds of doubt crept into her brain. A mental debate rolled through her head as she measured out an arm's length of the smooth rope.

What the hell am I doing?

I can do this.

The for-and-against deliberation sucked so much mental ability that she struggled to concentrate.

Oliver may've sensed her ineptitude, because he reached for the rope and showed her where to thread it through. Her breath caught when his fingers skimmed hers. Milton was the only man who'd ever touched her tenderly. Until now. While her heart skipped a few beats at his close proximity, Oliver seemed completely oblivious. She watched his hands, torn between concentrating on what he was doing and appreciating how manly his fingers were.

He pulled the rope tight, signifying the knot was ready, and stepped back, grinning. "Got it."

She nodded and cleared her throat. "I think so."

"Good." He unraveled the knot and handed the rope to her. "Your turn."

As she measured out a sufficient length of rope, the weight of succeeding was like a ton of sand, and she felt every single grain. The test became of life-and-death importance. Given that it was designed to keep her from falling off the wall, maybe it was.

Holly took her time, following the rope around itself to create a double figure eight, and to her surprise it looked right. She tugged on it, securing it tight, then looked up at him.

"Well done. You're ready… but unfortunately time's up."

"What?"

"It's past eight o'clock. Lesson's over."

She clenched her jaw. "I'm paying you to teach me to climb."

He crossed his arms. "I am teaching you to climb. Some things took a bit longer than they were meant to." She had no doubt he was referring to how long she took to tie the climbers knot. "Besides, you haven't actually paid me a cent yet."

"Is that what you're worried about? Payment?"

His eyebrows bounced. "It wasn't. But should I be?"

"No. Don't worry, Mr. Nelson. You'll get your money's worth."

His chest rose and fell with a deep breath, then his shoulders softened. "Look, Amber. I'm sorry, but it really is past eight o'clock, and I'm hungry. I haven't eaten since eleven this morning. We made some real progress today. Next session, we'll have you on the wall within five minutes, I promise."

Unclenching her jaw, she nodded. "Okay, that sounds good."

"Come on, let's get you out of this harness."

He stepped forward and leaned over so close that she placed her hands on his shoulders. As he demonstrated how to release the harness, his breath floated across her neck and her heart thumped out a reckless beat. When the apparatus fell to her feet, she let go of his shoulders, stepped back, and stared up at him, blinking. Holly tried to ignore the butterflies that danced in her stomach when he smiled at her. His tenderness somehow made him seem strong, and she was stunned by how comfortable she felt in his company.

"See? Easy." He looped the rope around his shoulder and elbow and stepped away to hang it on the wall. "Don't worry, I'll show you again on Monday."

She cleared her throat. "May I take some rope home please?"

He turned to her, frowning.

"I'd like to practice."

"Oh, okay, as long as it's not to hang yourself."

Her eyes bulged.

"It was a joke, Amber. Unless..." His eyes drilled into her. "That's something I should worry about."

She bit her tongue, because if he'd asked her that anytime in the last three years, he probably wouldn't have liked her answer.

Not now, though.

Now everything had changed.

KENDALL TALBOT

CHAPTER NINE

Regi knew struggling was pointless, yet he still wrestled against the ropes that kept his wrists restrained behind his back. He'd been in this situation before. Twice. The first time, though, it'd just been a warning. It'd still scared the crap out of him. They'd kept him tied up in a dark shed so long he'd shit his pants. He'd often wondered if that embarrassing moment was why they'd released him without a single bruise.

The second time, after slapping him around a bit, they snapped his pinky finger. He'd never forget the pain, nothing like he'd ever felt before. It never did heal properly, and when his hands were really cold his finger throbbed like a bitch.

This was the third time they'd brought him back to the same empty factory. At least, he assumed it was the same building, given the rotten fish smell. Each time they let him go, they blindfolded him and tossed him out of a moving van like a dead body.

Regi didn't fear for his life. If Carson wanted to kill him, he would've done it already. Carson wanted money. Money that Regi didn't have and would never have.

He accepted that he had to pay off his debt. It'd been over three years since he'd crashed into Carson's Stingray, and he'd been at the man's mercy ever since. Problem was there was no formal arrangement that detailed how the debt was being reduced.

His duties had been as easy as they'd been varied, and on the odd occasion he'd actually considered himself lucky to have crumpled Carson's car. He'd been Carson's chauffer dozens of times. Most often in the middle of the night, when Carson and a scantily clad young woman needed a lift to or from an exclusive engagement. Sometimes the command had been during the day, and Regi had to sneak out of work to perform his duty. One journey had been just three streets in total, and Regi had to crawl out of bed at three in the morning to complete that one. Another had taken hours, and he was pretty sure Carson had received a hand job along the way.

Regi had also played waiter at least a dozen times at Carson's exclusive mansion in Broadmoor, a gated community overlooking Union Bay. Those were the times Regi had felt blessed to have met the man. While he cruised the crowd with trays of drinks and miniature treats, he'd had the pleasure of being extremely close to some of the most beautiful women in the world. Most of them exposed ample cleavage and didn't seem to mind one bit if Regi's eyes wandered.

Problem was, Regi had no idea how much of the debt he'd repaid. He'd started tabling the unpaid work about fourteen months after the crash. Not that it helped. He wouldn't dare voice his tallied total to Carson anyway.

A loud crack and a bolt of light across the concrete floor signaled the opening of a door. He squinted against the glare and noted two men silhouetted against the light.

"Well, if it isn't my old friend Regi the Rat."

Regi recognized the voice: Pope. The man had made Regi his personal punching bag after Regi had triggered his fall in that alley all those years ago. If Regi could turn back one moment in his life, it'd be a strong debate between crashing into Carson's car and dodging Pope's tackle that time.

The blow to his jaw came out of the darkness. Regi's neck snapped with the force and he tasted blood. Carson never did his dirty work. If he did, Regi was certain the blows wouldn't be anywhere near as powerful as Pope's.

He had no idea why they called him Pope. The man was far from a saint.

The second blow burrowed deep into Regi's gut, slamming his breath out of him. He howled at the pain, yet tried to keep focus. If he could see where the punches were coming from, he could prepare. Boxing had taught him how to deflect and how to clench his muscles to diminish the blow. Trouble was, in the dark like this, he had a millisecond to counter the attack. It wasn't long enough, and his body suffered.

"What d'ya want?" Regi spat the words out and they bounced around the empty space.

"Carson wants his money." Pope followed up his demand with a kick to Regi's thigh. The chair toppled and Regi's head slammed onto solid concrete. Stars danced across his eyes, bringing a glittering display to the blackness around him.

He groaned at the pain belting his temple. His hip took the brunt of the fall.

Regi was airborne for a heartbeat as he and the chair were dragged upright again. He shook his head, trying to ward off the fog that threatened to consume him. "I don't have any money."

"Not the right answer." A fist shot through the ray of light and Regi clenched his stomach before the blow connected. It still hurt like hell, but this time it was muscle rather than kidneys.

"I am paying him back." Even to his own ears, his voice sounded shrill, desperate.

"Oh, really? That's interesting, I haven't seen a single dollar from you."

The slap across his face stung like a thousand wasps, and in that instant Regi knew he was never going to be free. He spat a wad of bloody spit and the red globule lit up briefly in the bolt of light. Tears stung his eyes, and he was torn between fighting them back and sobbing like a baby. "Just go ahead and kill me."

"What'd you say?" Pope leaned in close and his rancid breath nearly choked Regi.

Regi was a heartbeat away from head-butting the asshole when Pope pulled back, maybe sensing Regi's thoughts. "Kill me," Regi said. "Just get this shit over with."

"No can do, Regi the Rat."

Regi will never forgive his mother for naming him Reginald Aaron Tate. His initials created an acronym that'd followed him around like a bad smell for as long as he could remember.

Footsteps indicated that a second man had moved behind Regi, and he braced for a blow from behind. Seconds passed. A minute. But nothing happened.

"Mr. Carson has a proposal for you." Pope's voice boomed off the concrete.

Regi swallowed the blood in his mouth. "What?"

"How'd ya like to be debt free?"

KENDALL TALBOT

CHAPTER TEN

When Holly returned home after her first session with Oliver, she used that high to push onto the next step in her crazy plan: learning to ski again. She'd booked the nearest ski resort and planned to drive up on Friday night.

But her strategy to drive to the resort after work had been obliterated by too many lost hours staring at her computer. Her overactive imagination had her riding from one stressful thought about the upcoming weekend to another, and she'd tried to talk herself through the unease by reflecting on how well yesterday's session with Oliver had gone.

It didn't work, though, and she had to ward off a throbbing headache with two Advils.

Unable to put it off a moment longer, and for the first time ever, she shut down her work computer four hours early. Not that it mattered; the unfinished reports were for doctors who didn't apply strict deadlines. They knew she'd get it done as quickly as possible, and that seemed to be sufficient for them. She was the one who put pressure on her work performance. It was another one of those distractions that kept her sane.

Before she changed her mind, she strode to her bedroom, shoved the last bits and pieces into her suitcase, locked up her apartment, lugged the suitcase down to her car, and, with the music blaring from her car's ancient radio, she headed north on the road that divided the town in two.

Since moving to Brambleton, Holly had barely ventured outside her home, let alone beyond the city outskirts. Online shopping had become her norm. In fact, other than going to Upper Limits, the only time she'd had to leave her apartment in the last three months was to collect her mail or post a letter. It was amazing how easy being a recluse was.

She was surprised at how quickly the mountains came into view. Her first peek at the snow in the distance had her heart thumping in her neck and shivers prickling her spine.

According to her research, Altitude Mountain Resort was just a ninety-minute drive from her apartment, but each mile she crossed had her questioning what the hell she was doing. At every turn in the road, the instinct to turn back was like forked lightning in her brain. The forks shot off in two opposing directions: one saying she should be at home hiding and the other saying, damn it, she had to do this.

She never thought she'd return to snow again.

A vision permanently etched into her memory zipped across her brain. She was on her back, looking up at sheer ice peppered with charred helicopter debris. A jagged gash of blue sky ran through the middle of the icy walls, and plumes of her ragged breath punched out of her, clouding her vision. It was the very moment she'd realized she was all alone, deep in an ice crevice. It was the moment she'd accepted that she was going to die.

But she didn't die.

Somehow, she'd survived the nightmare.

Her mind flashed to the frozen lovers. Maybe they were the reason. And Dorothy, the elderly woman, desperate to prove her son's innocence.

Was this her destiny? She chuckled at that stupid concept.

But whatever it was… she'd started this quest now. And as ridiculous as it sounded, it was something she had to do. Holly clenched the steering wheel harder, cranked up the music, and helped Robbie Williams realize how much life he had running through his veins.

The song couldn't have been timelier. Holly had been trapped in her home for so long, she'd forgotten what it was like to breathe fresh air. She wound down her window and allowed the wind to whip her hair back. But a minute later, the cold breeze nearly had her ear snapping off and she reversed that decision.

She turned up the heater and fought with the windshield defogger as the car began its climb up the mountain. Dirty snow lined the black asphalt that cut a snaking path upward. Halfway up, tiny snowflakes began to hit the windshield and the wipers swiped them away with a noisy screech. The grating noise reminded her that she needed to get the twenty-year-old car in for a service soon. But that would require leaving home. She didn't leave home.

Unless it was for a quest to save two people who were already dead.

The absurdity of it hit her square in the chest when she arrived at the ski resort parking lot. On the drive up the mountain, snow-laden Douglas firs had blocked her view skyward. Not now, though. Not in the resort parking lot. The vista beyond the resort was supposed to be breathtaking. But not in the way Holly felt it. The mountain loomed, like a giant white monster about to devour the building and everyone in it.

She'd already been swallowed by a mountain once.

Sucking in a shaky breath, she counted to five and let it out in a huge huff.

But her brain was a frozen vault that'd trapped snapshots of her nightmare, and when she wasn't vigilant, they'd haunt her. They came back now. Ice. Blood. Bodies. Ten images. Twenty. Flickering like a faulty video.

Squeezing her eyes shut, she clenched her fists, plonked her head on the steering wheel, and rode out the onslaught. Her therapist had taught her this technique. Instead of fighting the barrage, she'd go with it. Eventually the images would stop and she'd still be there and nothing would have changed.

Facing her fear. That's what Dr. Andrews had call it.

Today's fear was dominating the windshield: the snow-covered mountain.

Her windows had completely fogged out her view by the time she peeled her fingers off the steering wheel. "I can do this. I am Amber Hope, and I can do this!"

Mentally repeating the mantra, she opened the door and stepped from the car. Four layers of clothing did little to stop the frigid air from seeping into her bones. It was like liquid mercury, leaching in, aching. Especially the bones she'd broken. They seemed to have their own gauges for cold and warm.

Furious that she hadn't thought to bring gloves, she tucked her hands into her pockets, put her head down, and aimed for the resort's stone steps. Halfway across the asphalt, her feet slipped on ice, and she only just managed to stay upright. With her hands out sideways, she made it unscathed, and at the top of the steps she pushed through the door.

She entered a large wood-lined room with a high vaulted cedar ceiling. A fireplace, nestled into an enormous hexagonal-shaped stone chimney, was the center of the room. In front of the fire, a man and a woman, occupying two overstuffed chairs, glanced her way, but only fleetingly before turning their attention back to the fire. Holly welcomed the warmth, yet her fingers maintained a painful throb that she attempted to massage away.

As she rubbed life back into her hands, she fought the anxiety mushrooming in her brain and walked toward the reception desk that spread the length of the far wall.

The young woman beamed at her. "Good afternoon. Welcome to Altitude, heaven at the top of the world." Her eyes bounced to the burn scar on Holly's cheek and her jaw dropped a fraction.

Holly should have expected this, but she'd been so worried about the mountain, she hadn't given any thought to her scar. A chunk of her resolve snapped off at the woman's reaction. It was a jolt. It always was. It was like her brain had her remembering what she used to look like, and then a complete stranger would bring that reality crashing into focus.

Holly flicked her hair forward, attempting to dislodge the woman's lingering gaze. "I'm Amber Hope. I'm checking in for two nights."

"Okay, let me get your paperwork." When she strolled to a table at the back, Holly studied the giant schematic that detailed the mountain, resort, and facilities that adorned the wall behind her. According to the diagram, Sienna Mountain, where Altitude Lodge was situated, had a highest peak of just nine thousand three hundred feet. The mountain where she'd lost Milton was nearly thirteen thousand feet high.

She pictured the mountain, with its dueling monoliths and shark fin peak, and a shudder rumbled through her. The temptation to turn around and run was crippling. She gripped the counter instead, determined not to give that thought any more attention.

"Oh, Miss Hope, you're going to be so happy." The young lady's voice lured Holly away from the black hole she'd tumbled into. "You're staying in the best chalet on the mountain." She gazed at Amber with a look of expectation.

"Thank you."

"Have you been here before?"

She shook her head. "First time."

"Wonderful. And I see you've also booked for ski lessons." She rummaged behind the counter, then placed a large white envelope on the counter. "Here's your welcome pack that'll explain everything." The woman placed a map on the counter and drew a line from the admin building to Amber's private chalet and explained where to park. Using her pen, she pointed out other significant aspects of the resort.

"Thank you." Holly clutched the envelope to her chest.

"You're welcome. If you need anything once you get to your chalet, you can call me by dialing number nine on your phone."

"Okay, thanks." Holly turned and braced for the cold as she stepped from the building. Her teeth were chattering by the time she slipped back behind the steering wheel. Her mother's old car coughed to life, and she followed the map to her chalet.

Five minutes later she parked in her designated space and, leaving all her luggage for later, she went to investigate her accommodation.

As they had offered when she'd made the reservation, the fire had already been ignited, and the flames spilled warmth and light into the cabin. Holly drifted from room to room like she'd fallen into a fairy tale. Whoever had decorated the chalet had an obsessive attention to detail and, unlike her home, trinkets and art adorned nearly every surface. It was quaint, tasteful, and perfectly suited the alpine setting. Her bedroom was located up a narrow set of stairs, in an open-air loft that was positioned over the lounge. She could look over the balcony to the area below, where heat from the fireplace radiated upward.

After retrieving her suitcase and unpacking her things, and sipping a glass of wine by the fire to settle her nerves, she pulled on her gym shoes, dressed in her four layers of clothing, and braced to step back outside.

A brilliant spectrum of citrus colors bounced off the low-lying clouds, and the setting sun had the sky looking like it was on fire. Holly locked the door, shoved her hands in her pockets, and stepped onto the snow. The white powder crunched beneath her feet as she made her way toward the village center.

When she arrived at the main building, the subzero temperature had her exhaling into the frigid air and pushing through the glass door without any hesitation. Two things hit her like slaps to the face: the warmth, and the abundance of people inside. Dozens of them. She'd expected to see people, but never this many.

The temptation to flee was so strong, an instant headache nipped behind her eyes. She stepped back and bumped right into someone. "Sorry." Gasping, she spun around and her eyes met a broad chest. She looked up.

The man was tall and beautiful, and he radiated youth and life and everything she didn't. His eyes leapt to her scar and away again in a nanosecond. "It's okay." He patted her shoulder, moved around her, and walked away.

Her feet were frozen. Her brain was too.

The reality of her mission sunk in. She was in a room full of strangers. Strangers who were likely to stare at her wounds with a variety of reactions. Living like a recluse had done two things: limited her exposure to strangers and amplified her response to their reactions.

But if she was going to do this, really truly do this mission to save Dorothy and bring closure to those people in the ice, then she needed to forget about her stupid embarrassment.

With hands curled into fists, she urged her brain to come to a conclusion.

Realizing that people were starting to look at her standing frozen in the doorway, she gulped down the indecision along with a bucketload of dread, unfurled her fists, and forced her feet to move.

To her right was a large store that sold clothing and equipment. A general store was beside that, and an equipment rental place was next. Two restaurants and a bar made up the left-hand side of the building. The bulk of the crowd noise was coming from those areas.

Centered in the middle of it all was a circular information desk with three staff members standing behind it. She headed that way. On her approach she adjusted her hair over her cheek and tilted her face so it stayed there.

"Hello, can I help you?" The young lady who spoke had long blond plaits that fell from her fluffy pink beanie. Her eyes were bright, her cheeks were flushed, and she was stunning enough to be the January model in an annual ski-bunny calendar. Holly couldn't remember ever meeting a woman so beautiful.

"Oh, um, hi," she stuttered. "Um, my name is Amber Hope, and I have lessons booked for tomorrow."

"Oh, hi, Amber. I'm Kelli. I'm your instructor. It's so nice to meet you." Kelli offered her hand, and when Amber shook it, the woman's grin made her model looks legendary. "Follow me. We'll get your gear sorted."

Together they walked toward the equipment rental shop. "So, this's your first time here? You're going to love it. We've had some fabulous snow over the last three days, so you have perfect conditions." Kelli carried on talking until they reached a rack of padded jackets that lined the wall. "You need all the equipment, right?" She pulled a red jacket off a hanger.

"Yes, I don't have anything."

"Oh, that's a nasty scar on your cheek. How'd you get that?"

Kelli's brazenness punched the wind out of Amber. No stranger had ever been so direct before. Her hand automatically went up to the raised lumps lining her cheek. "I—um, had an accident a few years ago."

"Wow, you poor thing. Must've hurt like hell."

Amber nodded. However, ironically, it'd barely hurt. Not compared to her other injuries anyway. She could vividly recall the moment the red-hot metal had hit her cheek. The chunk from the wreckage was on her flesh for just seconds, yet it'd been long enough to cause third-degree burns that'd killed her nerve endings in a flash.

Kelli handed Amber a jacket and a pair of padded pants. "These will fit; try them on if you like." She led the way to the change room, chatting nonstop about anything that popped into her brain.

Once the clothing was sorted, they moved to the equipment rental. "Have you skied before?" Kelli flicked her right braid over her shoulder.

"Yes, but only a few times, and it was a few years ago."

"Alrighty, well, I'll have you back up to speed before the weekend's over."

Amber didn't hold the same optimism. Especially since she couldn't shake the sense of dread snaking into her thoughts.

Fifty minutes after walking into the building, Amber had her clothing and ski equipment organized, and Kelli hadn't stop yakking the whole time. But after the initial bewilderment, Amber had found the young woman's flippancy refreshing. It'd been a long time since she'd had idle chitchat with someone face-to-face. Way too long.

Amber put her gear in a locker but kept her clothing with her. She shoved on her new gloves and beanie.

"Right," Kelli said once they were finished. "I'll meet you here tomorrow morning at nine. Does that work?"

"Sounds good."

"Excellent. And don't forget sunscreen. You can get pretty burnt up here. Oh," she giggled. "Not as bad as that, of course." She bulged her eyes at Amber's cheek.

Amber tensed at the callous comment, but as she studied Kelli's face, she realized that she'd meant no malice whatsoever. Kelli simply spoke her mind without any thought to the consequences.

It was going to be an interesting weekend.

Amber returned to her chalet and heated up one of the precooked meals she'd brought with her. Later, after two glasses of wine, she crawled into bed, and the crackle and pop of the fire below lulled her to sleep with a promise of peaceful dreams.

She woke the next morning with two burning questions frying her brain: the first asked if finding those bodies in the ice really was her destiny, and the second questioned if she could actually go through with her crazy mission.

They were stupid questions, really. Questions she couldn't answer.

But as she rolled out of bed and into a hot shower, she realized she could answer one of them. It was just going to take everything she had to go through with it.

After a quick breakfast, she donned her ski clothing and walked out her door. As she crossed the distance from her chalet to the village center, a line of children skied past, following a young man who sashayed effortlessly from side to side. The kids couldn't be any older than ten, yet they handled the slope like experts.

The warmth of the main building was almost suffocating. She zipped open her jacket and pulled off her beanie and gloves as she strolled toward the information counter. Kelli popped up from behind the desk, saw Amber, and smiled. Kelli's long hair fell in a blond cascade over her shoulders and back, and somehow, she looked even more beautiful than she had yesterday.

"Hey, you're here. Glad I didn't scare you off with all my jabbering. You'll have to get used to it. My dad calls it 'verbal diarrhea.' But what would he know?" She giggled. "Hey, Erik, here's the girl I was telling you about." She tapped the shoulder of the man behind her, and when he spun toward them, Amber was flustered beyond blinking. Erik looked like he'd stepped from the set of an action movie. Chiseled jaw, molasses eyes, perfect three-day growth, hair that flicked in all the right directions. "Check out her scar." Kelli's statement shattered Amber's veneer and her legs teetered.

"Show him, Amber," she insisted. "He didn't believe me."

In a stiff reluctant movement, she tilted her head to the model-like couple.

He whistled. "Holy shit, that's *way* worse than mine." Erik seemed impressed, thrusting Amber into whole new territory.

"I told you." She turned to Amber. "Erik's got a scar on his ass. He likes to show it off."

"Only to sweet cakes like you." He beamed a brilliant smile at Kelli.

"Yeah, yeah." Kelli rolled her eyes and came out from behind the counter. "Come on, let's get your gear and go have some fun." She reached for Amber's arm, leaving her no time to analyze what'd just happened. Kelli hugged her so close their hips bounced together as she led Amber to her locker. "Let's get you changed and go hit the snow."

She talked nonstop about all sorts of trivial things, like how good the coffee was here compared to the resort she'd worked at in New Zealand, and how bloated her mother's ankles were now that she'd given up tennis. Amber had no hope of navigating Kelli's conversational direction.

Amber's boots were firm, mid-shin high, and had her leaning at such an awkward angle that when she tried to stand she reached to Kelli for support. That simple move had a long-forgotten memory fluttering into her mind: a happier time, when Milton was helping her into ski boots. They'd laughed themselves silly as they'd clomped together, hand-in-hand toward the snow.

"Feels weird, huh?" Kelli plucked Amber from her rare cheerful recollection. "Don't worry, you'll get used to it. It's designed to propel you forward. Okay, put your beanie on, grab your poles, and let's go."

Kelli clutched both their skis and walked ahead in her boots with ease. Amber, however, stomped like she was wearing four-gallon drums that'd been set with concrete. Once on the snow, Kelli led her to a fenced-off area to the side of the central complex. Amber was already exhausted by the time she got there. It was going to require some serious mental focus to get her body through this. She visualized Dorothy and decided that the elderly woman's mournful image would be the inspiration to get her through. She just hoped like hell she wouldn't let her down.

The next couple of hours were consumed by Kelli demonstrating the basics. Clipping in and out of her skis. How to go. Stop. Turn. Walking sideways up a hill. And, of course, how to get up when she fell over. Which she had no doubt she'd do.

"Ready to give it a try?"

"Oh." Kelli had caught her off guard. The first rock climbing lesson she'd had with Oliver had been all theory, and Amber had assumed this would be the same. "Do you think I'm ready?"

"Of course, you're a natural." Now she knew Kelli was lying. "Come on."

Kelli led the way, gliding her skis across the snow with ease. Amber had no hope of speeding up; she was too busy concentrating on keeping upright. Kelli chitchatted the whole time she led her toward the chairlift, and Amber learned that Kelli's childhood home was in San Diego. That she ran away from home at seventeen and it'd been the best and worst decision she'd ever made. And that she'd lost her virginity in a cemetery. When she saw Amber's jaw-dropping reaction to that titbit, Kelli doubled over laughing. "I love telling that story. It's true by the way."

Amber had no doubt.

She was certain they were going to ski right on past the lift, until Kelli stepped in line with all the other skiers.

"Give me your poles." Kelli indicated for Amber to slip in beside her.

Amber's heart thumped in her neck as she handed over the sticks. She wasn't ready. But then people fell in behind them, capturing Amber in the middle of the crowd, and there was no backing out, not even if she wanted to.

Kelli seemed to know everyone, and not just the staff. The people in front. The people behind. Everyone was laughing, having fun. "Show them your scar," Kelli said, grinning at her.

Amber had been so caught up in Kelli's entertaining banter, she scowled at Kelli's request.

"Oh, sorry." Kelli slapped her hand over her mouth like it was the only way to stop her talking.

But with everyone looking her way, Holly had no choice. She inwardly cringed as she tilted her head to give those who wanted it a better view. After a variety of comments, most of them stating how much it must have hurt, they all seemed to lose interest as quickly as they'd started.

Kelli touched her elbow, indicating their turn to shuffle forward. "I shouldn't have done that, right? You don't like to draw attention?"

Amber shook her head. "No. I don't."

"I'm sorry. I'm a ditz like that. Don't be mad at me. Verbal diarrhea, remember?" She put her arm across Amber's shoulder and pulled her in for a hug. "Sorry."

"It's okay." She had no idea what else to say.

Every shuffle toward the spinning turnstile had Amber's knees trembling more. With each rotation the chair swung around the terminal, she studied each skier's process to mount the seat. Couple after couple repeated the process, progressing them farther in line. The pair in front jumped on and took off in an easy, practiced movement, and the moment they were gone Kelli grabbed Amber's hand and dragged her forward. "Place your skis on this line and turn so you can see the chair coming. Quick."

Amber followed her instructions, and had no choice but to fall onto the chair as it pushed into the back of her legs. Moments later her skis left the ground, and Kelli lowered the safety bar as they cruised up the mountain.

Kelli raised her mask onto her forehead, pushing her blond waves back from her face. "Having fun?"

A chill ran up Holly's spine as she realized Kelli had just spoken exactly the same words Milton had said before the helicopter crashed. It was the last thing he'd ever said to her. She hadn't recalled that until now. And no, she wasn't having fun then, and she wasn't having fun now. Realizing Kelli was expecting an answer, she decided to say the truth.

"Actually, I'm petrified."

Kelly tapped Amber's thigh twice and grinned. "No need to be. I'm going to be with you the whole time. I promise you'll have fun." She pulled her mirrored mask back into position and Amber snapped her eyes away. Milton had been wearing mirrored glasses too.

Amber hoped Kelli's promise was one she could keep.

Below them, dozens of people swished from side to side on their skis and snowboards. Some kicked up powder in their wake. They made it look graceful as they glided down the steep slope. The dark mountain looming on the horizon had as much black rock as pure white snow on its peak, and Amber was cast back to the last image she'd had of the mountain in Canada before the helicopter crashed. The blade of rock shaped like a shark's fin would be forever etched in her brain.

The chair bumped over one of the towers, making her jump, and she clamped her gloved hands over the safety bar, strangling it as they continued their journey upward.

"I really am sorry." Kelli touched Amber's thigh.

"It's okay."

"You know what? You should be proud of that scar."

Amber's eyebrows shot up. "What? Why?"

"'Cause it shows you've been through something horrific, yet here you are, getting out, enjoying life. Not everyone bounces back like that."

Amber huffed at the absurdity of her comment. She had not bounced back. It'd been more like crawling through a pit of sewerage, bumping shit at every opportunity. But... she *had* made it through the medical miracle and, despite all the odds against her, she'd learned to walk again. Maybe there was some truth in Kelli's insight. She glanced over at the stunning young woman. "It's embarrassing," she finally said.

"Why? Bullshit. If you'd done it to yourself, that'd be embarrassing. But what happened to you wasn't your fault." She paused and frowned. "Was it?"

Holly's heart spiked. For years Victoria and her tribe of ardent followers had blamed her for Milton and Kane's deaths. And it didn't matter how many times Dr. Andrews had assured her she wasn't responsible; the poisonous seeds of guilt needled their way in anyway. Realizing Kelli was expecting an answer, she faked a chuckle. "Of course not."

"Right. Then, so like I said, be proud of that scar. Oh, here we go, we're coming up to the top now." Kelli lifted the safety bar and explained the process for disembarking the ski chair.

The steep incline leveled out and the ground rose up fast. Amber's skis touched, the chair slowed, Kelli stood, and Amber forced her body to do the same.

Seconds later, she became a tangle of arms and legs. One ski snapped off and she sprawled face-first across the trampled ice. An alarm sounded, the lift shunted to a halt, and the chair swung over Amber's head. Kelli chuckled and glided over to help her stand. She grabbed her wayward ski and led Amber aside, out of the chairlift's path.

"Yay, you've got your first stack out of the way! Now you can relax because you know it doesn't hurt. The first one's always the scariest, right?"

Amber rolled her eyes. She'd never met anyone as painfully positive as Kelli.

"Clip your ski on, we've gotta get down this mountain now."

"Great," Amber groaned.

"It sure is."

Kelli glided over to the side and turned to watch Amber. "You're doing so well."

"Yeah right!" Amber cocked her head and gave a you've-got-to-be-joking look.

"You are." She chuckled. "Are you always such a negative Nelly?"

Once again, Amber had no idea how to respond. In a heartbeat, the young woman could flit from insensitive to blindingly insightful. And each one was as shocking as the other.

She made it to Kelli's side and they stopped to admire the view at the edge of the slope. Spruce trees loaded with white powder lined the sweeping slope and the sun was a giant white ball high in the sky. Amber remembered she'd forgotten to apply sunscreen, and she didn't know whether the biggest problem with that was getting sunburnt or Kelli learning of her mistake. She decided not to mention it.

Kelli stepped in front of Amber. "Okay, get your feet into the snowplow position, just like I showed you."

Amber slipped her heels apart, forming her skis into a triangle, and they tilted over the edge. It was awkward and uncomfortable but thankfully slow. Backward and forward they went, working on Amber's technique. Kelli was very patient and as the sun crept slowly over the towering trees, they progressed from one ski lesson to the next. Amber was surprised when the village center came into view; she hadn't realized they'd made it down the ski run.

Her body did, though. Her muscles were aching as much as her bones were by the time she clipped out of her skis for the last time that day.

Kelli helped Amber back to her locker, and after arranging a time to meet again in the morning, she hugged Amber in a way that indicated they'd become inseparable. The warmth of her embrace had Amber choking back tears. She hadn't been hugged by a person who'd moved her so much in years.

Kelli placed her hand on Amber's arm. "Remember, be proud of that scar. It shows how strong you are. Oh, and don't forget how impressed Erik was. Guys dig scars." She winked and spun on her heel, leaving Amber to watch the young blonde bound away, waving at anyone who caught her eye.

Kelli's parting comment had her both confused and elated, and a smile simmered on her lips.

Amber had brought enough food with her to eat alone in her chalet. It was her preferred choice of eating. Alone. In private. But capitalizing on the good vibes coursing through her, she let the aromas of coffee and melted cheese lure her to the restaurant.

She ordered a vegetarian risotto and a glass of wine and found a table at the window. Alone with her thoughts, she replayed Kelli's parting comment. Should she be proud of her scars? That was a new one. Not once had she considered that anyone would find it impressive. Although Erik had certainly seemed impressed. Either that, or he was an exceptional actor.

She'd never considered herself strong either. Surviving that crash had nothing to do with strength—if it had, Milton and Kane would've survived. Her survival was dumb luck.

In fact, Amber was the epitome of weak. A reclusive, twenty-eight-year-old, single woman, who changed her name rather than face her fears.

She was light-years away from being strong. Kelli had misjudged her.

Sighing, she studied the view that spanned the entire southern face of the mountain. Four chairlifts snaked their way upward, and she followed the one she'd traveled today from bottom to top. At the top, the blue sky was dotted with a few fluffy white clouds and the sun bounced off the snow, making it glisten like crystals.

It was a perfect postcard setting that could fool anyone into believing it was harmless.

She had firsthand experience at how quickly that could change.

CHAPTER ELEVEN

Oliver glanced at the clock and noted Amber was ten minutes late. Two minutes later she entered his office. "Oh, hey, Amber." He glanced at the clock for emphasis. "You're a bit late today."

"Actually, I've been waiting out front." She blinked a few times and he had a feeling she wanted to retract the statement.

"Huh? Why?"

She lowered her eyes. "I was waiting for everyone to leave."

"Oh right." He clicked his fingers. "Absolute secrecy."

"Are you mocking me, Mr. Nelson?"

"Of course not." He cleared his throat and stood. "You ready to climb?"

"Yes."

She'd remained standing in the doorway, but as he approached, she backed away. Amber was either incredibly nervous or she was terribly afraid. Either way, it wasn't pleasant to witness. He offered her what he hoped was a comforting smile. "Okay, let's get started." He turned and aimed for the beginner's wall at the back of the gym. "Did you practice the climber knot?"

"Yes."

"Good, let's see how it went." While she put her bag down and zipped out of her jacket, he went to fetch a climbing harness from the equipment room. By the time he returned she'd pulled her hair back and was tying a rope into a climber's knot. When she finished, she held it up for inspection.

It was perfect. "Hey, well done."

A small smile curled at her lips. Progress.

"Okay, let's see if you remembered the harness details." He handed her the harness and she loosened the clips, but as she went to step in, she winced.

"Oh, are you okay?"

"Yes." She clenched her jaw, and he was certain she was fighting back pain as she stepped into the leg loops. Amber pulled the harness to her waist and tugged the belt tight. He handed her the belay rope from the wall, and within a minute she'd tied a perfect double eight climbers knot. When she glanced up at him, her expression was a baffling mixture of uncertainty and pride.

"Fantastic, let's get you up that wall."

He stepped into his own harness and passed the opposite end of her rope into the belay device. "Okay, I want you to see this." He explained how the belay device worked. "So trust me, no matter what happens once you're on the wall, you can't fall. Okay?"

She nodded and her eyes traveled from him to the wall. He not only sensed her nervousness, he noticed her trembling. Once again, he questioned her motivation. She wasn't anything like his usual demographic. Amber was tiny, not just in height but in body mass too. He'd say she was undernourished. She seemed feeble. Her wrists and fingers were delicate. Her frame was slender. But none of that mattered. It was her obvious anxiety that was concerning.

Nobody *needed* to learn rock climbing.

He cast the troubling observations aside and demonstrated the basic technique by climbing a couple of the holds on the wall himself. "Okay, your turn. Now remember, if you fall, I've got you."

Again, she nodded without saying anything.

He stepped back and shortened the slack on the rope as Amber approached the wall. She paused there for a moment, sucked in a huge breath, and then let it out slowly. When she went to reach up for her first hold, he heard her flinch again.

"Are you okay?" He repeated his early question.

"Yes, I'm good." She put her other arm up and again winced when she raised her foot to the first hold. But whatever the pain was that'd evoked the groans from her, it didn't stop her progression up the wall.

"You're doing so well, Amber. I'm impressed." He meant every word. He'd seen many, many clients fly up these walls without any thought to what hold they'd reach for next. Amber, on the other hand, paused often and studied the way before she made her next choice.

She was halfway up the wall when he called up to her, "Okay, Amber, I want you to let go."

"What?" She pressed her body against the wall as if trying to hug it.

"I want to demonstrate how you get down, before you get too far up."

"Why?" Her voice was borderline shrill.

"Because I've had many clients who get to the top easily enough, but then they're too petrified to let go once they get there. Many of them opt to climb down instead. Trust me, climbing down is much harder than going up, because you can't see the holds properly."

She squealed and released without warning. Oliver caught her in the belay and she spun in lazy circles as he lowered her to the mat. Most people announced when they were going to let go. Her decision to jump showed a dangerous recklessness that he hadn't expected.

She placed her feet on the padded mat. "I made it." For the first time, she was smiling. It changed her appearance dramatically, and Oliver saw a truly stunning woman beneath the troubled facade.

She beamed. "Can I do it again?"

"Of course."

This time she approached the wall with zero hesitation. She did, however, wince again as she raised each limb to climb. Just like her first time, each step was taken with measured control. She studied each move, and once she seemed to have made her decision, she committed to it fully.

He let her get right to the top this time. "Hit the bell."

She didn't just hit the bell, she slammed it with her fist. Again, she let go of the wall without warning and Oliver silently admonished himself for not instructing her on the safety protocol.

He lowered her to the ground and her beautiful smile was even broader. "Again?"

"Sure. Hey, this time, just let me know before you let go."

"Why? You going to drop me?" The twinkle in her eyes was the first sign of mischief he'd seen from her, and he liked what he saw.

"No, but it's a good safety step to follow."

"Okay." She nodded. "Makes sense."

Amber stepped to the wall, and as she crawled up this time, he noticed that she took exactly the same holds as the previous two times. She'd memorized the route. There were dozens of different options to take a climber to the top, and memorizing wasn't an easy task. He was so impressed that all the original apprehension of taking on Amber as a climber had now vanished.

Her one-hour lesson went quickly and Oliver was disappointed when it came to an end. When he lowered her to the ground for the last time, he touched her shoulder. "Okay, that's it for today."

She seemed as disappointed as he was.

"You did fantastic. We'll move along the wall tomorrow night."

She nodded. "Okay, sounds good. Is there anything I can practice at home?"

He frowned at her. This sense of urgency was as mysterious as it was strange. "Um, I guess you could watch a few YouTube videos on climbing techniques."

"Okay, I'll do that." She stepped out of the harness, handed it to him, then pulled her hair from the band and tousled it forward. "Would you like to charge my credit card now?"

He snapped his fingers. "Good idea." He'd completely forgotten about that, which was strange. Getting money from people was usually one of his main business focuses.

After they finished the payment process, he walked her to the door. "See you tomorrow night."

"Thank you."

Oliver watched her walk up the street and was surprised when she didn't get into a car. He locked the door, returned to his office, and pulled her paperwork from his folder.

Amber Hope. He checked her address. She lived right in the center of town. Again, he questioned who she was. He was pretty certain she was new to Brambleton; he would've recognized her if not. Oliver was a social guy, and there weren't too many parties he missed. She'd never been to any of them.

He fired up his computer and typed "Amber Hope" into Google. Besides an interior designer in New Zealand and an Amber Hope in Illinois who looked nothing like the Amber he knew, there was no record of her. He didn't know whether that was normal or not; he'd never googled anyone before.

Out of curiosity, he typed his own name into the prompt. He was listed several times. His business was detailed, and he was mentioned for being coach of his kid brother's baseball team, which won the championship last year. There were plenty of photos too, most of them rock climbing related. None of it was surprising, but still... he was visible.

He typed in her name again, just to be sure. But there was nothing.

It gave him a terrible feeling she was hiding something. Or from someone.

CHAPTER TWELVE

It had been two weeks since Holly had first walked into Upper Limits, and she realized that the mental battle to leave her apartment was no longer nauseating. Between Oliver and the staff at the ski resort, Holly had met more people in the last two weeks than she had the entire year.

She hadn't realized how much she'd missed being with people. But that wasn't her only revelation… she'd come to enjoy her workouts too. Not only was she feeling better, but she was sleeping better too.

Instead of dragging her feet to Upper Limits, Holly arrived much earlier than she needed, just so she could watch Oliver in the shadows. But it wasn't just her joy over the rock climbing that surprised her—she enjoyed being with Oliver. He was fun and funny and laughed a lot. She found herself looking forward to his smiles. Each one was a dose of elixir that relaxed her. He had a kindness that made her feel safe, even when she was a dozen feet in the air.

It was so lovely to admit that.

Oliver had eased to the side wall with one of his clients, who she recognized as one of the regulars, and the two of them seemed to be having an in-depth conversation. His brows drilled together, and when he placed his hand on the man's shoulder, his concern was touching. Yet even as they continued chatting, Oliver still managed to say goodbye to each patron that walked past.

He seemed to know everyone. Holly reflected on the gym she'd frequented back in Seattle. Despite going there for nearly three years, she was pretty sure most of the trainers hadn't known her name. Until it was a headline in the papers, that is.

That flashback was the jolt she needed to remind herself that she was Amber Hope. *Amber Hope.* She repeated the name over and over as she waited for everyone to leave Oliver's gym.

Once all of his clients had gone, Oliver disappeared into his office and she waited a minute or two before she entered the building. Oliver stepped from the doorway, and she had a funny feeling he somehow knew she'd arrived. He gave her a smile that seemed so genuine an unexpected rush of familiarity blossomed within her. It was like they'd known each other forever. No, not just known each other—it was like they knew every little intimate detail about each other. It was such an intense feeling that Holly had to convince herself that they'd known each other for barely seven hours.

Oliver didn't even know her real name.

As he strolled toward her, her heart skipped a beat over the unfounded feeling he was about to lean in and kiss her. Instead, he touched her shoulder and walked right past. "I'll just shut the door."

Furious at her foolishness, she tugged her hair back into a hairband that'd been on her wrist and strode for the line of harnesses hanging on the wall. She plucked one off the hook and as she adjusted it to fit, she used the distraction to force any more irrational ideas from her mind.

She had a mission to do. And she was a long, long way from achieving that goal.

Oliver stepped up to her. "How was your day?"

She shrugged. "Same as usual. How about you?"

His quizzical expression indicated he wanted more from her answer, but after a moment's pause, he sighed. "Not too bad for a Tuesday." He reached for her rope and hooked it into his belay device.

Holly had become the master at brief responses, and she was sure Oliver was growing tiresome over her minimal banter. But she had secrets to keep. Lots of them. By not engaging in conversation, she was less likely to mess up.

No matter what, she could never reveal her identity. Nobody—not Oliver, not Kelli, not anyone—would ever have the opportunity to rummage through the wreckage of her past life.

Secrecy was paramount to her mental survival too. By assuming the identity of Amber Hope, she'd officially buried Holly Parmenter, along with all her rotten baggage.

At least that's what her therapist had said.

Besides, she had a job to do.

Forcing the tumbling thoughts from her brain, she stepped up to the wall, placed her fingers into the nearest hold, and wriggled her right foot into position. "Climber ready."

"Up you go then."

The gloomy nuance in Oliver's reply ignited a flame of guilt in her mind. It was raw. It was justified, and it hurt like hell. She used that fire to drive her limbs. With a clenched jaw and dogged determination, she clawed her way upward. Her breath shot in and out in ragged breaths as her arms and legs pushed on. Adrenaline coursed through her veins unchecked, giving her the now familiar rush of the challenge.

She didn't pause this time. She didn't look down.

Her concentration was on gripping one hold after the other and moving upward. She arrived at the top so fast it shocked her, and she cheered as she slammed her fist onto the bell. "Releasing," she called out, and a heartbeat later she leaned into the harness and Oliver gently lowered her to the padded mat.

"Good work." He looped the rope as he approached her. "That was your fastest climb yet." He placed his hand on her shoulder and her brain swam with reckless intoxication when she inhaled his musky scent.

She stepped back and wanted to slap herself. His smile was so genuine, so real, that he seemed as proud of her achievement as she was. "Thank you." A pleasant flush of triumph washed through her, but before she did something silly, she dragged her gaze away from Oliver's stunning eyes.

Oliver was a nice guy, and the brutal reality was that she was confusing his professional attention with affection. Yet despite accepting that her confusion was justified, she still had to fight the blaze of heat curling up her neck.

She'd survived a tornado of life changing events that'd ripped everything she'd loved from her grasp. Top that with her reclusive lifestyle and nearly zero personal contact and she'd created her very own perfect storm.

It was a storm that she needed to quell before she'd be forced to lock herself away from the world all over again.

* * * *

Regi adjusted his rearview mirror and tried to ignore his pounding heart. His fingers strangled the steering wheel. He turned to look out his side window at his opponent. Pope's grin was that of the devil. His stubble gave the lower half of his face a dark stain, his teeth were yellowed and crooked, and his thick black eyebrows cast a shadow over coal-black eyes. But it was Pope's I'm-gonna-kill-you glare that'd have any sane person running in the opposite direction.

But Regi wouldn't run. Not this time.

As he experienced that glare for the hundredth time, Regi wondered how he'd got himself into this situation. Although for the first time in years, he was finally doing something that'd get him out of his mess.

According to Pope's proposal, if Regi won this race, he'd be debt free. If he lost, he'd owe twice as much. Double or nothing. Losing was not an option, and Regi planned on putting everything he had into this race. He'd done some illegal street racing in his teens. But that'd been in beaten-up old cars on a dirt track.

This was very, very different.

The car Carson had given him to drive was worth at least a hundred grand. The Audi R8 was powerfully engineered and took to the road like an animal that was born to run. He'd already taken six laps around the impromptu track in an attempt to familiarize himself with both the lay of the land and the high-powered car. Regi had done the car little justice the first time around. His gearshifts were clunky, and he was so fucking nervous he had trouble breathing, let alone concentrating.

Forcing himself to calm down, he focused on the feel of the engine. By the fourth lap, it was talking to him. He accelerated around the corners and the wheels hugged the asphalt like it was glued down.

When he truly floored the accelerator, pushing the car to its 196-mile-per-hour limit, g-force wobbled his cheeks. The car was built to race, and when he forgot about the reason he was there and the looming ultimatum, he'd once again considered that crashing into Carson was a blessing.

But now, as Pope glared at him from the Porsche 911 Turbo, Regi hated that he'd ever met Carson and his bunch of thugs.

This was his chance to eradicate all the shit from his life forever, and he had every intention of doing it—or he'd die trying.

"Good luck." Carson's appearance at the driver's side window was as sudden as it was unexpected, and Regi jumped.

He swallowed the lump in his throat. "Thank you."

"Watch out for Pope; he races dirty."

Regi frowned. He had no idea what that meant, but it didn't sound good. A woman stepped into the headlights wearing only bikini bottoms and very high heels. She had the biggest tits he'd ever seen and, given that he'd had a year of playing waiter at Carson's wild parties, that was saying something. Her breasts wobbled when she raised the green flag above her head and he was annoyed at the distraction.

Pope revved the Porsche and the sound jolted Regi out of his trance. In his rearview mirror he saw Carson stand before the hundred-strong crowd and accept a wineglass from another topless woman.

Regi revved his engine, squeezed the steering wheel until his knuckles were white, clamped his teeth, and tried to stare at the billowing flag rather than the woman's bulging boobs.

She swung the flag down.

He stomped the accelerator and the car catapulted forward. About one second into the race he knew Pope had jumped the start. The yellow Porsche was a full car length in front before he'd even put the R8 into third gear. Regi's foot was to the floor. He didn't care about his safety, or about damaging another obscenely priced car.

Winning was all that mattered.

They flew up the warehouse-lined alley that was bathed in temporary floodlights. Litter scattered everywhere in the wake of the Porsche. Regi knew the turn up ahead was a tight one and expected Pope to brake in five hundred or so feet. He'd be ready; it was one of the few chances he'd have to get around his opponent.

Pope's brake light flared, but he was early—way too early.

"Fuck!" Regi stomped the brake and missed careening into the ass of the yellow car by barely an inch.

The Porsche's brake light blinked out and the car accelerated ahead. Pope had done that on purpose; he'd expected Regi to crash into him. That's what Carson meant about racing dirty.

"Fuck you, Pope." Regi slammed the R8 into third, floored the accelerator, and clamped his teeth as he aimed the Audi at Pope's rear end. The R8 was designed for this; it responded to every move with efficient deadliness and put Regi right up Pope's ass again.

Pope made his first mistake, and Regi didn't miss a beat. He pushed up on Pope's inside and they took the corner together, side by side. Once they were around the bend, Regi was in front. He floored the accelerator again and shot into the lead.

Regi was flanked with darkened warehouses one side and nothing but black water on the other. It was like looking into space. One wrong move and he'd be in the water. The Porsche was right behind him. He'd put his brights on, but Regi couldn't afford even a second to adjust his mirrors to deflect the glare. The hum of his tires over the uneven concrete was lost under the pounding of his own heart.

Pope was so close on his tail the Porsche's headlights disappeared. Regi decided to give Pope a taste of his own medicine. He clutched the steering wheel, tapped the brake, and braced for the impact he knew was coming.

But the squeal of tires ensured it didn't happen. Pope must've known Regi's intentions, and when he saw the Porsche's headlights again, he knew he'd backed off. Regi dropped the R8's gear and revved the engine to max before he pumped it up again. The next corner approached quickly. He readied to take it fast and tight.

He counted down the approach: five, four, three—

Suddenly he was flying through the air. The impact nanoseconds earlier had connected with the R8's back left corner. The Audi spun twice, clipped something, and the moment it flipped Regi knew he was a dead man.

He didn't even have time to scream before the car tumbled onto the roof and careened into a concrete barrier. The windshield exploded, and the airbag ballooned in a flash of white.

The ensuing silence was brutal.

A loud buzzing stung his ears, and his chest hurt so badly he could barely breathe. It took him a moment to realize he was upside down. The seatbelt had trapped him in place.

The sound of pounding feet forced him to move. He hadn't died in the crash, but if he didn't get out now, Pope would surely kill him. Desperate to escape, he punched the airbag, forcing the air from it. When he had wriggle room, he pressed the buckle and the belt released. He fell in a crumpled heap and howled at the pain in his chest.

Spots blurred his vision, but his brain forced him to keep moving. He shoved the door open and spilled from the car. His head was filled with static and the buzzing in his ears grew louder. Regi crawled from the wreck, and when he glanced sideways, he saw the leather boot about a second too late. It connected with his stomach and barreled him over. If he thought he was in pain before, that was fucking excruciating.

He sucked in air and his lungs burned with each breath.

"Looks like this's the end of the line for Regi the Rat." Pope had left the Porsche headlights on and the glare silhouetted his bullish frame. His opponent loomed over Regi, and he knew he had one shot at saving himself. He groaned, imitating intense agony, which wasn't hard. Regi rolled to his feet, pretending to be wobbly, then, the second Pope was within spitting distance, he balled his fist and with all the strength he could summon plowed it upward into Pope's chin.

The thug groaned, a tooth went flying, and Pope hit the ground in a full body slam. He didn't even use his hands to break his fall.

One look was enough for Regi to know that Pope was either out cold or dead.

CHAPTER THIRTEEN

It'd been four weeks since Amber forced herself to enter Oliver's gym. That decision had been one of the best ones she'd made in her new life. In fact, she'd been progressing so well she'd begun to believe she could truly go through with her mission. It'd been touch-and-go for a while, but the for and against debates in her head were leaning more toward the positive now.

It wasn't just her mental attitude that'd changed either.

Rock climbing three times a week and skiing every weekend had her body changing too. Her strength was gradually returning to her arms and legs, bringing muscle definition that she hadn't seen in years. She was eating more and sleeping better. Twice she'd actually slept right through the night.

She'd already motored through two doctor's transcripts, and, with her mission occupying the forefront of her brain, she decided she was ready to take her plan to the next step.

After making herself a peppermint tea, she settled in for an afternoon of research.

She'd resisted doing this research for two reasons. One was if she knew too much about the bodies in the ice and couldn't go through with her mission, then she'd be forever haunted with her failure to help Dorothy and the lovers. Somehow, not knowing their full story made it less personal. But after a month of training, both in the gym and on the ski slopes, she was almost certain she could now go through with the crazy quest.

Now she simply *had* to learn more about them.

There was no turning back.

The second reason she'd resisted the research was because she needed a goal. One month of training, then reassess. That'd been her first goal. Baby steps. Just like when she'd learned to walk again after the coma. Take a few steps and reward yourself. The dangling carrot was a great motivator. Today's carrot was learning everything she could about the frozen bodies.

Years ago, after she'd woken from the coma, she'd forced herself to read every article she could find on Milton's death. She'd been desperate for information. Anything that would help her piece together what'd happened and give substance to her missing eight months.

Now, though, she was scanning those reports for a very different reason: she needed to pinpoint the exact location of the helicopter crash. But it seemed that specific detail was an unnecessary waste of precious tabloid space, one they wouldn't print when they had so much other sensational media fodder.

Multibillionaire and son die in horrific helicopter crash.

Only survivor was Milton's young girlfriend.

Pilot way off course.

Yes, the tabloids had plenty to work with.

Victoria had spent years using Milton's wealth to climb the social ladder, so when her ex-husband died under such controversy, she had the ear of social media and the tabloids. She'd helped feed the media frenzy with her never-ending lies about Holly's relationship with Milton, the much older billionaire. Milton had always said his ex-wife was a heartless bitch, but Holly hadn't known the depth of her evil until after his death.

The fact that Holly had been willed a chunk of his money upon his death didn't help. Not when Victoria got nothing.

Holly would do anything to reverse that scenario.

She skipped over one report after another, searching for the exact location of the crash. The closest she could get was that it was somewhere on Whiskey Mountain and that the helicopter had been airborne for approximately thirty-seven minutes after departing the exclusive Miracle Lodge. Other than that, she had nothing.

This was where Mr. Carter Logan came in.

She typed "Carter Logan" into Google. The National Geographic photographer was featured in two headlining stories, the first being Carter's ordeal in Mexico with the drug runners. The second was his discovery of the plane wreck in the Canadian Rockies.

For Holly, the plane wreck was the direct link to figuring out more about the bodies in the ice. Carter had been in British Columbia to follow the trail of eighteenth-century explorer Alexander Mackenzie. Two weeks into the journey, he'd taken a helicopter ride as far as was permitted and was set down with an experienced mountain guide, Chancy Holden. Their plan was to reach the top of the peak and return within two days. What neither of them expected to find was the wreckage of a plane that'd been missing for nearly forty years.

Carter commented that the plane's cabin had been remarkably intact. They found one body—that of the Canadian pilot, Buddy Dickinson—but no other bodies were inside. But it was the discovery of a passport belonging to Mr. Frederick Pearce that had captured the world's interest.

Holly searched for information about Frederick Pearce. According to the first article that appeared, Fred was wanted in relation to the disappearance of the famous actress Angelique Forster. The fact that he was a police officer made Holly put her cup down and shuffle forward on her seat.

Angelique vanished on the morning of May 25, 1980, and her kidnapper had demanded five hundred thousand dollars in exchange for her safe return.

The next day, Angelique's husband David was apparently instructed to put half a million dollars cash into a suitcase and leave it at a bus stop near Seattle's famous Pike Place Market.

However, neither Frederick, Angelique, nor the money were ever seen again.

Frederick was consequently accused of Angelique's kidnapping and murder, and if the tabloids were to be believed he'd been sighted in London, Mexico, and Hawaii.

Frederick's mother was Dorothy, the elderly woman whose sad image had been flashing across Holly's mind for weeks. Dorothy had always maintained her son's innocence.

Holly flicked her television on and fast-forwarded to the footage she'd already watched dozens of times. She paused on the image of Dorothy holding up her son's photo, and the depth of her grief pooling in her graying eyes tugged at Holly's heart.

Until either Angelique or Frederick were found, Dorothy would never be able to prove her son's innocence.

Holly knew exactly what it was like to be blamed for another person's death. She was the one who'd convinced Milton to bring his son along on that fateful trip—Milton's ex-wife had never let her forget it. It was ridiculous, really. No one could've predicted that helicopter crash.

But it didn't stop the accusations that cut so deep she could barely breathe.

Holly cast Victoria's callous blame from her mind and googled Angelique Forster.

Angelique's rise to fame started at eight, when she'd starred in a series of Fluffo advertisements in the 1950s. Curious, Amber googled Fluffo and discovered it was once a popular vegetable shortening. After those commercials, Angelique changed her name to Angel Forster and went on to star in a variety of sitcoms before she landed her most prominent role. Unfortunately, halfway through the production of *Smokey and the Bandit II*, she was kidnapped and never seen again.

Holly scanned the internet for pictures of Angel. The actress had an evocative beauty about her. An elegance that radiated from within. Yet Holly couldn't help but notice the sadness in her eyes. She had the feeling Angel had upheld an appearance that her life was amazing, yet harbored a deep secret that was rotting her core. There were many photos of Angel, although very few had her smiling. As Holly enlarged one photo after the next, it cemented her conviction that it was indeed Angel's body she'd seen in the icy grave.

Her mind skipped to the frozen couple. Their embrace was nothing short of loving. She was curled up in his lap, leaning into him, and his arm was around her back so his hand rested on her hip. His other hand was on her waist, hugging her tight.

They were not kidnapper and victim—they were lovers.

Holly just had to prove it.

Two hours into her research, she found an article that slotted another piece of the puzzle into place. In January 1979, police were called to the home of David and Angel Forster after neighbors reported a disturbance. Angel was treated for facial bruising after she'd supposedly fallen down a set of stairs.

The attending police officer was Frederick Pearce.

Holly searched for more information, and one particular photo had hit the papers like a firestorm. She gasped at the image of Angel with a hideously swollen black eye. Holly was no expert, but she'd bet a million dollars Angel didn't get her black eye from falling down steps.

She was reminded of a similar photo she'd seen of herself. It was during one of her searches to piece together the missing eight months of her life. The photo was in a newspaper and had been taken just after she'd been rescued off the mountain. A broken eye socket was the reason for the mammoth bruise surrounding her left eye.

Fortunately for her, Holly had absolutely no recollection of that injury, or the subsequent pain it would've produced.

Frederick's mother had always proclaimed her son's innocence, and she'd referenced that particular photo often, proffering it as evidence that it was David who'd killed Angelique and disposed of her body, and not her son. Holly turned to the television and stared into Dorothy's eyes. "You may be right," she said to the still screen.

A scenario began to form in her mind. Angel had been in an abusive relationship with David. Being famous probably made it difficult for her to reveal this ugly secret. When Frederick Pearce had come to her home on the night of the incident, she may've confided in the handsome young police officer. Together, they hatched a plan to pretend to kidnap Angel so she could escape her very public life. They escaped with the money and somehow made it to Canada, but three weeks later their plane crashed.

They survived, only to fall into that crevice and freeze to death.

Holly's heart ached for them. They'd escaped one horror to fall into another.

Her heart also ached for Dorothy, that poor mother who never knew what happened to her son. Fred's father had died six years ago, never knowing either. Holly didn't want Dorothy to go to her grave with the same sadness.

While Dorothy was distraught over her son's disappearance and the endless cruel accusations, it appeared that both David and Angel's parents reveled in her misery. Every year on the anniversary of the disappearance they'd pop up in the media, pleading for someone, anyone with information, to come forward. By the looks of their abundant photos, they seemed to enjoy the annual attention. For more than thirty years, both sets of parents had worked together to host an annual ball that marked the date of Angel's disappearance.

Holly thought of Victoria, and imagined she'd do something like that too.

She clicked her mouse onto her calendar. The anniversary of Angel and David's disappearance was seven months away.

Seven months. *Could I have answers by then?* It'd be wonderful to save Dorothy from another year of hell. Seven more months of training. She was already surprised with what she'd achieved in just one month.

May 25. Seven months. It was the perfect deadline to aim for.

Her dangling carrot.

She tugged the keyboard forward, searched Google until she found what she was looking for, then picked up her phone and dialed the number on the screen.

"Welcome to National Geographic, how may I direct your call?"

"Hello, I was wondering if you could help me. My name is Amber Hope, and I'm doing an article on the plane wreck one of your photographers, a Mr. Carter Logan, found in Canada. I'd like to interview him. Is it possible to obtain his contact details?" After being put through to five different people and explaining herself each time, she was given an email address for Carter.

It took her a good forty minutes to construct an email that she hoped would incite a response.

Amber glanced at her watch and was surprised that it was already quarter past six. After shutting down her computer, she devoured a quick quinoa salad, dressed for rock climbing, and dashed out her door.

She fell into the shadows outside Upper Limits and waited for the last of Oliver's customers to leave. Two young women strolled up to Oliver. They stood close and openly flirted with him. He seemed to like their company and smiled and joked along with them.

The blonde said something to Oliver that Holly couldn't hear, and he gave the women an interesting expression. It was a mixture of confidence and cheekiness, but there was also a touch of detachment too. Holly thought it was strange given that both women seemed to be toying with him.

The blonde woman kissed his cheek and the other slapped his bottom, and when he flashed them a cheeky grin, a bolt of jealousy flared across Amber's mind. She smacked the ridiculous emotion aside. Oliver was well out of her league. To even consider that he may be interested was a rocky path to disappointment.

Amber studied the women as they ambled toward the exit. She guessed them to be about her age, but that's where the similarity ended. Both were beautiful and confident, and both had stunning figures. They were giggling as they stepped outside and climbed into a red Volkswagen Beetle parked in front of the gym.

A few more people left, and Amber recognized the last man as one of Oliver's regular customers. Because Oliver spoke so loudly when belaying for people on the wall, Amber had come to know a few of their names. This one was Neil, and based on how comfortable they were with each other, she believed he and Oliver were good friends.

Oliver walked Neil to the front door and said goodbye. But this time, after the customer had vanished from view, Oliver poked his head out the door. "You can come in now, Amber."

She inwardly cringed as she stepped from the shadows.

"There you are." Oliver's smirk confirmed he'd enjoyed catching her out. "How're you? Did you have a good weekend?"

He stepped aside and she walked through the front door. "Yes, thank you." She headed toward the side wall.

"What'd you get into? Anything exciting?"

She hated that he asked this after every weekend. Her response each time had been that she'd done nothing and it made her sound pathetic. So, deciding there was no harm in it, she said, "I went skiing."

"Skiing! Snow skiing?"

He seemed way too excited and she frowned. "Yes."

"That's excellent. I didn't know you were a skier."

She shifted her feet. "I'm learning."

"Well, aren't you Miss Adventurer." The delight in his eyes made her happy she'd told him. Now she didn't feel like a complete outsider.

"I haven't been skiing in months. I should come up with you sometime."

Her heart fluttered at his suggestion, but she quickly cast the foolish notion aside. He was just being nice. Oliver had young beautiful women falling all over him. He wouldn't have any interest in a disfigured freak like her.

Forcing her brain to focus, she pulled her hair back. It had become second nature to do this now, and she barely had two thoughts about revealing her scar to Oliver. He seemed to have accepted it too, as his eyes had rarely wandered over it since that first time.

They had an efficient routine going now. While he fetched their harnesses, she prepared their ropes, and within five minutes of her arrival she was usually on the wall.

"I think you're ready for the advanced climb." He gave a half smile, maybe assessing her thoughts.

"Okay." She didn't hesitate. Now that she'd decided to have answers for Dorothy in seven months, she needed to set some more goals with her climbing. This seemed like the perfect place to start.

"Let's do it then." The green in his eyes was a luscious shade, the color of new mint leaves, and they dazzled with what she thought may've been a little pride. His gaze had her stomach fluttering, like it was filled with butterflies.

They moved to the front section of the warehouse. Amber glanced up the climbing wall and her tummy did a little vertigo flip. She smacked the queasiness away by stepping back and forcing herself to look at it more thoroughly. The fact that she'd progressed to this level was a miracle. Much of it had been a battle over her mind as well as her body. Doing both skiing and rock climbing had her body improving, but it didn't stop her from feeling sore in nearly every muscle the day after each session.

Just like every Monday after her weekend skiing, she winced as she reached up to the first hold. But, ignoring the stiffness in her quads, she pushed on. With each grading progression she made along the climbing wall, the holds became smaller and farther apart. It required her to truly map out her route before committing to the next hold.

Halfway up, she reached a dead end. There didn't seem to be another anchor point.

"It's the pink one, to your right. You can do it, Amber." Oliver's encouragement floated up to her.

She loved and hated it.

Amber eyed the next hold. It was a pinch hold, which required her to squeeze the colorful lump between her thumb and fingers to keep her in position. To get to it, she had to stand on her right toes and counter her weight by extending her left leg out to correct her center of balance. Every muscle in her right leg trembled as she stretched her arm, her fingers, reaching… reaching. "Shit!"

She fell. As she swung back and forth on the rope, she clenched her jaw until her teeth hurt.

When she reached the mat, she stepped back to steady herself on the cushioning.

"It's okay." Oliver touched her shoulder. "You'll get there."

She glanced back up the wall and guessed it to be about forty feet to the top. That was farther than the fall she'd made into the frozen crevice. She shuddered at the memory.

"Hey." He touched her arm. "You've made excellent progress."

She shook her head. "It's not fast enough."

He frowned, and she instantly regretted her statement. "What's not fast enough?"

"Nothing," she snapped.

"I can tell it's something. Amber, remember my rule: you must be honest with me."

She glared into his green irises, silently pleading that he'd drop it. But Oliver wasn't like that. Something about him left her battling the urge to reveal her darkest secrets.

She'd managed to avoid catastrophe so far, but she wondered if it was only a matter of time before her ruse was over. It was a double-edged sword. As much as she stressed over her secret identity being revealed, she ached with the desire to divulge her true self.

"Amber..." Oliver's gentle squeeze on her shoulder lured her from her tumbling thoughts. "What is it? You can tell me."

She shook her head. "It's nothing."

"Does it have anything to do with your scar?"

She covered her cheek with her hand and a sob caught in her throat. The pity in his eyes cut like a thousand knives. She had to get out of there. Snapping the belt clips open, she let the harness fall to her feet.

"Hey, what're you doing? Don't go."

She stepped from the brace and kicked it aside.

"I'm sorry. Amber, please."

He reached for her arm but she yanked it away. "Don't." She blinked back tears, gathered her bag, and strode for the door.

"Amber, I'm sorry. It's none of my business. I shouldn't have asked."

Tears tumbled down her cheeks, and with each step toward her apartment she was torn between running home and running back to him, falling into his arms, and telling him every sordid detail about her wretched life.

CHAPTER FOURTEEN

Oliver waved at his mother, who was walking toward him from the opposite side of the field. The way she was holding her elbows and her slight limp confirmed her arthritis was giving her trouble again. In the last couple of years, the cruel disease had taken its toll and she'd given up her two favorite loves: golf and tennis. That, in turn, had her putting on weight that she couldn't shift, which only placed more pressure on her already crippling knees. It was a vicious cycle that looked to have no recovery point.

She opened her arms as she neared and Oliver squeezed her in a bear hug. Her breathing was ragged and he hated listening to the rattle in her chest.

"Is Dad coming?" Oliver's father wasn't as committed as his mother to watching Kurt practice his baseball, but he'd never missed a game.

"No, he's trying to fix the stupid dishwasher."

Oliver's eyebrows shot up. "Oh no." His father was well-known for his handyman mishaps.

"Yeah, so be ready to come to the rescue later."

Oliver chuckled. "Sure. Just give me a call. Okay, let me go sort this bunch out." He thumbed over his shoulder at the team of rowdy teenage boys gathering at home plate.

"Alright, you guys, let's go for a run." There were as many groans as there were kids who took off at a sprint. "Last ten boys to reach the fence will do ten more push-ups." That got them moving, and they roared together as they collectively ran toward the opposite end of the field. Oliver kept up with them, giving them as much gentle encouragement as assertiveness.

His brother Kurt was one of the stronger boys. Kurt had shot right past his mother in height before he was twelve and was already nearly up to Oliver's shoulders. He wouldn't be surprised if Kurt was the tallest in the family by the time he finished growing.

Oliver was sixteen when his mother sat him and Dane down and told them she was having another baby. He'd been horrified at the time. The concept of having a snotty screaming baby in the house was his worst nightmare. But right from the moment Kurt was born, Oliver had felt a special bond to his kid brother. Despite the seventeen years between them, they were best friends. And each year only got better.

Oliver went through the regular drills, working the kids into a sweat and improving their batting and fielding skills. But most of all it was about exercise, fun, and camaraderie. Oliver's philosophy was that developing lifelong friendships was just as important as hitting a home run.

He separated the boys into two teams and put half on the field and the other half into a batting order. Oliver was adamant about letting all the kids have a turn, regardless of their ability. Some of the parents didn't agree, but it was always the ones who thought their boys were better than the others. But Oliver stood his ground, and in his four years of coaching he'd only had five kids removed by parents who didn't support his coaching style.

He blew the whistle. "Batter up."

Joshua stepped forward, swinging the bat back and forth. He was a little kid, one of the smallest on the team. Joshua had a nervous stutter and preferred to slink into the shadows rather than get involved. But put a baseball bat in his hands and he could belt that ball better than some of the boys twice his size.

The pitcher wound up and let the ball fly. Joshua released his fury, connecting to the ball in the sweet spot. The batting team cheered as the ball sailed over the top of the center fielder. As Oliver followed the ball's trajectory his eyes fell on a jogger making slow progress across the darkened paddock in the distance. He squinted, blinked, and then frowned. The jogger looked like Amber.

As Joshua skipped to home plate, already cheering his home run, Oliver made up his mind to go investigate the jogger for himself. He removed his whistle from around his neck and handed it to Joshua. "Great hit, buddy. You did so well, you're in charge for the next four batters."

Joshua's eyes lit up. "Me?"

"Yep. Don't take any crap from them, okay?"

"Okay."

"Let me hear you blow the whistle."

Joshua inhaled a deep breath and made the whistle screech. "Listen up, boys. Joshua's in charge for next four batters. I don't want to hear any trouble. Got it?"

There was a mumble around the field.

"I can't hear you."

"Yes, coach," most of them yelled in unison.

Oliver didn't explain where he was going, he just took off at full pace, trying to catch up to the mysterious jogger before he missed her. He left the field, crossed beneath a row of oak trees, and reached the walking path that stretched from one end of Brambleton to the other. He spied the jogger in the distance. Their gait was rough, as if they'd hit absolute exhaustion, yet they kept right on going. As he neared, he convinced himself that it was indeed Amber.

She didn't strike him as the jogging type.

When he was close enough, he cupped his hands around his mouth and yelled, "Amber!"

The person continued on and he wondered if she had music buds in her ears.

He called again, closer this time, but again she didn't stop.

Oliver was barely sixty feet away when he called her name the third time. She jumped and looked over her shoulder.

He waved, and as she slowed to a stop and bent over, resting her hands on her knees, he strode right up to her. "Hey. I didn't know you were a jogger."

She shook her head. "Not." She huffed a few breaths. "See?"

Recognizing that she'd truly pushed herself to the limit, he rested his hand on her shoulder. "Deep breaths, nice and slow. Good for you. How long have you been doing this?"

She swallowed and inhaled a few deep breaths. "First time."

"You're doing so well." As she tried to catch her breath, he saw a woman who was drawing on some kind of dogged determination, but beneath that was an equally strong veil of insecurity. Not for the first time, Oliver wondered if Amber was in a situation she was trying to claw out of.

"Not really." Again she shook her head, and he noticed her burn scar was flushed even redder than usual.

"Well, I think you are."

Amber released her clasp on her knees and gradually stood up.

When she seemed to be coping better, he said, "You didn't come to rock climbing yesterday."

She gave a little shrug and looked to the ground in a way that hid her scarred cheek.

"I'm really sorry about what I said. It's none of my business." He placed his hand on her arm and for the first time she didn't pull back. His heart skipped a beat and he had to resist the urge to pull her to his chest and hold her tight enough to extinguish her troubles.

For Amber's sake, he had to be patient.

She puffed out her cheeks and, with a roll of her eyes, let out a long slow breath. "It's okay. I overreacted."

Despite the dimmed light, he was once again captured by the color of her eyes. He'd never seen such an intense shade of blue. "So, do we have a truce?" He held out his hand.

When she placed her palm in his, a wave of relief swept through him. When she kept it there, he recognized it as a huge step forward for her.

"We have a truce."

"Does this mean you'll be back tomorrow night?"

When she released his grip, it was like a piece of him had been torn away. "As long as I can move I will."

"You'll be able to move so well, I think you'll smack that bell at the top in no time."

She smiled, and the transformation was spectacular. An unexpected warmth flooded him and the desire to hug her had his heart thumping.

Their eyes met, and for once she seemed to let her guard down. For a couple of heartbeats, he had a feeling she wanted say something. He waited, holding his breath, urging the moment to linger. But as quickly as it appeared, the cloud of sadness crossed her stunning irises and she lowered her gaze.

"Okay… well…" She pointed at the path.

"Yeah, I've gotta get back to Middle League. I'm so glad I saw you."

A small frown rippled her forehead but swiftly dissolved. "See you tomorrow."

"Tomorrow," he agreed. "Don't be late."

"Never."

He took one last glance at her before he set a pace back toward the baseball field. Just before he crossed the line of trees, he turned to jog backwards and noticed Amber was still watching him. He waved, and his heart skipped a beat when she waved back. Spinning on his heel, he picked up his pace and sprinted to his position behind home plate.

He spent the next half hour with one eye on the baseball action and one eye looking for Amber's return jog. But either he missed her or she took a different route.

After the training session, he curled his arm over his little brother's shoulder and walked him back to their mother, who was chatting with some of the other women.

She turned to him as they arrived. "Who was that?"

"Who?"

"That person you raced over to." She pointed across the field.

"Oh, that's a new client at the gym."

"Hmmm." She raised her eyebrows.

"What?"

"You seemed pretty happy to see her."

He cocked his head and rolled his eyes. His mom had been trying to match him up for years. And ever since he'd hit thirty, she'd been in panic mode. "She's a client, Mom. You know how I feel about that."

"Yeah, yeah."

He shook his head, hoping she'd drop the subject. Although, if she was as intuitive as she usually was, she'd be able to sense his interest in Amber was more than just fleeting.

Once everyone had gone, he slipped into his car. As he drove the short distance home, he found himself scanning the jogging path for Amber. When he nearly went through a red light, he told himself to settle down.

But his mind still wandered to her. When they were together, he felt on top of the world. Like he could accomplish anything. It was strange—frightening even—because he'd thought his life was complete. Now, though, when he wasn't with Amber, he felt hollow and alone.

He'd had three serious girlfriends in his life, and several casual dates. His longest relationship had lasted nearly three years. But he'd never felt like Becky was *the* one. It'd been hard breaking up with her when neither of them had actually done anything wrong. It was just that they were too comfortable. Like an old married couple. They'd become boring. They had no spark, not even in the bedroom. He'd wasted too long to admit their relationship had run its course. Becky didn't speak to him for nearly three years after he broke up with her, but now she was married with two children and seemed blissfully happy. Oliver was happy for her too.

Amber was far from boring. Since the moment she'd walked into his gym he'd been drawn to her mysteriousness. But her eternal sadness squeezed his heart. Clearly she'd been through some horrific things. And not just physically—her hurt was deep. And if his gut instinct served him right, it was probably a bad relationship.

Every time he tried to learn more about her she changed the subject. Her sadness came in giant waves and her resistance to discuss it showed how deep that ocean was. He'd have to take his time. Amber struck him as a woman who would run away and never look back if he pushed too hard. But she'd captured his interest…. hell, it was more than that. He was fascinated by her. So as difficult as it was, he was willing to wait.

He parked his car on the street and climbed his front steps two at a time. When he opened his front door, the sound of the television was a sure sign his brother was on the couch. Again.

"Hey, bro. How's baseball?" Dane didn't bother turning down the volume.

"Good. How're you doing?"

"Same as usual."

That'd be an understatement. Dane had been living in Groundhog Day for years. He was an accountant by day, couch potato by night, and the routine never altered. Visiting his parents was about the only deviation Dane managed. Oliver had given up trying to explain to his brother that he was wasting his life. Dane seemed quite content to while away the hours. He never partied, never dated, and never had friends over. He was as stable as a pyramid, and that made him the best roommate anyone could ask for.

Oliver grabbed a Budweiser from the fridge, twisted the lid, and headed for the bathroom. He scrubbed off a day's worth of sweat and grime and washed his hair. Once he'd finished, the sound of a woman giggling caught his attention. He wrapped a towel around his hip, grabbed his beer, and strolled back out to the living room.

"Oh, hey, Olly."

"Larissa! What're you doing here?"

"Well, hello to you too." She was way too happy and way too loud. One glance was enough to know she'd been drinking. "You didn't come to Baxter's." She curled her long blond ponytail around her wrist.

"You know I do Kurt's baseball on Wednesdays."

She slipped off the sofa and sashayed toward him. "I know that. But I thought you'd come after training."

Oliver slid in behind the kitchen counter, trying to keep a little distance from her. But he realized his mistake when she came around with him, blocking him off, and rested her hand on the counter, maybe for support.

"I didn't feel up to it tonight."

She stepped forward and placed her hand on his chest. "That's a shame." He clutched her hand. "Larissa…"

"What?" She tilted her head and fluttered her eyes at him.

"I think you've had a few too many drinks."

She fell forward, maybe by accident, maybe on purpose, but when she wrapped her arms around him, he decided it was the latter.

"Come on, you need to go home." He tried to unhook her arms from around his back and after a little wrestle, in which he won, she stepped back and yanked the towel from his hips.

"Oops." She giggled and blatantly stared at his groin.

Oliver snapped his hands over himself. "Righty ho! Give me the towel." From the corner of his eye he saw Dane watching them. It was probably the most excitement he'd had since his graduation party.

"Nope." She stepped back and wriggled her eyebrows.

"Larissa, nothing's going to happen."

"Oh, you don't mean that." She curled her bottom lip between her teeth.

"Yes, I do. You're drunk."

"Not too drunk." She pouted her lips.

"Yes, you are. I'm going to get dressed and take you home."

"But I don't want to go home. I want to stay riiiiight here." She jumped up, placing her bottom on the kitchen counter, and opened her legs, inviting him to step in. "Give me a hug."

Instead, he strode past and went to his room. He tugged on a pair of track pants and a t-shirt. When he stepped back out, she was down from the counter.

"What's wrong with me?" Her chin dimpled.

"Come on, I'll drive you home." He decided to ignore her question. "How did you get here anyway?"

"I drove."

That wasn't good. He placed his hands on her shoulders and guided her toward the front door. She turned to Dane. "Bye, Dane. It was nice seeing you again."

"You too, Larissa. See you soon."

"I hope so."

Oliver didn't want to risk her falling down the steps, so he scooped her into his arms, and she squealed and wrapped her arms around his neck. She planted a kiss on his cheek and nuzzled in. "You're so lovely."

Ignoring her comment, he crossed the distance from the bottom step to the car in a couple of strides and plonked her down. He pressed the button to unlock the car and opened the passenger door. "There you go, climb in."

She closed her eyes, clenched her jaw, and Oliver knew he was about to get it.

Her eyes snapped open and the fire behind them was dangerous. "You're such an asshole." She slapped his cheek. The blow came out of nowhere and stunned him beyond thinking. He'd never been hit by a woman before. It didn't hurt; it was a shock more than anything. But he was pretty sure she'd regret it in the morning. He was certain she'd regret the whole incident come morning. She'd always had a fiery tempter, but this time she'd gone too far.

Opting to ignore her aggression, he helped her into the car without even a comment.

She was sobbing by the time he slipped into the driver's seat.

She was asking his forgiveness by the time he pulled up to the curb outside her house four streets away.

Oliver helped her out of the car and led her up to her parents' front door. She could barely stand, and based on her jumbled monologue she was unable to form sentences either. He knocked on the door and heard the television volume dial down. A couple of seconds later the door opened.

"Hi, Mrs. Rogers. I've brought Larissa home."

"Oh jeez. Thanks, Oliver. Frank, give us a hand."

Frank appeared from around the corner, running his hand over his bald head. "Shit, what's she done this time?"

"I think she had a few too many drinks at Baxter's, that's all."

Oliver allowed Mr. and Mrs. Rogers to take Larissa from him, then he said goodbye and shut the door. He hoped Larissa wouldn't be in too much trouble. After all, she was twenty-eight; she could get drunk if she wanted to.

He climbed back behind the wheel and drove home.

Dane raised his eyebrows at Oliver's return. But before he got ready for his brother's grilling, he fetched his unfinished beer from the kitchen counter.

After one long gulp, he plonked himself on the sofa.

"What's going on? It's not like you to turn down a woman."

He rolled his eyes. "She was drunk, Dane."

"I know, but my question still stands."

"I'm not interested."

"She sure is."

"I know." He swallowed a mouthful of beer. "I wish she'd let it go." He shook his head and huffed.

Dane frowned then cocked his head. "That's not all, is it? Cough it up, buddy. What's going on?"

Oliver suddenly felt torn. He'd promised Amber absolute secrecy. But this was his brother; he could trust him not to tell a soul. Oliver downed the rest of his Bud in one gulp, plunked the bottle on the coffee table, and turned to his brother. "There's this new client at the gym."

"And? What's her name?"

"Amber Hope. She's… different." It was the worst word to describe her, but he couldn't pinpoint the perfect one.

Dane frowned. "Different how?"

He pictured Amber's thick dark hair that she deliberately tumbled forward, hiding her stunning blue eyes. Eyes that reflected intelligence and sadness with equal intensity. "It's hard to explain, she's not like any other client I've had. She's shy, insecure, yet incredibly determined. She treats climbing like it's the answer to a life or death situation."

"Sounds weird."

"It's so hard to explain. She demanded private lessons."

"Oh, so that's why you're getting home later."

"She's paying extra."

"So she should."

His mind drifted to his first glance at her. She'd seemed almost like a child who'd crawled out of a closet after years of abandonment. "Have you ever googled yourself?"

"Nope."

"I googled her; there's not one mention of her on Facebook or anything."

"Is that strange?"

"I don't know. I googled my name and had a good bit of stuff come up. Pictures of me doing baseball, my business, a few party snaps."

"Maybe she doesn't get out much. Did you google me? I probably don't exist either."

Oliver chuckled. "That's a point." Other than never missing a day at work, his brother was practically a hermit.

He pictured the scar on her cheek. He didn't know much about burn scars, but the size of Amber's had him convinced it was life changing.

"You're frowning," Dane pointed out.

"Amber has this terrible burn scar on her cheek, right across here." He drew a rough circle from his earlobe, along his jawline, up toward his nose, and back to his ear.

Dane sucked the air through his teeth. "Shit, that would've hurt like hell."

"I know. She's always trying to conceal it behind her hair, but the scar's so big you can't miss it."

"How do you think she got it?"

He sighed. "I don't know, but I have a terrible feeling it was abuse, and not that long ago."

"Oh jeez."

"I'm not sure. She just seems a little scared. A lot scared, actually. Yet determined to fight it too." He sighed. "She's really interesting."

"Well, any girl who has you turning down a woman in your own home captures my interest too."

He grinned. It was nice having his brother around. "Thanks, bro."

"Maybe you're finally growing up."

Oliver lightly punched Dane on the shoulder. "Now you're being mean."

CHAPTER FIFTEEN

The second the bus doors opened, Regi jumped out and ran full speed toward home. His heart was in his throat and his mind was a fucked-up scramble as he tried to prepare for the mayhem he was about to see. If his mother's hysterical tirade could be trusted, then someone had messed up their home, big time.

And Regi knew exactly who that someone was.

Carson.

Well, not exactly Carson—he'd never lift a finger. It'd be Pope and his band of goons. He'd been both relieved and pissed off when he'd found out he hadn't killed Pope with that brutal uppercut.

After the crash, he'd shot out of there like a pellet-shot rabbit. But the location of the race track had him trapped between a mile of warehouses and endless ocean, and there was nowhere to run. He'd found a metal-rung ladder that led down to the water's edge, and as he'd clung to it, trying not to pass out from the pain in his ribs, he'd watched people flock to the wreck and Pope's lifeless body. It was a good forty minutes before Pope sat up. The whole time Regi was torn between horror that he may've killed someone and joy that the asshole was dead.

That was three weeks ago. Trouble was, Pope's vendetta was now personal. He'd been stalking Regi like a famished hyena, and he'd used Regi as a punching bag at every opportunity. Ironically, Regi was pretty certain Carson was the only thing keeping him alive, because Pope could've killed him a dozen times over since the night of the race.

Regi smacked his tumbling thoughts aside, fisted his hands, and pumped his arms in perfect coordination with his feet. He'd had good practice running for his life in the last couple of years. Even though there was no one on his tail right this minute, he felt the same life-or-death pressure. Regi had convinced his mother not to call the police until he got there. Whether or not she'd listened was another question.

About ten minutes after he'd started running, he was relieved to see his street free of police cars. He raced up his driveway and pushed open the front door. It slammed so hard against the wall one of the paintings fell off and shattered onto the tiles. But then he noticed the other four pictures were in broken bits on the floor too.

"Mom? Mom, where are you?" He stepped over splintered wood and glass shards.

"I'm in here."

He followed her voice to the kitchen, and along the way gawked at the damage around him. Furniture was upturned, ornaments and pictures were smashed. Stuffing from cushions was strewn everywhere. The extent of the mess had him wondering if the intruders had been looking for something, though he had absolutely no idea what that could be.

Long dark streaks of makeup stained his mother's cheeks, yet she appeared to have stopped crying. He wrapped his arms around her. "Are you okay?"

She squeezed him and shook her head. "No. I can't believe it."

"I know. Did you call the police?"

"Not yet, I was waiting for you." His relief made his knees wobble. The last thing he needed was the cops breathing down his neck too. Carson had made enough threats about what would happen should Regi ever contact the police.

And Regi was pretty certain Carson had a few cops on his payroll.

Every cupboard in the kitchen was open, and it looked like the thugs had just shoved their hands in and scooped everything onto the floor. Broken china littered the tiles.

Her handbag was on the table, and Regi spied the small plastic bag open in an inside pocket. Whatever pills she'd taken had probably helped her stop crying.

"Sit down, Mom." He directed her to a chair. "I'll have a look around. Did you notice anything stolen?"

She sank into the dining room chair and tugged her bag forward. "All my jewelry is gone. Except what I was wearing." She twisted the diamond rings around her fingers and stared at the jewels like she was seeing them for the first time.

Regi had seen this expression on his mother dozens of times. She was close to falling down the rabbit hole. Maybe this stint would be a blessing. By the time she woke up, he could have everything cleaned up. He could even call the insurance company and see about making a claim. Maybe they could get a new TV. That'd be sweet. Something good to come of something shitty.

"Hey, Mom, what's the name of our insurance company?"

She blinked at him as if she'd forgotten he was there. Then her mouth twisted into a scowl. "No insurance."

"What? Why not?" He knew for a fact that his mother used to have insurance, because she'd claimed on it when their roof was messed up in a storm last year.

"No more money." She did an overexaggerated shoulder shrug. "All gone."

As far as he knew, his mother had never had money troubles. She'd always had work, and even when she didn't, money was never in short supply. They didn't live extravagantly, they were just… comfortable. "What're you talking about?"

"He stopped paying."

He frowned and touched her shoulder. "Who?"

"Milton." Their eyes met and she let out an enormous sigh. "Your father."

Regi did a double take. This was the first time she'd ever mentioned his name.

"He paid you money?"

She nodded and opened her eyes wide. "But we were bad."

He pulled out a chair. The ransacked house was about to take a back seat. If his mother was ready to chat about his father, then he was ready to listen. He placed his hand on her forearm, hoping the touch wouldn't heave her from her talkative mood. "Tell me, Mom."

"I loved him, you know."

"I know," he lied. He knew nothing about him, let alone their relationship.

"He was so handsome, and smart. Rich too. A man who was truly going places."

It was funny, for years Regi had formed a mental image of the scumbag "sperm donor." He'd pictured him nearly bald and overweight. Not just fat, but really pudgy and unhealthy, with pasty skin that he hid beneath brown baggy clothes. He'd pictured him working away in a dingy office with no windows and suffering through a lifetime of boredom. Regi had thought the image was perfect for a man who didn't want anything to do with his own son.

"What happened?"

She shrugged and rolled her eyes. "His wife happened."

"He was married?"

"Yep."

He frowned. "Did you know that?"

She squeezed her eyes shut. Her chin dimpled. "Yep. But she was really mean to him."

Regi cringed at how pathetic she sounded. "How'd you meet?"

She smacked her lips together and glided her hand across the table, then sat back in her chair as if she'd come to a conclusion. But it was a long moment before she eyeballed him and cleared her throat. "I was just eighteen. Milton was much older. Eighteen years older, actually. I thought he was the most incredible man in the world. He was my boss. He owned the company and he was very successful. Really going places." She sighed.

Regi thought about Thomas, her new boss, and how ironic it was that history was repeating itself.

"Milton traveled the country, you know, flitting from one fancy hotel to the next. He took me with him when he could. Vegas, New York, LA." She heaved another sigh, as if struggling to feed her lungs. "We were so in love."

Regi tried but failed to picture his mother with a man that she truly loved. It seemed to him that Milton was a user and she'd fallen for his fancy shit. He resisted commenting, though, and waited for her to continue.

"His wife caught us. She showed up at our hotel in Chicago. It was horrible."

Regi touched her arm, trying to portray sympathy he didn't feel.

"She told Milton to get rid of me or she'd take him for everything he had. It wasn't fair—he'd built the business from scratch and she just wanted to waltz in and take the whole thing."

Regi refrained from pointing out that she probably had every right to do that.

"But then I found out we were pregnant. It was the best and worst day of my life." When she looked at him, Regi saw distress in her eyes, but for the first time he didn't pity her.

"You deserved so much more," she said. "I wish you'd had a chance to know him; he would've been the perfect father. But Milton and I made a pact. He looked after us, making sure we always had money. We were careful too; he paid me every month in cash... so there was no paper trail."

Every month. Cash. His mind spun. Then it hit him. "You kept seeing him?"

She nodded and lowered her eyes. "Right up until he died." Tears spilled down her cheeks.

"He's dead?" Not once had Regi considered that his father would be dead.

"Yes. He died in a helicopter crash in Canada."

"Canada?"

She sighed and wriggled her head like it was all floppy. "He took his fiancée and son for a vacation."

"What the fuck? He was engaged, and had a son? I have a brother?"

Her eyes rolled and Regi feared she was about to fade away.

"Did. You *did* have a half-brother, but Kane's dead too. They're all dead."

As he glared at her, a million questions bolted through his brain at once. "When? When did they die?"

She went cross-eyed. "About four years ago. That's why I have no more money. It's all gone."

Regi clutched her wrist and shook it. "What money?"

"The cash he gave me, silly. Five thousand every month. He never missed a payment."

"Five thousand," he gasped. "Holy shit, where is it?"

She pointed to the decorative tin that was now on the floor in the corner.

96

The lid was nowhere to be seen. Regi had been walking past that tin for years and had never thought twice about it. He turned back to his mother and her eyes grew so wide he was worried they'd pop right out of her head. "Seven thousand. That was all I had left. Now it's all gone."

Regi frowned at the tin, trying to comprehend that she'd been stashing money in there all this time. He turned back to her. "You kept money in that stupid tin?"

"Yep. Milton said no paper trail. Always a secret." She put her finger to her lips. "Shh." Her head flopped to the side and her eyes fluttered closed.

"What about his estate? Did he leave you anything?"

"No paper trail, remember? You're so silly."

"But… did you fight it?"

"No proof." She wobbled her head side to side. "Not even a photo. Now he's dead."

Regi shook her arm. "Mom. Mom."

But she'd slipped into drug-induced oblivion.

Regi got up and paced the room. His boots crunched on china shards as he strode from one end to the other. His brain flew from one thought to the next. This revelation created as many questions as it did answers.

Now he understood how his mother always had money. It also explained why she'd hit a whole new level of depression four years ago.

Five thousand dollars! Each month. Cash!

Bitch.

Half that money was his. And she'd snorted it up her nose. If she'd been awake, he would've shaken her until her bones rattled. Not that it would've mattered. The money was gone.

His mother groaned, rolled her head sideways, and smacked her lips together. He'd always thought of her as the victim. In his mind, she'd been the innocent one in the relationship with his father. But she was just as much to blame as he was. To have kept their affair going all these years, especially when Milton was married, then engaged, and had a kid? It was totally fucked up.

I have a half brother? Had *a half brother.*

Regi strode to her bedroom with the intention of going through her drawers to find something, anything, to confirm her statements were true. He couldn't even push her door open. There was shit everywhere. Clothes, shoes, underwear, papers. Every drawer had been upended and the clothes in the closet tossed out. The pillows had been slit open and bits of fluff covered everything. He once again wondered if the thugs had been looking for something, and now that he understood the extent of his mother's lies, he wondered if they'd found it.

Five thousand dollars every month.

He couldn't get the figure out of his mind. Milton was rich. That's what his mother had said. To have a wife, a fiancée, and a mistress that he'd paid off for twenty-odd years… he must've been extremely wealthy. And the helicopter ride in Canada. That wouldn't have been cheap.

An idea hit him like a thunderbolt. If Milton *was* his dad, then surely Regi had a claim to his estate.

All he had to do was prove Milton was his father.

CHAPTER SIXTEEN

Four months later

Amber breathed in the crisp air, let it out in a cloudy plume, and tried not to focus on the flurrying snow crystals that landed on every available surface. She'd given up wiping it from her legs. Instead, she wedged her hands between her thighs, trying to ward off the cold that was determined to invade her fingers.

In the five months she'd been coming to Altitude Mountain Resort, she'd grown accustomed to the cold. Not her feet and hands, though—they still felt frozen to the bone every time. Maybe it was the expensive thermal clothing she had beneath her ski gear, which Kelli had helped her choose. Or maybe it was her determination that had put her body's issues aside so she could concentrate on her mission. Either way, she'd come to enjoy her weekends on the mountain with the eternally effervescent Kelli.

The chairlift they were riding was the longest on the mountain, taking them up to the only black run, and Kelli had been speaking almost nonstop since their chair had left the terminal eight minutes ago. Amber had no idea how Kelli did it. If her stories were to be believed, and Amber did believe them, then Kelli partied until nearly four o'clock this morning. Yet she somehow managed to be outrageously excited to see Amber at their regular nine o'clock start.

Amber would have been in bed at nine, ensuring she was ready for the next day. Although Kelli was only two years younger than her, she was a thousand years away in every other aspect. By the time they reached the top, Amber was exhausted just listening to what Kelli did up until just five hours ago.

They pushed off the chair and settled at the edge of the slope to survey down the mountain toward where the resort should be. But it wasn't there; a cloud as thick as sponge had shrouded it completely.

"Looks like we're in for a bit of a snow storm." Kelli said it ridiculously chirpy, like she'd been talking about a nail polish color rather than something that looked like it'd give them a good lashing.

Amber had only experienced two days of poor weather since she'd started visiting this mountain, and both of those she'd spent inside, curled up by the fire, scouring the internet for information about Angel and Frederick.

"Ready?" Amber adjusted her ski mask.

"I guess so."

"Course you are, we've done it tons of times."

That was true. This five-mile ski run was classed as black at the top because of its initial steep vertical descent, which included a few moguls. It leveled out to a cruisy red run that took a wide berth around the resort and hit black run steepness again. At the bottom they'd ride a surface lift back up to the resort. The first time she'd done it, Amber had been petrified and had spent most of the descent on her bum. But thanks to Kelli's insistence she'd done it at least a dozen times since then, and each time was an improvement on the last.

"Come on, I'm getting hungry." Kelli gave Amber a playful shoulder nudge.

Side by side, they glided their skis over the edge and set off down the slope. The familiar rush of adrenaline coursed through her as the wind lapped at her ski jacket. Powdered snow inches thick blanketed the run, making it as smooth as water. Amber hit the moguls in no time and guided her skis through them with a series of quick flick-back turns.

"Beat ya," Kelli yelled as they popped out the bottom of the moguls. Amber laughed with the crazy young woman as they flew toward the next turn.

Her clouded breaths shot in and out in rapid succession as her energy level hit maximum. She wished Oliver could see her now, tearing up the snow-burdened slope like an expert. He'd smile at her, with that look of pride that she'd come to love.

She was so lost in thought that when she reached the bottom of the black run she was surprised at how black and burdened the sky looked.

When she glanced at Kelli, who'd paused at a line of trees, her usual smiling face was gone and Amber thought she saw terror written on her features.

"What?" Amber scooted across the snow toward her.

"I think I heard the siren. That's not good. We've gotta get off the mountain."

"What siren?"

"Storm siren. We need to do this fast and hard. I know you can do it, Amber. Let's go." Kelli shot forward, heading toward a cloud that seemed to be sitting on the snow. It was the first time Kelli hadn't let her lead the way, and that one simple action highlighted how serious this was.

Bolts of fear shot up Amber's back, and her heart was in her throat as she drove her poles into the powder and chased after Kelli. She tucked her sticks under her elbows, hunched over, offering as little wind resistance as she could, and let gravity take over.

The ski run's vertical descent was over one and a quarter mile and, being south-facing, it held the snow well. Sometimes too well, and they'd have to wade knee-deep to get through it. Not today, though. It was an ideal four inches or so, which gave little resistance. Amber guessed she was flying at about thirty miles per hour and that scared her more than the black clouds swirling overhead.

Kelli was a red blur in the distance, cutting through the white haze with a series of tight swishes. Amber couldn't tell, but she was certain Kelli would be taking frequent glances over her shoulder to confirm she was still behind her.

The wind screamed rather than howled and struck her at every angle; it was an effort just to remain upright. Sleet and snow attacked in a relentless torrent, and the icy needles pounded her only exposed skin—her face.

A clap of thunder pierced her eardrums, and when a fork of lightning cut through the clouds, she reached up to shield her head. It was the wrong move.

Her face hit the snow and Amber tumbled over and over, cartwheeling down the slope. Her skis flung off and her body nearly snapped in half when she hit a tree.

The wind punched out of her and her ribs suffered the full brunt of the impact. She crumpled into a heap at the base of the tree, and it was a couple of frantic heartbeats before she realized what'd happened.

Giant trees above her bent and moaned, spitting clumps of heavy snow from their overburdened branches. She searched for Kelli, praying she'd appear out of nowhere. But visibility was barely three feet. After straining to see through the whiteout, her heart sank as she conceded Kelli was gone.

Amber was alone. Scared and alone.

Suddenly she was back on that icy ledge. Battered and broken. Frozen to her core, and so scared she could hardly breathe. Dread crawled up her spine as she remembered the terror that'd numbed her brain. She felt that now. Not from the deafening cracks of thunder that split through the menacing cloud. Not from the ice that pummeled from the sky like bullets. It was the fact that she was alone. Freezing, terrified, and alone.

The moaning trees took on a life of their own, and brittle limbs were torn from the trunks, adding extra ammunition to the ice-laden gale-force winds.

A tree limb crashed at Amber's side, and it was the jolt she needed to get moving. She dragged her body upright, and that's when she remembered that her skis had snapped off in the fall. If she was to get out of this, she needed them.

She pushed off the trunk and, after a frantic search, found evidence of the path she'd tumbled down. It was nearly obliterated by the snow and wind. Using her poles for support, she tracked her path uphill. Each pace was a heavy step upward, and as she contemplated crawling on her hands and knees a sense of urgency gripped her like a full-blown fever. One ski appeared out of nowhere just eight steps away, and she plucked it from the ground.

Continuing upward, she lost all sense of time. She lost all sense of direction. All she had was uphill or downhill. Her heart thumped in her ears with both exhaustion and panic.

The second ski was nearly buried, and it was by pure luck that she stood on it. Shattered, she crumbled to the snow.

It'd be easy to stop. To crawl into a ball and wait for it to be over.

But, for the first time in years, she wanted to live.

An image of Oliver pitched into her brain. He was smiling at her—not just smiling, he was so proud of her he was bursting. She loved that look. But it was more than that. So much more. Oliver was entering her heart. Little by little. Filling her heart with a want she'd never felt before. Never. Even with Milton. This was deeper. Right into her soul. And each time she resisted Oliver's advances she saw the confusion in his eyes… and the hurt. She hated herself every time. She desperately wanted to tell him her feelings, and everything else too. Most of all, she needed to be with Oliver.

She pushed up from the snow. Dying here was not an option.

Oliver drove her to succeed in the gym. He drove her to succeed now too.

The blizzard was merciless, buffeting her with invisible fists that packed a punch, but she forced her mind to concentrate on getting down the mountain. She angled her body sideways and clipped on her skis.

Debris tumbled in the vortex, peppering the whiteout with chunks of black, and it was impossible to differentiate sky from ground. Gravity was her only certainty. With that knowledge, she inhaled a deep shaky breath and angled her skis downhill.

Although she couldn't see them, the trees that lined the ski run were her only hope to keeping on track, so she glided to the left until they came into view. Tempering her speed with the angle of her skis, she counted her turns as a way of keeping her mind off the insanity around her. At one hundred, she started again.

Progression was slow. Not the blizzard, though—the ferocious wind seemed to get stronger around every turn. But she pushed on. A couple of times she recognized different aspects of the run, but it was when she saw the marker indicating she was near the surface lift she just about cried with relief.

A wire above caught her eye, and she yelled for joy at the sight of it. It was the cable that pulled the T-bars up the hill. But her joy was short-lived when she realized it wasn't moving.

Her one and only way to get up to the resort had stopped.

Without any other choice, she forced the tears from her eyes and used the overhead wires to guide her to the turnstile that powered the T-bar up the mountain. At the very least, she could hide in the turnstile shed until the storm was over. With a bit of luck, there may even be a phone inside.

She passed the stationary T-bars that were positioned at regular intervals and was grateful just to have something to follow. The bright yellow building that housed the turning circle for the T-bars appeared amidst the whiteout, but it was the presence of Kelli, who came running with open arms, that had tears of relief springing to Amber's eyes.

Kelli wrapped her in a bear hug and openly wept as she apologized a thousand times.

"It's okay." She squeezed Kelli to her chest.

"No, it's not. I'm so sorry. I couldn't find you. I've been going out of my mind."

"I crashed when that lightning hit. Did you see it?"

"Way up the top?" Kelli hugged her again. "You're amazing. Come inside, you must be freezing."

She turned and clomped ahead while Amber skied the final couple of yards to the shed. And that was all it really was: a shed, with only three walls because the wire fed in and out of the open side. But after what Amber had just been through, it was a mansion.

She clipped out of her skis and joined Kelli in the corner.

"You must've been scared outta your mind." Kelli wrapped her arms around Amber again.

She shrugged. "I've had worse."

"Oh god, girlfriend. You're the strongest woman I know. Here, sit down." Kelli guided Amber to the corner and tugged a metallic blanket over her. Then she plucked a two-way radio off the wall.

"T-bar trap to base. T-bar to base. This is Kelli, do you read?"

The speaker crackled to life. "Yes, Kelli. We hear you."

"Amber made it; the crazy woman just appeared right out of the storm."

There were cheers on the other end of the line and Amber's heart swelled at the sound.

"That's great news, Kelli. Now for the bad news. You'll have to hunker down for an hour or so, till the storm blows over."

"That's cool. Us girls have got some catching up to do anyway. Right, Amber?"

Amber grinned and nodded. As Kelli finished up the call and fussed about finding emergency supplies of water, energy bars, and space blankets, Amber realized how lucky she was to have found Kelli. Their friendship had grown to be one of the most powerful relationships she'd ever had. Kelli was both a source of fun and a wealth of inspiration. And even though she was a nonstop chatterbox, she was also a great listener. Not that Amber talked much. But as they settled into the corner that offered the most protection from the wind, Amber realized that this was the perfect time to tell Kelli some of the secrets that'd been crushing her for what seemed like ever.

Outside, the storm raged and wind slammed into the sides of the shed with such force that Amber wouldn't have been surprised if the roof ripped off. Inside, snuggled up against each other, she told Kelli about her injuries, her coma, her recovery, and her mother dying.

During the story, they'd cried together, and Kelli hugged Amber often. There were many things she couldn't mention, though. She never elaborated on the crash, and Kelli most likely assumed it was a car crash. She didn't mention her fiancé or his son. She left out her name change, the bodies in the ice, the murderer label that Victoria had given her, and Milton's inheritance. She hated that she couldn't tell Kelli everything. She loved Kelli, there was no doubt about that. But she wasn't sure Kelli could keep anything a secret. After all, verbal diarrhea was Kelli's thing. She wasn't malicious, she was just a chatterbox.

By the time the T-bar lift shunted to life, Amber felt like an enormous concrete blanket had been lifted from her body. It'd been cathartic to reveal some of her burdens, and Amber believed her friendship with Kelli had launched to a whole new level. And it was perfect.

When they finally arrived at the resort, the cheers from the waiting crowd were overwhelming. A party struck up almost instantly, and the second a woolen blanket was draped over Amber's shoulders, a wine was put into her hand. Kelli was the life of the party, and during her retelling of the drama in the storm, she made Amber out to be some kind of mythical being that amazingly emerged from the whiteout.

She hugged Amber to her side. "She's incredible."

The crowd lapped it up, and Amber's embarrassment over the attention hit maximum capacity. Yet for the first time in years, her hideous wound took a back seat.

It was like releasing the elephant in the room. And now that it was done, nobody seemed to notice. Maybe all these years of hiding behind it had been the wrong choice. People were more interested in what they couldn't see. Once she got that initial exposure out of the way, it was like they no longer cared.

Like Oliver. He didn't seem to notice it anymore either. Nor Kelli.

The whole concept was like a brilliant light. Focused, daring, enlightening.

By the time she'd had her second wine, she was totally relaxed, and for the first time in as long as she could remember, she was enjoying being in a crowd of strangers.

Once again, she found herself wishing Oliver could be here to see her.

It seemed like an eternity before she was able to leave the celebration, and

Erik was a gentleman and walked her back to her chalet. Once safely at her door, he pulled her in for a hug and kissed the top of her head. "So glad you're okay."

"Thanks." She was beyond flustered as she listened to his thumping heart.

He pulled back. "Okay then, see you tomorrow." He turned and set off back toward the party.

She was glowing inside and out by the time she stepped into the cabin.

In her bathroom, she stripped out of her clothes and reluctantly glanced in the mirror. She already assumed she'd have bruises, but the quantity and the severity of them had her gasping. It looked like she'd been shoved in a cocktail maker with chunks of ice and shaken like crazy. The bulk of her bruising was on her hips, buttocks, ribs, and shoulders. A couple on her thighs and shins were straight lines, and she assumed they were from the dislodging skis.

Pain had been her constant companion for many years now, but that didn't mean it hurt any less. She was eternally grateful her body had slipped into a coma after the chopper accident, because she doubted she could have handled the pain she would've suffered.

But the pain she was feeling now took a back seat to another emotion: pride.

Her determination in the storm proved her strength had improved a thousand-fold from the woman who'd woken from the coma. And not just physically, mentally too. The fact that she chose life over death was truly empowering. She'd turned a corner and was now treading on exciting groundbreaking territory.

After a long hot shower, she pulled on flannel pajamas and fluffy socks and wrapped a woolen scarf around her neck. She'd taken to wearing a red scarf, similar to the one Angel had been wearing when she'd frozen to death in that crevice. Somehow it made her feel closer to the poor woman whose demise had been destined to remain untold. Amber planned on changing that, though. And she was pretty confident she was on track.

She poured her usual glass of wine nightcap, although with how exhausted she already felt, she doubted she'd have any trouble sleeping. Placing her wine on the side table, she switched on her laptop and curled up in front of the fire to go through her emails.

The very first message had her sitting up, wide awake.

Carter Logan had finally responded to one of her five emails.

KENDALL TALBOT

106

CHAPTER SEVENTEEN

The entire time Oliver was belaying for Peter, who was halfway up the rock wall, he shared his concentration between the climber and the blackness outside. He knew Amber would be out there, hiding in the shadows. It no longer seemed strange that she did this. He'd come to accept her secrecy. He just hoped that one day she'd feel comfortable enough to confide in him. And when she did, he hoped he'd react in a way that didn't scare her off.

The bell sounded, signaling Peter had reached the top, and Oliver scolded himself for missing it as he lowered Peter to the mat. "Good work, buddy."

"Felt great up there tonight."

"Excellent, that's how it's meant to feel." Oliver clapped Peter on the shoulder.

"Yeah, it doesn't always, though."

"If it was always amazing, you wouldn't recognize the good times."

"You, my friend, missed your calling." Peter unclipped his harness.

"Really?" Oliver chuckled. Intrigued, he asked, "What should I be doing?"

"Priesthood, or something just as godly."

"Oh jeez, Pete, I think you went too high on that climb."

Peter laughed. "It's true, you're a miracle worker."

When he'd first come into Oliver's gym, Peter had just separated from his wife of seven years. He was a broken man who'd devoted his life to his work and left little time for his marriage or his health. To his credit, Peter had since turned his life around. He put the balance back into his work/life equation. He dedicated a chunk of his schedule to getting fit, and he'd put a concerted effort into fighting for his marriage. His efforts had paid off—he was back with his wife and he looked incredible.

"You did all the work, Pete."

"Thanks to you." Peter tapped Oliver on the shoulder. "See you next week."

"Sure thing."

Oliver followed Peter to the front door, and after he left, he searched the shadows. Amber appeared out of nowhere, and he couldn't stop the smile blazing across his lips. "There you are. Quick, get in before anyone sees you."

She chuckled as she slinked beneath the arm he was using to hold the door open. As she strolled toward the office, he shut the door and twisted the sign around to closed.

Amber flipped the bag off her shoulder and turned to him. "How was your day?"

"Same, same." A potent mix of hormones dosed his veins when he inhaled her delicious scent. It was floral, spicy, and familiar. It was Amber. "How about you? See anything interesting in those reports?"

"Well," she said, "one of the doctors is treating a woman who eats dry dog biscuits to keep in touch with her dog that died."

Oliver's jaw dropped. "Tell me you're joking."

"Nope. The dog died ten years ago."

"That's disgusting. And weird."

"And very sad." She scrunched up her nose, and when she tucked her hair behind her right ear, he had to resist pulling her into his chest and squeezing her tight. When he'd first met her, she did everything possible to drape her hair across her scar. Now, though, she wasn't as self-conscious. He liked to think he'd helped with that transformation.

"Actually, they probably taste better than those vegetarian sausages you eat." Oliver was a devoted meat and vegetables man. Throw in a beer and he was as happy as the winner of the World Series. He couldn't comprehend how someone could live on vegetables alone. He wondered how Amber had any energy at all.

She playfully slapped his arm. "You should try them, they're good."

"Oh, no no no. Bring on the big fat steak for me." He chuckled and liked the easy grin lighting up her face. She smiled freely now. And laughed. It'd been a full six weeks before he'd heard her laugh. Now she was the one cracking the jokes, and he loved every minute with her—so much so that he'd become a constant clock-watcher, counting down the minutes to her next session.

"You ready to break your record?"

"Sure am." Amber's climbing ability had not only surprised him, it'd made him rethink the way he assessed new customers. Never before had he underestimated someone so completely. She'd taken to the sport so well that he occasionally wondered if she'd done it before. If she had, she did an amazing job of faking her inexperience. He doubted she was lying. Oliver had always considered himself an expert judge of people. He'd know if she were lying.

If it was competition rock climbing Amber was seeking, he was certain she'd be capable of winning gold soon. Although she'd never actually voiced that as her goal. At this point he had no idea why rock climbing was so important to her.

"Climber ready," Amber announced as she paused at the base of the wall. "Up you go then."

She smacked the timer and launched up the wall with the confidence of an expert and the agility of a cat. Unlike his earlier customer, he couldn't take his eyes off her. Amber was born for this form of exercise. She was tiny and slender, and since she'd started climbing, new muscle definition was noticeable despite the full-length clothing she wore all the time.

He'd give anything to see more of her. Her arms, her legs—hell, he'd like to see all of her flesh. He swallowed hard at that thought, but he couldn't deny it. His attraction to Amber had gone beyond fleeting. He wanted to learn everything there was to know about this beautiful yet mysterious woman. Amber's insistence on covering herself had him convinced she had more scars.

He didn't care.

He'd dated gorgeous women before. Women who spent more time in the mirror than their beauty warranted. But they became so caught up in their looks that it cost them in personality.

Amber's understated ordinariness made her simply stunning.

There was a shyness to her too, an uncertainty in her body movements that he sometimes thought was the result of constant pain. Yet put her near a climbing wall and she was a demon. And with each progression she made up the skill levels, she came more out of shell.

She was like a butterfly emerging from an oppressive cocoon.

When she smiled, something radiated from within her that rendered him useless.

Amber was nearly at the top, and he could already tell she was about to smash another personal best. She had yet to progress to the final level, but it'd been him holding her back.

It wasn't that he didn't think she was capable. Oh hell no.

He was more worried about where she'd go after that. Her progression through the levels had been so swift, she'd no doubt smash through the next level too. Then what would she do? Find another sport? He had no idea. One thing was certain: he couldn't hold her off for too long.

Amber was on a mission, but he had yet to establish what that mission was.

She smashed the bell and the timer confirmed another personal record. Amber whooped as she fell into the harness. As Oliver lowered her to the ground, he couldn't wipe the grin from his face. This was another aspect about her that'd blossomed since their first meeting. It'd taken her weeks to show any emotion. Not anymore, though.

Seconds after her feet found the padded mat, he loosened the rope and stepped forward to touch her shoulder. "You're on fire tonight."

"Must've been that herbed tofu I had before I came." Her eyes twinkled.

"Oh god, stop it, you'll make me sick just thinking about it."

"Exaggerator. How can you complain if you've never tried it?"

"Is that an invitation to dinner?" He wriggled his brows.

The smile curling her mouth was so genuine and sweet, his breath caught.

He grumbled at the tinkle of the bell and turned toward the door. His heart sank as he watched Larissa stride toward them like a marauding bull. "What's going on here?" She stopped two feet from Oliver, but glared at Amber.

Out of the corner of his eye he saw Amber pull the band from her hair and tousle it over her scar.

"Larissa, this is a private lesson, would you mind—"

"Is this why you've been ignoring me, 'cause of her?" The words snapped off Larissa's tongue like they were laced with poison.

"I haven't been ignoring you."

"Bullshit." She spun to Amber. "Who're you?"

Amber had stepped back a few paces and lowered her eyes.

"Larissa, you have to leave." Oliver pointed at the door.

"I will not. I want answers, Oliver. You said you'd take me to the championships, but now I find you taking secret lessons with… with this."

"Hey, cut it out! You have no right—"

"Don't I? I was going for gold… for you. You, and your stupid gym. What's she doing for you?"

"Amber's a better climber than you'll ever be." He spat the words out.

Three things happened at once: Amber snapped her eyes to him, Larissa noticeably cringed at Amber's scar, and a look of absolute fear riddled Amber's features.

"Oh yeah? Prove it, bitch."

"Larissa, it's time for you to leave." He went to reach for her arm, but she snapped it away.

"No, Olly! We had an agreement."

"What agreement? You're a client—"

"A client! Is that all I am?"

"Yes. That's all. And I'm teaching you how to—"

"Oh, and I suppose she's *just* a client!" She aimed her finger at Amber.

He clenched his jaw, and maybe Larissa saw the fire in his eyes, because she stepped back.

"How do we prove it?"

Oliver and Larissa both spun to Amber's comment.

"What?" Larissa snapped.

"You wanted me to prove it. How?"

His heart squeezed at both the danger and determination simmering in Amber's stunning blue eyes. "You don't have to do this."

"I know." She squared her chin and glared at Larissa. "I want to. How's it done?"

Larissa's top lip twitched. "We race. If you're as good as he says you are, you'll beat me."

Amber frowned, and Oliver knew why she was confused: she'd never seen anyone race. "You go up one at a time, the one with the quickest time wins."

"Okay." Amber nodded and glanced up the wall.

"Oh, this just gets better and better." Larissa chuckled. "You've never even raced?"

"Shut up, Larissa."

"Don't tell me—"

"I'm ready." Amber glared at Larissa. Oliver had seen resolve in Amber's eyes before, but this was different. This look blazed with insane recklessness. He'd seen that look on her a few times too. It was like this was another test that she simply had to do. Like her life depended on it.

Realizing this had gone too far, he reached out to touch Amber's forearm.

"I'm doing this." She clenched her jaw, then, as she pulled her hair back into a band, she turned so Larissa could get a full look at her scar. Oliver had never felt such a strong sense of pride as he did at that very moment. His heart swelled to bursting, and all he wanted to do was wrap his arms around her and tell her exactly how he felt.

"I'll get my gear." Larissa's cocky smile indicated she thought Amber would be a pushover. She turned on her heel, jogged to the front door, and disappeared outside.

Oliver reached for Amber's hand, and when their palms connected it was like they'd been holding hands for years. "You don't have to do this."

"Did you mean what you said about me being a better climber than Larissa?"

"I meant every word. I've never taught a climber like you; you have a natural gift for this sport."

A flicker of triumph rippled across her eyes and her cheeks blushed. "So tell me how to win."

Aware that there was no talking her out of it, he switched to coach mode. "Take your time, and don't rush. Don't even think about the clock. You're good at this. Trust your instincts and concentrate on your core and balance. There's a slight overhang on this one, only just a bit more angle than what you've been doing. Nothing that you can't handle. Pivot your hips and reach, just like I've taught you."

Larissa slammed the door shut after she reentered the gym, and both Oliver and Amber turned to her. Larissa's expression was a mixture of cockiness and hate, and in that moment Oliver learned what it was like to truly despise someone. No matter what happened, after this, Larissa would no longer share time with him.

"I'll get changed and then we'll do this." Larissa strode into Oliver's office and shut the door.

Oliver turned back to Amber and their eyes met again. "You don't have to do this."

"Yes, Oliver, I do." She clenched her jaw and swallowed.

Her comment confirmed this was no longer about Larissa. This was about Amber. She needed to prove something. Maybe to herself. Hopefully not to him. He reached for her hand and squeezed. "You can do this. You're the best climber I've ever seen." He just hoped she could see how much he meant every word.

"Who's going first?" Larissa demanded as she strode from his office.

Oliver gave one last squeeze before he released Amber's hand, stepped back, and glared at Larissa. "You're the one who put out the challenge. You go first."

"I don't have a problem with that, do you?" If eyes were daggers, Larissa would've sliced Amber's face off.

"Not at all." Amber stepped off the mat, giving them room.

Larissa pulled a harness from the wall, tugged it on, and tied the belay rope into position. Oliver prepared his belay device and confirmed he was ready.

Larissa stepped up to the wall and her hand hovered over the timer's start button. "Climber ready."

"Safety ready."

She slammed her palm onto the clock starter and launched up the wall. Larissa raced up the first couple of holds like she was running on flat ground. Within seconds she was ten feet up the wall. But the higher she went, the more challenging the climb became, and Oliver knew she'd slow down—unless she became so flustered by the race that she forgot the basics, which she'd been known to do.

He was banking on that now.

Out of the corner of his eye he spied the intense look on Amber's face as she watched Larissa scramble to the top, and with a jolt he realized that he'd become so caught up in this stupid race that he hadn't stopped to consider the repercussions should Larissa win or, more importantly, Amber lose.

Would it deflate Amber, or motivate her more?

He had no idea. It was a pointless debate—he'd have an answer soon enough.

Larissa launched for a hold, but swore as she missed it. She regrouped and went for the hold again. She got it that time, but her feet swung off the wall, costing her precious time. Larissa yelled out, obviously aware that the mistake would cost her. But she swung her hips, repositioning her feet on the hold, and pushed on.

After a couple more holds, she reached the overhang. But, typical of Larissa's style, she didn't pause to assess the route. She plowed on, and Oliver hoped it'd be her defeat. She made it around the overhang, and less than half a minute later she slammed her fist into the bell.

Without announcing her release, she let go of the wall. Oliver caught her in the rope and lowered her down. Her cocky grin indicated she was happy with her time. It wasn't her best effort, though—that slip had cost her valuable seconds.

Oliver wasn't sure if Amber could beat it, but he was certain she'd give it everything she had, and that meant she'd get very close.

Larissa wriggled out of her harness and stepped back. "Your turn," she snarled at Amber, and if Oliver had thought he'd despised Larissa before, he hated her now.

Oliver stepped between the women, blocking Larissa's evil glare. He leaned in to Amber's ear. "Focus on your movements and find your flow. Do what you do best."

She simply nodded and set about tying the climbers knot.

Once she was done, she inhaled deeply and let out a long slow breath before she stepped up to the wall. "Climber ready."

"Safety ready." Oliver's stomach twisted into knots as he watched her steady herself. Her shoulders rose and fell with another deep breath. She closed her eyes, and when she reopened them, he saw the focus that he'd come to expect from her.

She slammed the timer and launched up the wall like a nimble monkey. Each movement was smooth; each hold she gripped was committed on her first go. She was fast—very fast—and Oliver was certain she was ahead of Larissa's time. He could feel Larissa's dagger eyes in his back but was grateful she remained behind him.

Amber reached the overhang but didn't slow her pace. She seemed to scan the route with the efficiency of a climber who'd been doing it for years. Amber was up and over the overhang and reached for the pinch hold to her right. Her feet slipped and swung out from the wall, but with a strength that belied her size she used only her arms to hurl herself at the next hold.

She made it and was able to reposition her feet. But she'd lost time.

Oliver's heart was in his throat as his eyes flicked from the digits on the clock to Amber's movements. His gut squeezed as he realized she wasn't going to make it. She was out by seconds, maybe even less than a second. With two more holds to go, Amber released an almighty growl and threw herself at the bell.

Oliver caught her in the rope and she swung from the wall in a pendulum.

There was a moment's silence before Amber let out a squeal of joy. She'd won by half a second.

"Fuck!" Larissa yelled, and out of the corner of his eye he saw her pick up her pack and storm away.

"See ya," Amber called from halfway up the wall.

"Fuck you, bitch!" Larissa yelled before she strode out the door, slamming it behind her.

The second Amber's feet touched the ground he went to her. They wrapped their arms around each other and he squeezed her tight. "You're amazing."

"I can't believe I won."

"I can."

She pulled back to look up at him, and Oliver knew without a doubt he was looking at the woman he wanted to spend the rest of his life with. He couldn't fight the feelings coursing through him. Her eyes flickered to his lips and, hoping he read the signals right, he leaned over. When his lips touched hers, he knew he'd read the signs perfectly. They melted into each other, their bodies aligned, her soft lips parted, and they tilted their heads. He'd kissed many women before, but this was different. Like two souls becoming one. A whimper tumbled from her throat, and it was the most glorious sound he'd ever heard.

He didn't want the kiss to end, but when they parted and he saw the longing in her eyes he knew she felt the same way.

Oliver reached up and cupped her right cheek. He barely noticed the raised scarring beneath his palm. "I'm so proud of you."

Her chin quivered. "Thank you."

He touched his lips to hers again. A brief kiss that said so much more. A strange feeling floated through his body. It was overwhelming, yet it felt so right. Oliver felt like he was about to step into a fire, yet at the same time he wanted to do it so badly it hurt.

"Let's get you out of this." He unclipped his belay rope.

"Okay, then we need to do something about this." She held up her hand.

"Holy shit." Her pinky finger stuck out at a hideous angle. "You broke your finger."

"Just dislocated, I think."

"It must hurt like hell."

She shrugged. "I've had worse."

He melted at her casualness. "I bet you have." Their gaze met and he hoped she'd elaborate, yet at the same time he knew this was neither the right time nor the right place for that discussion. When she finally opened up to him, he wanted everything to be perfect. "Let's get you to a doctor."

"Can't you just pop it back in?"

"What?" His jaw dropped. "You're joking, right?"

"No. I'm sure it won't hurt."

"It'll hurt like hell, and I have no idea how to do it."

She must've seen how adamant he was because she sighed. "I hate doctors."

Her calmness was crazy. "You're going to love this doctor, I promise."

He grabbed her good hand and led her toward the front door.

"Will the doctor's office even be open?"

"He's always open."

He helped Amber into his car, raced around to the driver's side, and jumped in. "Does it hurt?"

"Not really."

He kicked the car into gear and reversed out of the lot. "Did you do it when you jumped for the bell?"

She nodded. "Yeah."

"I can't believe you did that."

"I wanted to win."

"I can tell. Are you always this competitive?"

"No. I've never won anything in my life."

He chuckled. "Shit, you could've fooled me."

As the glow from the streetlights flicked past in alternating shades of light and dark, Amber lifted her hand and reviewed her dislocated finger with what looked like complete indifference. He couldn't believe how nonchalant she was. Every other woman he knew would be hysterical if it'd happened to them. Every man too. Not Amber, though. It was almost as if she'd done it a thousand times before. Maybe she had. Her soul was fragile, but her body was a machine. He cast the thoughts aside and turned onto Jordan's narrow street lined with houses on either side.

"So how do you know this doctor?"

"We went to school together." He pulled up outside a whitewashed Georgian colonial.

"Is this where he lives?"

"Yep."

"Are you sure he'll be okay with us going to his home?"

"Shh, stop complaining."

"I didn't think I was."

"Trust me. It's definitely okay."

She allowed him to help her out of the car and they walked up to the front porch. Oliver knocked on the front door.

A few moments later, a young boy opened the door.

"Hey, Max."

"Uncle Olly!" The kid opened his arms and Oliver lifted him up and squeezed. "Boy, have you grown up." He carried Max across the threshold. "Where's your daddy?"

"He's watching hockey."

Ice hockey was Jordan's first love. His wife and child came in a very close second and, much to Helen's disgust, Jordan wasn't scared to admit it. "Who's winning?" Oliver said as he stepped into a cozy lounge with two brown leather chesterfields, a large brick fireplace, and an enormous television centered on the wall.

"Oliver, how're you doing, man?"

"I'm great. I'd like you to meet Amber. She's had a bit of an accident."

Amber held up her hand.

"Oh wow, okay then." Jordan pushed off the couch.

"Owee." Max's eyes bulged at Amber's finger and Oliver put the boy down. "Does it hurt?"

"Not really." She held it forward so Max could get a better look.

"Come into the kitchen." Jordan led the way. "Put your clothes on, honey, we've got visitors." Oliver knew he was joking. Jordan had a wacky sense of humor.

Helen was smiling when they entered the kitchen but it quickly changed to a look of horror when she saw Amber's finger. "Oh my god, what happened?" Helen pulled out a chair and demanded Amber sit.

"Hey, Helen." Oliver kissed her cheek. "This's Amber. It was a rock-climbing incident."

"Wow, you sure know how to show the ladies a good time." Helen grinned, picked up Max, and sat him in a chair opposite Amber.

Jordan thumped Oliver in the shoulder. "Yeah. No wonder you're still single."

"You guys are a laugh a minute."

Amber stayed silent, but a grin remained on her face as she followed the banter from one person to the next.

Jordan looked to his wife. "Honey, can you get me some ice, please?"

"Sure." She turned to the freezer at the end of the kitchen.

Jordan sat beside Amber and reached for her hand. "Is there any tingling?"

"No."

"Can you feel this?" He pinched the end of the finger.

"Yes."

"That's good. It looks like it's dislocated, not broken."

"Can you pop it back in?"

"I can, but I'll give you a local anesthetic first." He turned to his wife. "Honey, can you grab my bag?"

"Sure." Helen plonked a bag of ice on the table and strode from the room.

"It's going to bruise and be sore for a few days."

"I'll be fine," Amber said matter-of-fact.

Jordan's lips formed into a thin smile. "I'm sure you will. But it'll still be sore. No rock climbing for a week or so."

Her eyes shot to Oliver.

Oliver winked. "We'll just have to find something else to keep you busy."

"Watch out for this guy," Jordan joked.

Amber smiled. "Don't worry, I'm keeping an eye on him."

Helen placed a well-worn leather bag on the table and Jordan stood and pulled apart the two sides. He rummaged around for a moment, then removed a syringe and small vial of clear liquid.

"Can I get you two a drink?" Helen was the eternal host, even in a time of crisis.

"After this." Oliver touched his hand to Amber's shoulder. "We'll need a good dose of whiskey, I think."

"I'm fine," Amber said.

Jordan filled the syringe, cupped Amber's hand in his, and turned it over so he could access the underside of her finger. "Just a little sting."

"Okay." Amber didn't take her eyes off the needle piercing her skin, nor did she flinch as he injected her in three different locations on her pinky finger.

After a minute or so of more lame jokes, Jordan pinched the end of her finger again. "Can you feel that?"

"Not this time."

Helen gathered Max into her arms. "Come on, little man. Let's go see how the hockey's going."

"Aw, Mom." Max glanced over Helen's shoulder as she carried him from the room.

"Okay." Jordan gripped the tip of her finger. "Ready? One… two…" He snapped her finger, and the sickening crack made Oliver's stomach flip. Amber, however, showed no sign that she'd felt or heard a thing.

Jordan plucked a roll of tape from his bag and strapped her pinky finger to her adjoining finger. Then he handed her the tape. "Keep them piggybacked together for a few days for support."

"Okay."

"So, now that you're here, you can save me." Jordan looked up at Oliver with pleading eyes. "Helen was about to make me change the channel. We can pretend it was your idea."

"I heard that," Helen said.

"Shit," Jordan whispered.

Helen walked in, grinning. "You can have your stupid hockey. As long as Amber agrees to share a glass of wine with me."

Oliver would normally jump at the chance to watch hockey with his friend, but he felt terrible about Amber being put on the spot. He turned to her, curious about her reaction. So far, she'd gone out of her way to avoid being near people.

To his surprise, she smiled and nodded. "Actually, I could use some wine."

"That settles it then." Jordan smacked his hands together and stood. "Come on, before they change their minds."

Jordan pulled a beer from the fridge and handed it to Oliver, then led him to the sofa and directed him to sit. The sound was turned up, but the whole time he tried to concentrate on hockey, Oliver was actually trying to hear how Amber was doing.

When the two ladies burst out laughing he wanted to run to them and see what they were cackling at. As the game clock ticked down, he spent more time analyzing how he felt about her than watching the action. For the first time in years, he found himself mesmerized by a woman. He just hoped she felt the same way. If their kiss earlier was any way to judge, he believed she did.

After the game, he couldn't get off the sofa quick enough. He strode through the kitchen and found the ladies sitting in a couple of chairs in the back room. Amber had an empty wineglass in front of her.

"Who won?" Helen asked at the men's appearance.

"Not the right team."

"Wondered why we didn't hear you cheering."

Oliver pulled out the chair next to Amber and touched her arm. "How's your finger?"

She shrugged. "It's fine. I don't think the drugs have worn off yet. Ask me tomorrow."

"What've you ladies been talking about? We heard you laughing."

Helen touched her nose. "Secret women's business."

"Yeah right. You've probably been telling Amber lies about me."

Helen clutched her chest in mock hurt. "Never."

Again Amber followed the banter with her intense blue eyes. At a pause in the conversation, he squeezed her forearm. "You ready for me to take you home?"

"Yeah." Amber nodded at Helen. "It was lovely meeting you."

"Likewise."

She turned to Jordan. "Thank you for fixing my finger."

"My pleasure," he said. "Just don't make a habit of it."

"You don't have to worry about that," Oliver said.

"Yeah right." Jordan rolled his eyes.

Oliver kissed Helen goodbye, and after shaking Jordan's hand with a clap on the back, he and Amber headed out the front door.

The drive to her house was short. Way too short for Oliver's liking, and he wracked his brain for a way to prolong the journey. But it wasn't to be. At her address, he climbed out and again helped Amber from the car.

"Can I walk you to your door?"

Her eyes softened and she chewed on her bottom lip. "It's just up there."

"It's no trouble."

Her cheeks blushed. "Okay, that'd be nice."

Positive a ripple of delight had flickered across her eyes, he bent his left elbow. She pushed her good hand in and as they walked side by side up the path, Oliver couldn't decide if it was the heat of her body or the flush of desire blazing through him that filled him with warmth.

"Well, this is it." She stopped outside a door with the number four centered on it.

He turned to face her. "May I take you out to dinner on Saturday night?"

She seemed to deflate and shook her head. "I'm skiing again this weekend. At Altitude Mountain."

Her decline had him heading into uncharted territory. Never before had he felt so disappointed about being let down. "When do you leave?"

"First thing Saturday morning."

"Damn." He felt like a wrecking ball had slammed into his chest.

Something flickered across her eyes. It was like she was on the verge of taking a giant leap but didn't know how to make it. Silently praying that it was a leap his way, he reached for her hand. Their fingers entwined like they'd done it thousands of times before.

But she didn't leap. She didn't do anything but chew on the inside of her lip. He decided to take the jump himself.

"I haven't been skiing in a while. Maybe I could come with you?" His heart thumped in his ears as he waited for her response. "If you want, of course."

"Really?" She tugged on her lip as if trying not to smile. "You can get out of work?"

"Of course." Oliver felt like he could fly. "I'll check for accommodation in the morning. See if they have a spare cabin."

A twinkle danced across her beautiful blue eyes. "My cabin has a comfy sofa. You could sleep on that."

Oliver couldn't stop the grin blazing across his lips. "Sounds perfect."

KENDALL TALBOT

CHAPTER EIGHTEEN

For more than a day, Amber had been checking her phone with the expectation that Oliver would call to say that he couldn't make the trip up the mountain. But there'd been no such call, and as she attempted to keep her mind on packing, she'd begun to wonder if his offer had been a dream.

Her brain was like the giant pirate ship at the fair, smashing through one emotion after the other: fear that spending two whole days with Oliver would make her accidentally reveal who she really was, excitement about getting to know him better, and worry that he'd see more of her scars and be as disgusted by her body as she was. But the overriding emotion was curiosity about how a man like Oliver could be even remotely interested in a girl like her.

She was introverted, insecure, and… average.

Oliver was the exact opposite. Confident, charismatic, and stunning.

He could have any woman he wanted.

Of that she was certain. He was funny and successful too. Everyone loved him, men and women alike. They were drawn to him like metal to a magnet. She'd seen it many times while hiding in the shadows waiting for everyone to leave the gym. His customers idolized him; his staff respected him.

Yet for some reason he seemed to be interested in her. She hoped like hell she was reading the signals right or she'd have some serious mental backtracking to do.

She packed her bag into the trunk, and without any other reason to delay she jumped into her mother's car and headed toward the address that Oliver had scrawled down two nights ago.

Her heart skipped a beat when she spied him waiting at the curb. He waved at her, then bent over to gather the handle of the bag at his feet. His jeans were faded and worn thin at the knees, but the way he wore them, with a white t-shirt and a tanned leather jacket, had the words "rock star" blazing across her brain. This was the first time she'd seen him out of his gym uniform, and his appearance wasn't just seductive, it was charismatic and stylish, and if she wasn't careful, she'd probably drive right off the road.

Avoiding catastrophe, she managed to pull the vehicle over to the side and pop the trunk. Before she'd had a chance to unbuckle and step out to greet him, he'd tossed his bag in, slammed the trunk shut, and raced to the passenger door. He slipped into the seat, leaned over, and kissed her cheek like it was something he'd done a thousand times before. "Hi."

"Hi." The flush of heat coursing through her body was delicious, and she savored every pulse of it. She hadn't felt this confused about her emotions in years. On one hand, she was as giddy as a schoolgirl. On the other, she was petrified that she was reading the signals all wrong.

"How's your finger? Do you want me to drive?"

"It's not too bad. Throbs a little. But I'm fine to drive." With all the emotion running through her brain, she hadn't given her finger any thought at all.

"Okay, but I'll drive home." He buckled up and she put the car into gear.

She had no intention of letting him drive—that would mean he'd have full view of her scar the whole way—but she didn't see any need to argue about it now. She changed the subject instead. "Did you have any trouble getting out of work?"

"Nope, I'm the boss. I just told them what to do."

"That's good."

They cruised through town and were amongst rolling green pastures within minutes. As the miles coasted along, they covered superficial topics like favorite foods and types of music. Their conversation flowed so freely she was fooled into believing they'd been friends forever.

But of course, if they had, he'd know her real name.

Her deception ate away at her soul. As much as she desperately wanted to tell him everything, she didn't want to scare him away. The longer she left it, the harder it was.

As much as she felt complete in his presence, she felt incomplete too.

Fulfilled, yet hollow.

It was a weird sensation. Other than her therapist back in Seattle and the lawyer who'd changed her name, not one person knew who she was. And that's the way it was meant to stay. But it didn't stop her from feeling guilty about it whenever Oliver was around.

The mountains came into view and, like every other time she'd spied them, the sense of foreboding was almost crippling. Today was no different. Because of a mountain, the life she'd known as Holly Parmenter had changed forever.

Oliver shifted in his seat, angling himself so he could see her better. "How long have you been skiing for?"

"Oh, um... same amount of time I've been rock climbing."

"Same? As in exactly the same?"

"Yes."

"Wow, you're on a mission, huh?"

If he only knew. She shrugged, trying to downplay it. "What about you? How long have you been skiing?"

"Ever since I was a kid. Our parents took us skiing all the time."

"Lucky you."

"Yeah, I haven't been for a few years, though. We're pretty lucky having the mountains so close. Where'd you grow up?"

Realizing she had to be careful, she paused. But then, conceding how foolish the pause was, she decided to answer truthfully. "Seattle."

"I went to Seattle once, a few years ago, for a mate's wedding. It's nice. So, what made you move to Brambleton?"

"I don't know. Wanted a change, I guess." She needed to move the conversation away from her before she said something she couldn't undo. "Have you always lived in Brambleton?"

"Yep. I'm fifth-generation Brambleton. We're born there and usually die there. Not too many of my family have ventured out. Those that did usually came back."

"You're happy with that?"

"Of course. I wouldn't mind doing some traveling, but I think I'll always come back home. Besides, my mother would drag me back by the ears if I left."

She chuckled. "Tell me about her."

"Oh, you'd love her. She's a strong woman who rules with an iron fist, but she's also the biggest softie."

Thankfully she'd chosen a subject that kept Oliver talking most of the way up the mountain. His love for his mother, and the rest of his family, was incredible. They were close, something she'd never had a chance to experience.

She pulled into the covered car space outside her cabin. The resort had come to expect her every Saturday morning, and in addition to lighting the fire and leaving the lights on, they also left the door unlocked and the keys on the kitchen table so she didn't need to check into reception first.

Oliver helped with the bags and she showed him into the cabin.

"Is this your place?"

"No." She explained how they looked after her.

"Wow. Talk about luxury." His eyes scanned the downstairs area and then looked upward toward the loft that jutted out over the lounge. "Shall I take your bag up?"

"Yes, please."

As he carried her case up the stairs, she couldn't tear her eyes away from the bulge and flex of his muscles beneath the fabric of his jeans. The flush coloring her cheeks was hotter than the blazing fire and she quickly told herself to calm down.

"Holy smokes. Look at this place." He leaned over the railing. "I've never stayed in anything so fancy."

She smiled up at him. His boyish exuberance was impossible to resist. "I get the same cabin each weekend."

"Must cost a fortune. Sorry, you don't have to answer that. It's none of my business."

He must've seen the smile fall from her face. The last thing she wanted to do was explain her financial situation. She couldn't believe it herself.

He bounded down the stairs. "I don't know about you, but I'm starving."

Grateful that he'd changed subject, she nodded. "Me too. After we unpack, we'll get your skis sorted and then get a bite to eat at The Summit. They make a good omelet."

"Excellent." He rubbed his stomach. "With bacon, right?"

She chuckled. "For you maybe."

"I don't know how you get through life without bacon."

"It's not that hard."

"Hard? It'd be impossible."

"Exaggerator."

He feigned shock. "Have you even tasted bacon?"

"Yeah, I didn't become a vegetarian until my early twenties."

He whistled and shook his head. "Crazy woman."

She laughed and then showed him around the rest of the cabin, including the hot tub that she'd never used and never would, especially not while he was there. After showing him where he could put his things, she went upstairs and unpacked her suitcase.

Once they were ready, they pulled on their ski clothes and headed back outside. Despite the sunshine, it was freezing. She pointed out one aspect of the ski resort after another: the chairlifts, the beginner run where she'd learned to ski, and the side of the mountain where the black run started.

They entered the resort, and as she peeled out of her scarf and beanie, she spied Kelli behind the information desk. When she'd called Kelli yesterday, the crazy woman had been so excited about Amber bringing a male friend that Amber thought she'd hyperventilate. Then again, Amber could've said she was bringing the plague with her and Kelli would have emitted the same childish glee. It was in her nature, and Amber couldn't image anything that would perturb the young woman. Amber liked to think she'd been like that once. But it was impossible to remember back to that time.

"Hey, Amber!" Kelli waved at her and she headed in her direction.

"Kelli, this is Oliver."

Kelli held her hand forward. "It's always nice to meet a new victim." She giggled.

Oliver shook her hand. "Victim, huh? Nice."

"Yep. Amber told me you haven't skied in a while. How long's it been?"

He rumbled his lips. "Oh, about five years."

"That's nothing." Kelli flicked her hand. "You'll be on the slopes in no time. Let's get you geared up."

Half an hour later, Oliver had rented his equipment. They'd arranged to meet Kelli in an hour, which was just enough time to get something to eat.

There were plenty of tables available, and she chose one in a corner next to giant windows that offered a magnificent view up the mountain. She ordered the asparagus and mushroom omelet and Oliver ordered bacon and eggs with extra bacon. Once again, their conversation flowed. She was getting good at directing the conversation toward topics that kept Oliver chatting.

She ate only half the omelet before she'd had enough and picked up her coffee. Oliver may've underestimated the meal sizes, as he seemed to be struggling to finish his. She decided to save him by checking her watch. "You finished? We've got just enough time to brush our teeth and get back to Kelli."

He stood. "Yep, don't want to keep her waiting."

Twenty minutes later, they were on their skis at the top of the beginner run.

"Okay, big boy, show me what you've got." Kelli flashed her dazzling grin at Oliver.

Amber watched as he pushed over the level platform and headed down the hill. She couldn't stop giggling as his knees wobbled, his skis gradually grew farther and farther apart, and his elbows stuck out like chicken wings. To her surprise, he completed the turn and quickly shot back across the slope.

But his speed gathered and his arms began to backpedal. He was losing it.

She burst out laughing when Oliver plowed headfirst into a mound of snow. Kelli was instantly at his side and Amber scooted down to him too. "Are you okay?" she said.

He came up smiling and brushed away snow lacing the couple of blond curls that'd escaped his beanie. "Yep, all good. The first tumble is always the worst." He chuckled, and Amber and Kelli laughed with him. Oliver removed a glove to fix his goggles back into place, then made easy work of getting back up on his feet.

Amber recalled nearly being in tears the first time she tried to right herself after falling.

"Let's try that again." Without hesitation he pushed off, scooting crossways over the slope. He did a tentative turn, with his elbows a bit closer this time, and looked to be finding his balance. After a couple more turns, he increased his speed.

Maybe it *was* like riding a bike, because he improved greatly in the space of a few minutes. She left the safety of the deeper snow and scooted down toward him. Her turns were smooth and she felt the now familiar rush of adrenaline as she glided down the ski run with ease.

She came up beside Oliver and with the flick of her skis cast a wave of snow over him. "Finally, I'm better than you at something." Laughing, she skied ahead.

"Is that the way it's going to be?" His laughter seemed to echo off the trees as she continued to sashay from side to side down the hill. At the bottom, she slid to a halt and watched Kelli mirror Oliver's every move down the slope.

"How'd he do, Kelli?" Amber asked when they were within earshot.

"He's ready for a green run."

Oliver's smile beamed. "I'll catch up to you in no time."

"We'll see," Amber said, but she had no doubt he would.

Kelli led the way to the chairlift and then stepped aside. "You two lovebirds go first."

Amber's heart fluttered at the reference and she turned to Oliver. When they smiled at each other, something teetered between them. It was fresh, exciting, exquisite. And as his eyes bounced from her lips to her eyes and back again, she was certain he felt it too.

Their turn on the chair came quickly and they jumped on and lowered the bar together. The chair swung back and forth with their weight a couple of times before it steadied. Rising quickly, tiny flurries of snow fell upon them, peppering their legs in a layer of white. Twenty feet below them, a group of kids about half her size skied along in a smooth practiced line.

Oliver reached behind her back and placed his gloved hand on her shoulder. Her heart swelled as she wriggled over so their legs touched. It felt so natural to be in his embrace, and she curled her gloved hand over his leg and nestled it between his thighs.

It'd been an eternity since she'd felt so wonderful, and a sense of peace enveloped her as they rode up the mountain. "Thank you for coming."

"Thank you for letting me come."

She nestled in, and with her head resting on his shoulder she listened to the beat of her own heart in her ears.

All too soon, they crested the top of the ski run and the turnstile hut appeared. They raised the safety bar above their heads, and the second their skis touched the snow they pushed off the chair. She'd half expected both of them to end up in a tangle of skis, but Oliver handled the dismount with ease and they glided to the side and waited for Kelli in the following chair.

She turned to face the magical view. Trees, heavy with snow, lined the sweeping slope, and the sun painted everything pure white, creating a magical glow.

"Ready to go again?" Kelli's smile was extraordinary, and with the circle of fur from her hooded jacket surrounding her face she could easily grace the cover of a sports magazine. A pang of jealousy hit Amber out of nowhere, and for a brief second, she wished she'd never introduced Oliver to Kelli.

"I am." Oliver turned to Amber, and when he touched her elbow that bout of protectiveness vanished in a flash. Instead she found herself puzzled once again over how a man as spectacular as Oliver could want to be with her.

"Sure am."

Together the three of them tipped their skis and glided down the slope. Oliver handled the turns well and became faster with each leg of the run. His quick learning surprised her, and it was hard to believe he hadn't skied in five years.

As the day progressed, his skiing ability improved extensively, and when they arrived at the bottom for the fourth time, she decided to let Kelli go for the day.

"Hey, Kelli, Oliver and I might do another run by ourselves. Is that okay?"

"Of course it is." Her high-pitched voice could dislodge icicles. "You two lovebirds enjoy yourselves. But stay clear of the moguls and the black run."

Oliver saluted her. "Yes, boss." With his ski mask covering most of his face, his distinct cheekbones and angular jaw made him look even more handsome—if that was even possible.

Kelli playfully slapped his shoulder. "You look after her." She indicated to Amber. "She's special."

"I know she is." When he gazed Amber's way, his eyes softened and a flush of warmth washed through her.

Kelli released a cute moaning sound before she skied away, heading toward the main resort building.

"What's the plan?" He rubbed his gloves together.

"Would you like to take the green three-mile or do the longer blue run on the west slope?"

"I liked the blue."

"Me too."

They turned and skied down to the chairlift in unison. Their turn on the lift came quickly, and as her feet left the ground Oliver draped his arm across her shoulder, and she pulled down the safety bar and nestled in beside him.

The sun had almost set and their view from the chairlift spanned the entire west face of the mountain. Brilliant orange and pink hues bounced off the low-lying clouds and reflected in the snow, creating a perfect postcard setting.

"This's magnificent." Oliver read her mind.

"It's the best time of the day."

At the top, they jumped off the chair, skied to the side, and paused with their masks pulled up to admire the stunning panorama. It was fairy tale perfection as the setting sun bounced off the scattering of clouds and filled the sky with a potpourri of oranges and purples.

"Wow, check out that sunset." Oliver's magnificent smile added to her already glorious view.

But, for the umpteenth time, the venom of deceit snaked through her. When Oliver turned to her, he may have sensed her turmoil, because the dancing pleasure that'd been in his eyes seconds ago morphed to concern.

He reached for her hand and his eyes softened like he knew exactly what was troubling her. A thread of desire ran through her. She inched closer and clasped his hand tighter and he leaned in, head tilted, lips parted, and when he closed his eyes, she closed hers too. Their lips met and every ounce of concern evaporated when she melted into him.

His kiss was brief, way too brief, and every part of her ached for more. That moment confirmed what she already knew: she was falling in love.

She had never thought she'd have that pleasure again. She'd always thought Milton would be her one and only, and when that'd shattered to a million pieces, she'd believed she was destined to be alone forever. But now, standing on top of a mountain with a man who made her heart sing, she was tempted to believe that she'd been wrong.

Except he didn't even know her real name.

That horrible detail had caused her countless sleepless nights. Oliver had been incredibly patient with her. Never pressing when she failed to elaborate on one of her quirky requests. He deserved her honesty, and as much as it terrified her to admit her deceit, she couldn't deny him any longer. She just hoped he'd still look at her with desire in his eyes once the truth was out.

Oliver playfully smacked her bottom. "Race you to the bend." He launched off the leveled-out snow and became airborne over a gentle mound.

"You little shit." Laughing, she pushed off and raced after him. It seemed a day of skiing was all he needed to perfect his skills. Oliver looked like a professional.

On a mission to catch him, Amber didn't sashay from side to side. Instead, she shoved off, rammed her poles into the snow a few times then tucked them up under her elbows, squatted down, and let momentum do the work. It was the same move she'd done on the day of the storm, except instead of being filled with dread, this time she was filled with exhilaration.

Oliver glanced over his shoulder and she heard his deep, throaty laugh as he drove the poles into the snow over and over in an attempt to increase his speed.

She shot right past him. "Come on, slow poke." Her heart pounded with both adrenaline and a delightful throb for him. Not just him, but everything he represented: stability, security, comfort, fun, and, most of all, passion.

At the bend in the ski run, she slowed and arced gracefully into a turn that flicked up a wave of snow. Oliver was seconds behind her. He reached out for her, but misjudged his distance. Their skis tangled, and as he wrapped his arms around her they collapsed, laughing onto the soft snow.

"Well, that didn't exactly go as planned." He chuckled. "Did I hurt you?"

"No, I'm fine."

"I think you'd say that even if I'd broken your leg."

She giggled. "Probably."

He reached around her shoulders and pulled her to his side. She rolled toward him, nestling into the crook of his shoulder and inhaling his spiced cologne. Delicate snowflakes floated onto them like sifted icing. The snow was cold on her back, yet she'd be happy to stay right there in his arms forever. She ached to stroke her hands over the muscles she felt beneath his padded ski jacket.

When their plumes of breath began to settle, he removed a glove and placed his soft palm on her cheek. "Don't know about you, but I'm exhausted."

Her heart swelled at his nonchalance over touching her hideous scar. "Me too, but we can't stop yet. We're not even halfway down."

"Let's get going then. I can hear a warm fire and a cold beer calling." When he withdrew his arm, she was dizzy with a want that'd eluded her for years.

She'd fallen into a powerful spell, and it was wonderful to be there.

They clipped their wayward skis back on and pushed off again. But this time they took it slow, gliding from side to side in synchronized turns like they'd being skiing together since they were kids.

The sun had disappeared behind the trees and nightfall was making its presence. They took turns going over small jumps that would have them airborne for a second or two, then Oliver led the way through a short track he'd spied through the towering trees.

It was the most fun she'd had in years, and she was disappointed when she paused over a rise and saw the resort in the near distance. Hundreds of twinkling lights outlined the building, and wisps of smoke trailed from the stone chimney and absorbed into the surrounding darkness.

As they approached, subtle music from speakers hidden somewhere within the snowcapped hedges filled the alpine silence. They glided right up the steps, removed their skis, and climbed up to the foyer. The warmth hit her like a balmy cloud and she wrestled her skis to one arm so she could remove her beanie. Kelli waved hello from reception but the mischievous grin on her face indicated she wanted to say so much more.

People were everywhere, and based on the excited banter, every single one of them was having a wonderful time. After shoving their equipment into their lockers, she unzipped her suit and pulled off her gloves.

Oliver strolled toward her, rubbing his stomach. "I'm famished. Does the restaurant do takeout?"

"I have no idea." She'd always brought her own meals, and today was no exception.

"Well, let's go ask. I'd rather sit by the fire at home than in here."

Amber's heart sang a beautiful melody at Oliver's comment. She loved that he'd called it home, and she'd also love nothing more than to sit around the fire with him.

Just him.

The bar was overflowing. Based on the raucousness, some people had been drinking there for hours. They walked past the bar and approached one of the restaurant staff. To her delight, not only did they do takeout, but they also offered to deliver it to her cabin when it was ready. They placed their orders: spaghetti Bolognese and garlic bread for Oliver and vegetable lasagna for her. After thanking the staff, they headed toward the exit.

Outside, radiant moonlight gave the snow an incandescent aura, and fresh snow like moonlit crystals fell upon them in a mystical dance. Their shoes crunching in the snow was the only sound. Oliver offered his hand, she clenched his palm to hers, and they set off toward the cabin as a couple. The moon was an enormous beacon, startling in contrast to its black velvet surroundings. It seemed extraordinarily close, and she could easily see hundreds of craters pockmarking its luminous surface.

At the cabin they stripped out of their padded ski gear and she told him to make himself comfortable while she showered. She cut her normally long shower brief, then pulled on leggings, a long-sleeved sweater, and pink socks that had a cat knitted into the pattern, complete with ears and whiskers. She was embarrassed to wear them and annoyed at herself for not thinking to pack anything else, but she'd been bringing the same clothes up here for months.

When she emerged from the bathroom, Oliver had the fire going and had filled two long-stemmed glasses to the top.

"I hope you drink champagne."

"Sounds lovely."

"I brought red and white wine too. And port." He shrugged. "I wasn't sure what your preference was."

She chuckled. "Champagne is fine." Their fingers touched as he handed her the glass, and her stomach fluttered. When their eyes met, she sensed he wanted to say something. He probably had a thousand questions, yet he'd resisted. His patience had her falling for him by the second.

"Okay." He dragged his eyes away. "Well, take a seat and I'll get showered too."

She sank into the corner of the sofa, curled her feet to the side, and watched Oliver pluck clothes from his bag. He gave her one last grin before he dashed to the bathroom.

Amber sipped her bubbles and stared into the dancing flames, accepting the warmth in the room like it was a welcoming hug. She was the most settled she'd been in years, and yet at the same time her mind was a battleground as she tried to strategize over how to tell her secrets.

Oliver opened the door to the bathroom wearing just track pants. "Ah, that's better."

When he ran his hand through his wet hair and strolled across the room to toss his clothes into his bag, she felt like she'd stepped onto the set of a sexy magazine shoot. She had to resist grumbling when he pulled a shirt over his torso.

He collected his drink from the coffee table and held it toward her. "Cheers."

"Cheers." They clinked their glasses, and as they each took a sip the front door chimed, signaling dinner had arrived.

They ate their meals and chatted about their day, but the whole time Oliver studied her with his inquisitive eyes, yet he didn't ask a single question.

She couldn't put this off a moment longer. Wouldn't. It was time.

Oliver made her heart swell with want and her soul feel safe.

She just hoped that revealing all her rotten secrets wouldn't scare him off.

After dinner, they cleared away their plates and returned to the fire. Oliver refilled their glasses and sat at the opposite end of the lounge, his knee up so he faced her. The spice of his cologne drifted between them and she inhaled his fragrance. She'd come to love his scent. She'd come to love a whole lot more about him too. The curl of his lips just before he smiled. The crinkles next to his eyes that deepened when he laughed. The intensity in his eyes when he looked at her. And he did look at her—really truly look at her, like he was reaching into her mind.

"Thank you for a wonderful day." He placed his hand on her leg. "I haven't had that much fun in years."

Her heart did a little dance. "I was thinking the same thing." She curled her foot up and rubbed her toes beneath her sock, trying to get some feeling back in. Since the accident, she'd had trouble with circulation in her left foot.

"Here, let me." Oliver put his glass down, and she had no time to pull away as he reached for her foot.

Before she knew what was happening, he began peeling off her sock. If he noticed the scar on her ankle, he didn't indicate, but she braced for the moment he saw her toes. However, at the same time, she knew this was the moment she'd been waiting for.

He gasped and his eyes flicked from her foot to her face. "My god. What happened?"

She too stared at her foot. Even after all these years, she couldn't get used to the absence of two toes.

Oliver reached up and placed his hand on her upper thigh. "Amber, I can tell there are things you don't want to talk about, but I'd like to know everything about you."

Little butterflies danced across her stomach at the sincerity in his eyes. "I don't want to ruin our perfect day with my shitty story."

"It's not going to ruin our day. I promise."

After a moment's hesitation, she nodded, finally ready. "It's a long story."

He reached over her thigh and grasped her hand. "Lucky for us then. We have an entire night. Not to mention loads of alcohol and a lovely fire."

He was right; there may never be a better time. Oliver released her hand and gently ran his knuckles up the instep of her foot. It was a caring sensuous movement and she sighed from his touch. It took a couple of thumping heartbeats before she found her voice. "Okay, but don't say I didn't warn you."

He tilted his head but remained silent. The time had come, and although she'd been dreaming of telling him for months, she still didn't know where to start. She decided to get one of the biggest shocks out of the way. "Have you ever heard of Milton Ashcroft?"

He frowned, but also nodded. "His name's familiar, but..."

"He was my fiancé." She waited for his reaction, but there wasn't one, so she continued. "Four years ago, Milton and I, and his son Kane, took a helicopter flight over the Canadian Rockies. The helicopter crashed—"

"Oh, that's where I know his name from. I remember now. It crashed into a crevice. Only one survivor."

She nodded. "Me."

The green in his lovely irises darkened but he remained silent.

"I fell from the helicopter and landed on a ledge in the crevice. Milton did too..." As she fought the dimpling in her chin, Oliver continued to massage her foot in silence, displaying extraordinary patience.

"Kane also fell from the helicopter, but he fell so deep into the crevice I never saw or heard him again."

"Was Milton alive?"

She shrugged. "I have no idea. He was on the other side of the crevice, about fifteen feet away, so I couldn't reach him. He didn't move, though, and there was blood on the snow."

"Oh jeez."

"You know what his last words to me were?"

Oliver frowned and shook his head.

"He asked me if I was having fun." She shook her head.

Oliver looked like he was as pained over Milton's last words as she'd been when he'd said them.

"But I wasn't," she clarified. "From the second I sat in the helicopter, I had this terrible feeling something bad was about to happen, but I couldn't say anything."

"Why not?"

"Because... death follows me, Oliver." She blurted it out.

"What do you mean?"

"Death follows me. My whole life I've been surrounded by it. When I was four years old my little brother was born, but he died three weeks later from SIDS."

"Oh, Amber, that's not—"

She cut him off. "My dad died when I was nine. In a workplace accident." She inhaled long and deep, ready to divulge the rest. "My best friend in college died in a freak Jet Ski accident. Even my first pet, Romper, died as a puppy."

Oliver reached for her hand and squeezed. "I can't imagine what you've been through."

"Then Milton and Kane, and then my mother. See? Death—"

"Your mother?"

"Mom died when I was in the coma."

"You were in a coma?"

She sighed. It was obvious she wasn't explaining herself very well. She took a big gulp of champagne and huffed out a breath. "Sorry, there's a lot to take in. I'll start again."

"Hang on, let me grab that bottle. We need a top off."

He pushed off the couch, then bent over and kissed her on the lips. "Thank you."

She blinked up at him. "For what?"

"For telling me. For trusting me." A lovely smile curled his lips. "For being you." He turned, and as she watched him stride to the fridge, she tried to catalogue all the retched events in her life into something that would make sense.

He returned with the bottle and topped off the glasses. "I can't believe you can rock climb without two toes."

She chuckled. "It's not that hard."

"I bet it's not easy either." He resumed his position on the couch and reached for her foot again. "Tell me about the crash."

She nodded. He'd obviously wanted some sort of order to her story. "Milton had decided that we'd do a mountain picnic."

"Sounds romantic."

She rolled her eyes. "Hardly. We had his son with us. He was seventeen and a spoiled brat."

"Seventeen?" His eyebrows bounced upward and she knew what he was thinking.

"Milton was twice my age."

When Oliver didn't comment she carried on. "Milton paid the pilot a ridiculous amount of money to take the helicopter to the western face of Whiskey Mountain so we could watch the sunset while we picnicked. It didn't matter that the pilot said no one had landed a chopper there before. Milton just paid him more."

"That's right. I remember there being a huge uproar about how stupid the pilot had been."

"Huh, was there?"

He frowned at her. "You don't remember?"

"I was in a coma, but I'll get to that. So, we took off and flew for just over half an hour, but while Milton and Kane looked to be having the time of their lives, I was petrified."

Oliver massaged her feet and toes. If he had any apprehension about her amputated digits, he didn't show it.

"We passed between these two rock towers." She used her hands to demonstrate the pillars. "But the second we crossed to the other side, the wind hit us. The pilot couldn't hold it and we fell from the sky like a brick. When we hit the ground, it opened a giant crevice and the helicopter fell into it."

"Jesus, Amber. I can't imagine it. What happened then?"

"Kane fell through the windshield. I can remember his screams like it was yesterday. But then I fell too. I thought I was dead, you know."

"No." He shook his head. "I don't know."

"No, I guess there aren't too many people who would."

"You were so lucky."

Lucky? It was a thought-provoking word. If she was lucky, she wouldn't have been in that helicopter crash.

She went on to explain where had Milton landed, and the fire in the helicopter, and how the pilot's screams were so piercing they echoed through the chasm. "I covered my ears; I couldn't stand it. That's when the helicopter exploded."

"Shit!"

In minute detail she spoke about finding Milton gone, and when a tear trickled down her mutilated cheek he nudged forward and pulled her to his chest. She sobbed in his embrace, and it didn't seem at all strange that she was crying for another man.

When she couldn't cry anymore, she pushed back and offered a lopsided grin. "So, there you go."

He blinked a few times. "That's not the end. You haven't told me about how you got your scar and lost your toes, or how you were rescued."

She chuckled. "Haven't we had enough misery for one night?"

"Not even close. It's time for port. Do you drink port?"

"I've never tried it."

"Perfect. I like that I'm showing you something new." While he went to the kitchen, she took the opportunity to go to the bathroom and check her eyes. She'd done her fair share of crying and knew exactly how bad she looked after it. Today was no exception. She washed her face, holding a cold cloth to her closed eyes for a few moments. It made very little difference. She dried off with a towel and when she returned, Oliver was placing another log on the fire. He'd also put a box of chocolates onto the table, with two port glasses that he'd filled to the brim. He raised a glass to her as she approached. "Here, try this."

She inhaled its sweet berry aroma, then sipped. "Yum."

"I know. It's even better with chocolate." He held the box forward and she plucked one with intricate gold swirls across the top.

They settled back on the sofa, facing each other, and sipped their port. "Okay," she said. "Ask away. What do you want to know?"

He ran a hand through his damp hair, then settled his palm on her thigh. His touch was as warm as the blazing fire. "I still don't understand how you got the burn scar."

"A piece of the burning helicopter fell onto my cheek. I flicked it away, so it was probably only there for a second or two." She touched her cheek, remembering the moment she'd been hit. She'd been lucky she was wearing gloves at the time. "But it was long enough to burn through three layers of skin."

"It must've hurt like hell."

She shrugged. "Not as much as some of my other injuries."

"Tell me about them."

"When the helicopter crashed, so much was going on that I barely even noticed my injuries. But after the explosion, when Milton... vanished, that's when the pain started to set in. I broke the ulna in my left arm." She held it up and indicated where the break was, between her wrist and elbow. "Broke two fingers, middle and ring."

"Shit. So you've hurt three fingers on that hand now."

"Yep. I broke my eye socket."

"Oh my god."

"Yeah. I couldn't work out why I blind in my left eye. Thought it was blood at first, but it was so swollen I couldn't see."

"Jesus. Anything else?"

"Yes. Fractured my left ankle and had cuts all over, including my left cheek, which—thank god—didn't scar, or I'd look like something from a B-rate horror movie."

"No, you wouldn't. You'd still look beautiful."

Amber's heart fluttered, and she could barely contain the smile shaping her lips. She sipped her port and, for the hundredth time, questioned how Oliver could possibly be interested in her.

"It's a wonder you survived."

She resisted telling him how many times she'd wished she'd died on that ledge. "The doctors called it a medical miracle. Oh, I nearly forgot. I also had two fractured ribs and a partially collapsed lung."

"You forgot about your toes too."

"Oh no, that didn't happen in the crash. Apparently, that was frostbite."

His brow furrowed. "Frostbite? How long before you were rescued?"

She huffed. "According to the report I read, we crashed about four o'clock in the afternoon, and I was pulled from the crevice about three o'clock the following day."

His eyes bulged. "Twenty-three hours! Holy shit. You must've been going out of your mind. Why so long?"

"Because remember I said the pilot wasn't supposed to fly there? Well, apparently he didn't register the exact flight path, so they didn't know where to look. Fortunately the explosion left a heap of debris on the surface, so a spotter plane saw it. But then it took a long time for a rescue party to reach the crevice."

"How'd you survive?"

She huffed. "I've been asking myself the same question ever since. Dumb luck, I think. I had one of those safety blankets down my jacket. Milton had given it to me as a joke, so I'd be warm during the picnic." Her survival had been predicated on so many miracles, it was no wonder people had trouble believing her story.

"Jeez. Were you conscious the whole time?"

She nodded. "I can recall every single second, until I heard the rescue party shout out if anyone was alive. I don't remember anything after that. Next thing I knew, I woke up in a hospital in Seattle eight months later."

"Eight months! Good god." His eyes widened. "Your mother…"

She let out a breath. "While I was in the coma, Mom developed pancreatic cancer. The last time I saw her she was happy and healthy. She died five weeks before I woke up."

Oliver hugged her to his chest again. But her tears didn't flow this time— she'd already cried a lifetime for her mother. It was time to tell Oliver about the bodies in the ice, and the thought terrified her. She'd lost lifetime friends over it. Three of them. They'd all thought she was crazy—as did some of the so-called experts who'd treated her.

But she wanted Oliver to know. No—she didn't just *want* him to know. She *needed* him to know.

Pulling back, she looked into his eyes. "There's something else."

His shocked expression was justified; she'd already overwhelmed him with too much. "Okay."

"When the helicopter exploded, it dislodged the ice shelf Milton had been lying on. But what I didn't realize until I rolled away from the ledge was that the explosion had also sliced off a chunk of ice near where I was lying. In doing so, it exposed… in the ice were…" She closed her eyes, and the image of the frozen couple appeared as if they were right in front of her.

Oliver placed his hands on her thigh. "It's okay, babe, you can tell me."

It was the first time he'd called her babe, and the wonderful connotation broke down the final barrier she'd been fighting.

She opened her eyes. "There were two bodies, frozen in the ice."

"Holy shit. I wasn't expecting that."

"Neither was I. Believe me, they scared the crap out of me when I first saw them. I wondered if I'd lost my mind. But I was stuck there with them so long I had time to debate whether or not they were real. The ice kept them in perfect condition, to the point where I half expected them to wake up."

"Jesus. Were they mountain climbers?"

"No, that's why it was so strange. They were a man and a woman—a couple, I assume—and they had their arms around each other. The woman wore a full-length fur coat and a matching fur hat. She had a red woolen scarf around her neck that matched her red lips and nails. She didn't even have gloves on. Her shoes looked to be fine leather, and were trimmed with gold. They'd be hopeless in the snow."

He frowned. "That's weird."

"I know. The man was in a long brown leather trench coat. He had a black woolen scarf and his hat was a black felt trilby. *His* shoes were normal evening shoes, and looked to be made of crocodile skin. I was near enough to touch his right foot. It took me a long time before I did, but I had to know they were real."

She looked into Oliver's eyes, searching for the look she'd received from her friends that implied she was crazy. But, to her relief, Oliver didn't show that at all. His wide inquisitive eyes implied he was fascinated.

"How long do you think they'd been there?"

"I know how long."

"You do?"

"I know who they were, Oliver."

She told Oliver everything she knew about Angel and Frederick. She described how she found out about them and how sad Frederick's mother Dorothy looked over the accusations that Fred had kidnapped Angel. To bring it into perspective, she also told him about Victoria's never-ending accusations that she'd killed Milton.

"She sounds crazy. Why on earth would she think that?"

"Because I was the one who convinced them to go on vacation."

"Well, shit, it's not like you planned the crash."

She shrugged. She'd been playing the what-ifs through her mind since she boarded that helicopter.

Oliver shuffled over and wrapped his arms around her. "Thank you for telling me.

"So, you believe me?"

He pulled back with a jerk. "Of course. Why wouldn't I?"

"Because the people who rescued me never saw the bodies—at least, if they did, they never mentioned it, so no one ever believed me. And it was eight months after the accident before I even had a chance to tell anyone.

Everyone thought I'd lost my mind."

"I don't think you've lost your mind. You're a little crazy sometimes, but not in a bad way."

"You might change your mind in a minute."

"Oh god. Don't tell me there's more."

She nodded. "Dorothy needs to know what happened to her son. She needs to prove he's innocent."

"You mean you haven't told her?"

"No. Telling isn't enough. I need to prove it to her."

"Prove it!" His frown deepened. "How?"

"I'm going back there, to the bodies."

CHAPTER NINETEEN

Oliver stared at Amber, and the look in her eyes was both calm and resolute, convincing him she meant every word.

"You want to go back into that crevice? Do you know how dangerous that is?"

"I know. That's why I've been training."

"*That's* why you started rock climbing?"

She nodded. "And skiing."

He shook his head. "Why don't you just tell someone?"

"Tell who, Oliver? No one believed me back then, they won't believe me now."

"But now you know who the bodies are."

"And that makes it sound even crazier. They went missing nearly forty years ago, and everyone thinks Frederick killed Angelique and took off with the money. Besides, when I go to Dorothy, I want her to know the absolute truth and, believe me, when she sees the way Fred and Angel are holding each other, she'll know he didn't kidnap her. They were in love."

Oliver shook his head, trying to rattle all the pieces into place. "Do you even know where you're going?"

"That's the interesting thing. You know the plane I told you about, that'd been found by that National Geographic photographer, Carter Logan?"

He nodded.

"Well, I've been in touch with Carter, and he gave me the name of the guide he used. Chancy Holden. I've spoken to him."

"So, what? You told him you're getting Angel and Fred's bodies out of the crevice and he didn't—"

"No," she interrupted gently. "I told him I was retrieving Milton and Kane's bodies."

"What?" He frowned and shook his head.

"That's not what I'm actually doing, though." She placed her hand on his knee. "All I want is photos of Angel and Fred. I want to show Dorothy how loving their embrace is. But I couldn't tell Chancy about them, so I needed a more convincing reason to go back there. I told him I wanted to give Milton and Kane proper burials. It took some persuasion, but apparently he's retrieved bodies off the mountain before, so we went through the logistics and he's agreed."

"So he knows where the crevice is?"

"He's fairly certain."

Oliver leaned forward, ready to protest, but she held up a finger. "Please, just hear me out. Angel and Fred can't have traveled too far from the plane wreck. Think about it. The shoes they were wearing... what they were wearing, they couldn't have gone too far before they fell into the crevice."

Oliver was struggling to get his head around the plan. "So, what? You just fly up there, get down to the bodies and..."

"Well, um... it turns out we can't take a helicopter all the way. The western face of the mountain has this ridge that runs right up to the top. The wind chops and changes too much as it switches from one side of the ridge to the other, so it's too dangerous. We were never meant to go there in the first place." She rolled her eyes. "But Milton had bribed the pilot with a bucket of money and the stupid guy agreed. Anyway, they're not allowed to fly near there now, but the helicopter can take us most of the way, then he thinks it'll be about a two-day return trek."

"Two days? Amber, you're talking about climbing a mountain. No amount of rock climbing or skiing can prepare you for that."

"I know. That's why I've booked a mountaineering course too."

"What? When? Are you crazy?"

"I told you you'd change your mind about me being crazy."

He reached for her hand and clutched it between his. "I know how determined you can be. Hell, I've seen what you'll do to prove yourself, and I can't even imagine what you've been through. But this idea..." He shook his head. "It's dangerous."

She nodded and turned her gaze toward the fire. "I know. But I have to do it."

He cupped her cheek, desperate to get her full attention, and waited until she turned to meet his gaze. "Then if I can't stop you, I'll go with you."

She did a double take. "What? No. You—"

"I mean it." He truly did. As much as his offer surprised him, it also felt right. Amber had come into his life for a reason, and he'd never felt so connected to a woman before. The need to protect her was carved into his being now. "When are you doing the mountaineering course?"

"Oliver, I can't let you."

"Of course you can. I want to come, it'll be fun."

"It's not going to be fun."

"Sure it will. We'll make it fun. Just like today."

Her shoulders softened, but she still shook her head. "I didn't tell you so you'd—"

"I know. I'm glad you told me, 'cause I was going out of my mind trying to figure you out."

"You may never figure me out."

He huffed. "That's probably true. So, when do you start the mountaineering course?"

"First of next month."

That was two weeks away. "That soon, huh? And how long does it go for?"

"It's a twelve-day course. Full time."

"Full time? But what about your work?"

She shrugged. "I've already told them I'm taking a vacation. None of the doctors had a problem with it."

Oliver tried to run through all the things he'd need to do to get away for twelve days. It'd be a hell of a lot. He hadn't had a vacation since he'd opened Upper Limits for exactly that reason—and money. Even if everything worked out, the ability to pay for a mountaineering course would be an issue.

"What?" Amber must've noticed his apprehension.

"Nothing."

It was her turn to lean forward. "When I first met you in your office, you told me I had to be honest with you. I have been. Now it's your turn to be honest with me."

"I have."

"Then don't tell me you're thinking of nothing. After everything I've just told you, you'd be thinking a thousand things."

He chuckled. "You're right about that. Okay, I was wondering how much a mountaineering course would cost."

"You're not paying a cent."

"Excuse me?"

"If you really want to come—"

"And I do," he cut in.

"Then I'm paying. And that's not negotiable."

"Amber, I can't ask you to do—"

"You didn't. My mother left me some money when she passed, so I can afford to pay for both of us."

That explained how she could afford the private climbing lessons. Several times he'd offered to drop the price, but she insisted on paying the agreed-upon amount. "If you have money, then why don't you pay someone to—"

"No." She cut him off, and the resolution in her eyes surprised him.

He was certain there was something else she wasn't telling him. Considering what she'd already told him, he couldn't even begin to fathom what it could be. But as all her revelations rolled through his brain, he realized there was still something that didn't add up: her secrecy. None of what she'd told him explained why she hid in the shadows before every lesson, nor why she insisted he keep her lessons a secret. Nor why she didn't show up on a Google search. With what she'd told him, her name would be all over the internet. She wasn't being entirely truthful. The very thought cut deep. "We're being honest with each other, right?"

Her eyes shifted, and he sensed she was formulating the perfect response. "Everything I've told you is the truth."

He absolutely believed her. "But what about what you haven't told me?"

The flames from the fire danced across her wolf-like irises. "What do you mean?"

"Well…" He opened his hands and shrugged. "None of what you've told me explains why you wanted private lessons."

When she looked down to her lap and ran her tongue over her lip, he had a terrible feeling she was calculating her answer. "I wanted your undivided attention so I could learn as quickly as possible."

Her answer was plausible, yet… "So why did I need to keep your patronage a secret?" He used the exact same words she'd used when she made the odd request.

Amber seemed to shrink back into her seat, and she looked as scared now as she had when she'd first walked into his gym.

"Hey, it's okay." He placed his hand on her thigh, feeling her warmth beneath his palm. "You can trust me."

She picked at her fingernail. "I know."

"What is it then?" Contemplating that he was on the verge of something that was potentially even more shocking than all the secrets she'd revealed so far, he decided to back off. He'd wait for her to be ready. "It's okay, you don't need to say."

She deflated even more, and tears brimmed her eyes. "It's not that I don't *want* to. It's that I can't."

Can't? That confused him even more. But whatever it meant, he had to let it go… for now. Instead, he pulled her to his chest. She felt even more frail in his arms than she had earlier. When she reached up to touch her cheek, he assumed she was wiping away tears.

Her distress broke his heart. He wanted to take her pain away, but had no idea how. Tonight was a monumental step toward understanding what she'd been through, but it was obvious there was more.

He ached to kiss her. Hell, he ached to touch her. All of her. But he'd wait until Amber was ready. She deserved that much. Her life had been taken out of her hands so many times, he wanted their relationship to be on her terms.

It was an eternity before she pulled back to look up at him. Her chest rose and fell, and when her lips slipped apart, he was sure she wanted him to kiss her. Capitalizing on that belief, he leaned over and brushed his lips to hers. When she parted her lips farther his tongue explored, tasting chocolate and port, and he savored the excited beat of his heart, something he hadn't felt in a very long time... never with this kind of intensity.

She reached up and twirled her fingers through his hair, and that one simple move signified her want for him too. Their kiss was an explosion of passion that confirmed their mutual attraction was every bit real. When she caressed his neck, he wasn't sure his intention to take this slow could be preserved.

He was both grateful and utterly crushed when she pulled back from him. "Oliver..."

The way she said his name, choked with emotion and with a pleading lilt, indicated she felt the same turmoil. He touched her cheek, and the unspoken words between them said more than enough.

Oliver cleared his throat. "Would you like another glass of port?"

"I think it's time I went to bed."

He nodded, expecting as much.

Amber pushed off the couch and they stood at the same time. The momentary pause between them was charged with a palpable sizzle. In the end, it was Amber who made the first move. She stepped forward, placed one hand on his chest, and reached up on her toes to kiss his cheek. "Thank you for a wonderful day."

"Good night, Amber. Sweet dreams."

A glaze of sadness crossed her eyes and he wondered what had triggered it. She turned and headed for the bathroom. When she closed the door, the confusion he'd felt earlier came sliding back. Amber's reluctance to share another piece in her puzzle was unsettling.

He gathered the glasses and chocolate from the table, and as he washed up and put things away, he tried to picture lying on a narrow ledge in an icy crevice. It was impossible to imagine, let alone with all the injuries she'd suffered, and especially after the deaths she'd witnessed. Then there were the bodies in the ice. Everything about them was extraordinary, from how they got there to how they were discovered. He had to admit, the idea of being involved in their saga was as thrilling as it was daunting.

He'd done a few extreme sports—bungee jumping, skateboarding, free climbing, sky diving, mountain biking—but Amber's plans made them all seem like child's play.

She emerged from the bathroom and paused before the stairs. Her dark hair framed her angelic face, curling beneath her chin, and her stunning blue eyes, rimmed with lush lashes, were breathtaking. The sadness in her eyes made her hauntingly beautiful. He had a strong feeling she was torn between going to him and heading to bed. His heart skipped a few beats as he awaited her decision.

She tucked her hair behind her ear, placed her foot on the lower rung, and paused to glance his way again. "Good night."

Her overwhelming sadness seemed crippling. But, conceding his wishes weren't to be granted, he simply nodded. "Good night."

Five steps later she vanished from view, and when the floorboards beneath the loft creaked, it confirmed she'd reached her bedroom. A little piece of him wished she'd turned around. Actually, it was all of him that wished for that.

Take your time, he told himself.

He shoved two more logs into the fire and crawled onto the sofa. It was comfortable enough. He'd certainly slept on worse, having spent many a night at a friend's place, relegated to the floor or, if he was lucky, a bean bag.

Oliver rolled to his side, pulled the blanket up, and stared at the fire. The urge to go to her was extreme, and he had to force his brain to think of something else. Like two frozen bodies—and Amber's determination to bring them justice. It was a crazy idea, and yet at the same time it presented an opportunity like none other.

A log rolled in the fire, emitting a spray of embers and reigniting the flames. His thoughts went to how much that log replicated his life: one minute he was comfortable and stable, then Amber came along and ignited a fire in his soul like he'd never felt before.

Maybe this expedition was exactly what he needed. What Amber needed too. Should she succeed in her mission, it'd be a perfect way to put her past behind her. They could move forward together.

As long as they didn't die in the process.

CHAPTER TWENTY

Amber lay on her side, the feather comforter tucked right up under her chin. But while every inch of her body ebbed with fatigue, her mind was like an electric current, zapping through every word of their discussion.

She hated that she hadn't told him the full story, and the fact that he knew she'd resisted broke her heart. Her reason for holding back was a selfish one. Every one of her friends changed once they'd learned of her inheritance from Milton. Money changed people. Four billion dollars affected people in ways that was impossible to predict.

But she didn't want Oliver to change. Not one bit. She loved him exactly the way he was.

Loved him. Her heart fluttered at that admission. She'd pondered this feeling for weeks, but after tonight, after he'd learnt about her past, and in particular when he didn't press her for more information, she knew without a doubt that he'd entered her heart.

Oliver was just one floor below, and the urge to go to him was beyond powerful.

As much as she didn't want to reveal her final secret, she had no choice. It'd only take him a little bit of research to find out the truth, and she'd be devastated if he found out that way.

Something popped in the fire and it was like a trigger in her brain. She listened for signs of him sleeping, but other than the crackling fire and the wind singing outside the window over her bed, there was nothing. "Oliver, are you awake?"

"Yes."

She threw back the covers, and the creaking floorboards announced her progress across the bedroom and down the stairs. Oliver was sitting up. He was shirtless, and the glow from the fire highlighted every magnificent contour of his flesh. Her body was no longer weary; just the sight of him triggered doses of desire that coursed through her like adrenaline.

He moved over on the couch and she sat beside him. Their thighs touched and she placed her palm on his leg. She squeezed her eyes shut and inhaled, and when she opened them again, she looked up into Oliver's inquisitive gaze. "Before I moved to Brambleton, I changed my name to Amber Hope. My real name is Holly Parmenter."

He cocked his head and frowned. "Huh. That explains why you didn't show up on Google."

She gasped. "You... you googled me?" Her words stuttered out, unbelieving.

"Well, yes. I'm sorry, but I wanted to know more about you."

"You could've just asked."

"Every time I tried you shut me out. You were like a vault; you gave me nothing. I want to know you. I want to know everything about you."

His eyes were pleading, his voice was too, and until now she hadn't realized how much damage her secrecy had caused.

Her shoulders slumped. "You're right. I'm sorry. Well, now you know why Amber Hope didn't show up. She didn't exist until about eighteen months ago."

He nodded, then stopped to frown at her. "You're not an escaped criminal, are you?"

She burst out laughing. "No, it's nothing like that."

"Phew, that's good. Are you going to tell me why? Or do I have to keep guessing?"

She sighed and met his gaze. "When Milton died, he left money for me in his will. A lot of money." She paused, ready to catch his reaction to her next statement. "Four billion dollars."

His jaw dropped. His eyes bulged. "Holy shit." A whistle escaped his lips. Then he frowned. "Is that why you changed your name?"

She clasped her hands together. "That's one of the reasons. Once people learned of the money, they changed. My friends started asking for money. They were subtle at first, then not so delicate. Complete strangers would arrive at my doorstep or come into my work asking for money. Money I didn't have yet. I still don't have."

"Hang on a minute." He pushed back on the couch. "And you thought I'd ask for money? Is that why you didn't tell me? Is that what you think of me?"

"No. No, I don't think that, but I didn't want you to change! Everybody changed, Oliver." The horror in his eyes cut her to the core. "Money changes people, especially this kind of money."

He shook his head and she knew she'd hurt him.

"Oliver, please understand what I've been through. When I came out of the coma I had no family left. I only had my three best friends, women I'd known since we were kids, and all three of them changed. It was like the

146

money possessed them somehow. I couldn't trust anyone."

"I'd never do that to you, Amber—Holly—whatever your name is." He threw up his hands in frustration and the fire in his eyes was unmistakable.

She fell to her knees at his feet and wriggled up to face him. "Please, Oliver. Don't be mad at me. When I changed my name I was instructed never to tell anyone. No one was to know, and the secret has been eating away at me since the moment we met."

He lowered his eyes to her. "Your secrets have been eating me too."

"I know, and I'm sorry. Sorrier than you'll ever know. Please forgive me."

He pulled her up to her knees, and when he wrapped his arms around her, she did the same. They squeezed each other like their lives depended on it. After a long moment, she pulled back to look into his eyes. "There's something else I need to tell you."

"There's more?"

"Just one more." Her heart galloped in her chest and she fell into the mercy of his questioning eyes. The electric sparks that danced between them convinced her to say the words that'd been on her tongue for weeks. "I think I love you."

His eyes sparkled and his body seemed to melt. "I love you too."

Amber tilted her face up to him, closed her eyes, and silently begged him to kiss her. Barely a breath later, their lips met. She glided her hands around his back, exploring his warm flesh beneath her fingertips. Their tongues danced in a delicate tango, moving together as if they'd been kissing forever. His hand curled beneath her nightshirt and he pulled her closer, uniting them in a wild passion to explore each other.

When he tugged the fabric of her shirt upwards, their kiss released. "May I?" His voice was a throaty whisper, loaded with lust.

Amber paused. She hadn't been with a man since Milton's death. And other than her doctors, nobody had seen the hideous scars that marred her body. But for the first time in years, that no longer mattered.

The only thing that mattered was Oliver.

She raised her arms and he wasted no time drawing the fabric up and over her head. His chest rose and fell as he looked at her, really truly looked at her, her nipples peaked and hardened beneath his gaze. If he saw the hideous scar that zigzagged over her breast, he didn't indicate.

Oliver placed his hands on her waist and raised her to standing. She stood topless before him and he didn't miss a beat. He curled his hand beneath her breast and cupped it to roll his tongue around her nipple. When he sucked her hardened bud into his mouth, she gasped at the wonderful sensations flooding through her.

Closing her eyes, she tilted her head back and savored Oliver's hot tongue on her flesh. Electric pulses flashed through her, and she glided her fingers up his back and through his wavy hair. When he released her nipple and looked up at her, she studied his face, taking in every exquisite detail. She knew she was looking at the most stunning man in the world.

"May I make love to you, Amber?" The way he said her name was the perfect mix of love and lust, potent enough to make her glow from the inside out.

She nodded, and a couple of heartbeats later, he guided her onto the sheepskin rug nestled between the couch and the fire. Oliver hovered over her. His bulging biceps held him in place, and she flitted her gaze from his lust-fueled eyes to his cinnamon-colored lips and back again.

He lowered his mouth to hers and their kissing intensified, eager to taste, eager to explore. Their hands did the same, and as she discovered the muscles in his chest and back, he caressed and fondled her breasts.

Oliver pulled back and rested on one elbow, and she watched his eyes scan her body. According to the doctors, it'd taken one hundred and fifty-seven stitches to put her back together. If that wasn't enough damage to her flesh, keloid scarring raised the jagged purple lines, making them look like ropes had been threaded beneath her skin.

The blazing fire, whilst wonderfully warm and romantic, emitted too much light for her liking, and she was torn between hiding her body from him and getting this first reveal over with. As if he'd heard her tumultuous thoughts, he leaned forward and trailed kisses from the jagged scar over her breast to the tip of her nipple and down her torso. Each touch of his lips to her old wounds ignited something warm and wonderful inside her.

Taking the lead, she wriggled out of her pajama bottoms and watched in anticipation as Oliver whipped his track pants off too. His penis stood to attention, hard and proud.

Oliver lowered to his knees between her legs and leaned forward to position himself above her again. A dark vein pulsed at his temple, and when his lips parted his tongue lashed out to wet them. Her heart fluttered as he placed a hand on her scarred cheek and leaned in to kiss her again. She pushed her tongue into his mouth, eager to taste him. As their breaths mingled, a delicious pulse quivered from deep inside her.

She raised her knees, letting him know she was ready, and Oliver angled his erection to nudge her opening. He held himself there, teasing, and the sizzle of anticipation was as exquisite as it was agony. Slowly, he pushed forward, entering her, until he touched a wonderful spot inside her that begged to be pleased.

He felt so right, so complete, like he was a piece of her that she'd been missing for a very long time. His eyes flickered open, unseeing, and the raw passion in his glistening pools made her feel treasured.

They worked together as one, drawing out each other's pleasure like only lovers could do. He knew how to please her, and by the intense focus on his face, she believed she pleased him too. Every move was perfect, as if they'd been making love forever.

A light sheen glossed his flesh. His deep primal groans grew deeper, yet he clenched his jaw, squeezed his eyes shut, and continued to draw out her pleasure. Every nerve ending in her flesh tingled, begging for the delicious sensations to last a lifetime. She cried out when her body tipped over the glorious precipice, and she savored the exquisite tremors shuddering through her.

The groan that tumbled from Oliver's throat was music to her ears, and he plunged into her over and over. When he finally flopped onto her chest, his breathing was as ragged as her own pulse. She trailed her fingers up and down his back, and as they lay there, still united as one, her body pulsed with contentment.

When their breathing returned to normal, he pushed up onto his hands, and his arms trembled as he held himself above her to look into her eyes. "You're amazing."

She smiled and reached up to cup his cheek. "So are you."

It was an eternity before they were ready to move off the rug, but Amber didn't want to leave him even for a moment, let alone an entire night. "Would you like to come upstairs?"

His boyish grin made the invitation a thousand times better. "Absolutely."

After they each visited the bathroom, she held his hand and led him upstairs, and, following his lead, she didn't redress in her pajamas. Snuggling beneath the covers, they lay naked with her back to his chest and his arm curled over her torso so their hands entwined. It was perfect. He was perfect. Everything about her life right now was absolutely perfect. So perfect, in fact, that she wondered if risking everything to complete her mission was foolish. But then she thought of Dorothy and how imperfect her life was.

If she didn't do this, she was destined to live the rest of her life on that icy ledge with two frozen bodies.

CHAPTER TWENTY-ONE

It'd been five months since Regi found out who his father was, yet he was no closer to proving it. Whilst it was good to finally know the bastard's name, he'll never forgive his mother for keeping his identity a secret. As far as he was concerned, his mother had prioritized Milton's wish of keeping their ongoing affair a secret over Regi's continual requests to learn about the "sperm donor." She'd chosen sides, and Regi had lost. And that hurt deep.

As ludicrous as her story was, everything made sense after he heard it. It explained how she could afford their home and her expensive drug habit. It explained why she often vanished at a moment's notice, stating she was going on one work trip or another. It also explained why she'd hit rock bottom four years ago.

But in Regi's eyes, with the truth out, she'd gone from victim to selfish bitch in the space of an afternoon.

After he'd searched her bedroom for evidence of their affair, he'd scoured their already messed up house, combing for anything that proved Milton was his father. But he got nothing. Not a damn thing. So he'd sat and waited for his mother to emerge from her drug-induced stupor.

Not that it'd helped. The bitch was a thousand percent adamant that not one single photo of the two of them together existed. In addition to that, nobody—and she was adamant about that too, nobody—knew of their affair, even though it'd lasted for twenty-three years.

Twenty-three years. How in the hell someone could do that was beyond his grasp. It just proved how calculating his mother could be. It was another side of her that he never knew existed, and it hurt nearly as much as finding out his wealthy father didn't want anything to do with him. The asshole had plenty of opportunities too. Regi thought he'd hated him before—now he despised the fucking bastard, and was determined to get his hands on what was owed to him.

Since that afternoon, Regi had spent every available minute scouring the internet, researching Milton Ashcroft. Fortunately for him, the boring office job he'd snagged eighteen months ago gave him unlimited access to a computer. And his tiny cubicle meant he could do whatever he wanted without anyone seeing over his shoulder.

He'd taken up a routine. Mornings were for work, and damn if he didn't work his butt off to get everything done as quickly as possible. Afternoons were dedicated to research. Every photo of the smiling prick made him want to punch the monitor. But of course, that was a pointless waste of energy. He needed to be smart.

Surely it wasn't possible to have an affair for two decades and not leave a single trace of it? He'd scoured news reports of the helicopter crash and the aftermath. He'd read everything he could find on Kane, the half-brother he'd never meet. And there was loads of information on Milton's successful animal apparel empire, Creature Comforts.

Dog clothing! Regi couldn't believe his father's rise to success was on the back of a dog, literally.

He opened a report from Google that he'd saved, and as usual his eyes snagged on the estimated value of Milton's estate at the time of his death: twelve billion dollars. *Twelve billion fucking dollars.*

Reginald Tate, twelve-billion-dollar man. In his mind it sounded like he was being introduced for a world wrestling match.

Each day, he continued reading, devouring every article he could find. It seemed Milton's ex-wife had made a career out of playing the distraught widow. He googled Victoria Ashcroft again… she was everywhere. Society dinners. Talk shows. Facebook. She'd even survived six episodes on *I'm a Celebrity... Get Me Out of Here!*

Pausing on a photo of her with a blond reporter, he noticed the NBC Chicago insignia on the microphone and suddenly it hit him.

She knew of the affair. His mom had said Milton's wife had caught her and Milton in a hotel in Chicago. *She* was his proof. He went back to her Facebook profile and tapped on the message button. But then he paused. What the hell was he going to say? *Hi, I'm your dead ex-husband's bastard son and I want my fucking money.*

Somehow, he figured that wouldn't work.

He stood and paced between the partitions and back, trying to piece together a message. The insurance office where he worked was open plan, and a dozen or so other claims consultants were hunched over in their own cubicles. It was a solid ten minutes before even one of them seemed to notice him. And that's when an idea slotted into place. Ms. Ashcroft's thirst for attention would be his savior. He trotted back to his computer and attacked the keyboard.

Hello, Ms. Ashcroft. My name is Reginald Tate, and I'm a reporter from the New York Times. *Can I interview you?* He gave her two phone numbers, his direct office line and his cell number. His heart was in his throat when he clicked send.

He jumped when his cell phone rang barely a minute later. The number on the screen was blocked, but he didn't hesitate to press the green button.

"Hello? Ms. Ashcroft, is that you?"

"It is." The woman sounded posh, and he could barely contain his excitement.

"Thank you for calling."

"My pleasure. What exactly would you like to know?"

He cupped the phone, hoping to shield his voice from the prying ears of Telitha in the cubicle adjacent to his. "I'm following up on information I have regarding Milton Ashcroft. Do you have time to talk?"

"I do."

"Okay, good. I've been told Milton Ashcroft may have—" He paused, realizing he hadn't exactly thought this part through.

"May have what?"

He decided to go for broke. "Well, um, there's a woman who says she had an affair with him for over twenty years."

"Pfft. It's a lie. Milton loved me. We loved each other. Who is she?"

"Fiona Tate." He felt zero guilt dropping his mother's name.

There was a moment's pause. "She already tried years ago, but her case was thrown out. She had no proof. Just like every other bastard still trying to get their hands on his estate."

"You mean it isn't settled yet?" That was good news. He'd read a news report from six months ago that'd highlighted the long-drawn-out litigation over the estate. Hearing that it still wasn't settled had his heart racing.

"Young man, I suggest you do your research."

"My apologies. How awful for you; you've already been through so much." His fake sympathy was vomit-worthy.

"It's been hideous. My money has been tied up in court for years."

Your fucking money. He stabbed his pen onto his notepad and the blue plastic shattered to pieces. "Fiona says you found them together in a hotel in Chicago."

She huffed. "Well, unless she comes up with something solid, like DNA, she's got nothing."

The mention of DNA had the hairs on the back of his neck standing on end.

"Okay, thanks for calling, gotta go." Before she could reply, he ended the call and toggled the mouse to wake his computer again. Something was there, tickling the back of his mind, but he couldn't pinpoint it. His cell rang with a blocked number several times but, assuming it was Victoria, he ignored it as he read the headlines of report after report, trying to get to the bottom of his burgeoning excitement.

Afternoon rolled into evening and people around him packed up and left. The eternal drone of voices petered out until there was just the hum of the fluorescent lights overhead. And suddenly there it was, the headline he'd been looking for.

Multibillionaire Milton Ashcroft to remain in icy grave forever.

Regi stood, cheered, and fist-pumped the air. His manager in the far office stared at him through the slats of his window blinds. Regi waved at him and sat down again.

DNA.

That's what he needed, and he knew exactly where to find it.

He just had to figure out how.

Returning to the computer, he researched where Milton's helicopter crashed: Whiskey Mountain. He googled it and was surprised to find there were four of them. But it was the one in Canada that he was interested in. Another article captured his eye. It seemed Whiskey Mountain had more than one casualty to its name.

Twenty minutes later, he knew exactly what he was going to do. He picked up his phone again, and as he punched in the number from his Google search, he prayed he hadn't missed them for the day.

"Hello, and welcome to Helirides Canada."

"Hi, I'm calling about a plane wreck that one of your guides found on top of Whiskey Mountain. Can I speak to the guy who was there?"

"That'd be me. Chancy Holden, how can I help?"

Regi couldn't believe his luck. "I work for Heathcote Insurance, and I need to take more photos of the plane. There's a pending claim that needs solving."

"Well, it must be your lucky day. I had a call from a woman the other day, and she's hired me to take her to a crevice near the plane to retrieve a body. So I can take the photos if you want."

"A body?" Regi's mind raced.

"Yeah, apparently her fiancé died in a helicopter crash up there a few years ago, and she wants to give him a proper burial."

Holy fuck. It had to be Holly Parmenter, Milton's fiancée and the sole survivor of the helicopter crash. Regi could barely breathe, let alone speak. His lucky streak just hit the twelve-billion-dollar jackpot.

"You there, man?"

"Oh, yep." His mind rocketed a thousand miles an hour. He cleared his throat. "Can I join the group?"

"Depends. You got eight grand in your pocket?"

Regi just about swallowed his tongue.

"You there?" Chancy's gruff voice cut into his brain.

"Yes, it's just… eight thousand?"

"That's correct. It covers the cost to take the helicopter to the highest point, then it's about a two-day return hike on the mountain, depending on the weather. Then the chopper's gotta come back to get us. Costs money. Insurance alone's a fortune, though I'm sure I don't need to tell you that." He chuckled.

"No. No, you don't." Regi's glimmer of hope exploded like a grenade. There wasn't a chance in hell he'd get his hands on that kind of money. *Unless...* "I'll get back to you."

"Okay. But if you're coming, I need to know by"—There was a pause, and Regi assumed Chancy was checking for a date—"by April sixth at the latest.

"Thanks." He looked at his calendar. Two weeks. "Okay, I'll call you soon."

He didn't shut down his computer like he was supposed to. Instead, he grabbed his phone and strode for the exit.

For the first time ever, *he* was hunting Carson.

Four buses and a two-mile walk later, he arrived at the security gate at Broadmoor. He drove his fingers through his hair, straightened his shirt, and cleared his throat as he stepped up to the gatehouse. "Hi, I'm here to meet Mr. Carson."

"Is he expecting you?" Built like a fridge and with eyes that could cut steel, the guard was born for this job.

The entire trip here, Regi had debated how to handle this obstacle. "No, but he'll want to see me. I have his money."

After snapping the window shut, Regi watched the guard lift a phone to his ear. Following a brief conversation, he tugged the window open again. "Mr. Carson will be here soon. Wait over there."

Regi sat where indicated and stared through the wrought iron bars up the tree lined street. Carson liked to keep people waiting, and today was no exception. The sun gradually set behind him and the street lanterns lit up, as did all the million-dollar mansions beyond the gate. Not a single vehicle came or went, and the guard made a show of glaring at him every once in a while.

When a pair of headlights flooded the asphalt, Regi stood and awaited its approach. The guard went to the car, and then he must've pressed a button for a side panel in the gate that clicked ajar. Regi didn't wait for an invitation. He stepped through the opening and strode to the highly polished black Mercedes AMG S65 coupe. He was disappointed to see Pope behind the wheel, so Regi climbed into the back seat.

"Regi the Rat. I hear you've got the boss's money."

"I need to see him."

"Give me the cash."

Regi did a double take. He had no idea how much Carson wanted and was pretty certain Pope had just stepped into a hole. "How much?"

"What?" The torment on Pope's face confirmed he realized his mistake.

"How much does Carson want?" It was the one answer Regi had been seeking for years.

When Pope didn't respond, Regi decided to push his luck. "Just take me to him, dickhead."

The seething in Pope's eyes only proved what Regi had suspected all along: Carson was the only one keeping him alive. Problem was, Regi had no idea why.

Pope turned to the front, put the car into gear, and rolled up the asphalt with a calmness that was a world away from the Pope Regi knew.

They pulled into a driveway, and when the garage door eased up Pope drove down into the enormous parking bay beneath Carson's mansion. The garage was a car lover's wet dream. They cruised past a Rolls-Royce Wraith, a McLaren 650S Coupe, a Lamborghini Huracán LP610-4 Spyder, and a Ferrari 488GTB. Carson's Corvette Stingray was there too; the car that'd instigated his living nightmare showed no signs of the crash.

Regi had been to Carson's mansion several times, but never via this entrance. The darkened space and abundant shadows prickled Regi's brain with dread. Pope parked alongside a silver Aston Martin DB9 GT, and Regi readied his body and mind for a beating.

When Pope climbed out, Regi did too, and he stepped back to put distance between himself and the thug. Regi scanned the area, looking for the way out, but it was nowhere in sight, so he waited for Pope to lead the way. He did, and Regi followed behind, still maintaining a distance. Pope paused at a door to unlock it, then pulled it open and indicated for Regi to go first.

Regi clenched his core muscles, expecting a blow. The punch to his kidneys came before he was on the second step. Regi howled and crumbled to the ground. Nothing could've prepared him for that.

"Get up, *dickhead.*" Pope's breath fouled the air.

Regi groaned as he stood and clawed at the railing to drag himself up the remaining stairs. They entered the mansion, and Pope stepped in front again and led the way through the building and out to the pool area, which was lit up like a party was about to start. Even the water glowed from lights hidden below the waterline. Regi breathed a sigh of relief when he saw Carson lazing in a deck chair at the head of the pool.

He walked toward him and noticed a woman swimming beneath the water. She was naked. Regi decided then and there that once he got his hands on his billions, he too would have naked women swimming in his pool. Lots of them.

As he approached, Carson raised his eyes from the paper he was reading. "I hear you have my money."

Regi glanced at Pope, who was watching the woman backstroke across the water. "Mr. Carson, can I speak to you alone, please?"

Carson made a show of folding his paper and shoving it onto the table next to an open bottle of red wine. He picked up his wineglass and eyeballed Pope. "Give us a moment."

Pope nodded and obediently backed away.

"Speak." Carson commanded.

Regi's knees trembled, yet he remained standing. "Sir, can you please tell me how much I owe you?" His eyes shifted to the woman's ass as it bobbed up and down in time to her breaststroke.

"How much do you have?"

Regi was no longer the naïve twenty-two-year-old who'd crashed into Carson's Stingray. Back then he worked casual in a car wash. Now he was a claims assessor for an insurance company, and if his job had taught him one thing, it was that there was a fine line between knowing when to work with something and when to write it off altogether. His hope was that Carson's figure was high enough that he'd consider investing more. "I believe I have enough to pay you, but I need to know the figure."

"One hundred g's."

Regi had to resist sighing with relief. This was far from over. He nodded and made a show of implying it was a hard ask. "If I can get my hands on that kind of money, will you let me walk away?"

"Walking away will cost you another four hundred."

Half a million. It was way too much, and both he and Carson knew it. This was a test, and Regi had every intention of passing it. He clutched the back of a chair. "May I sit?"

"No."

Regi adjusted his stance so he couldn't see Miss Nude's tits wobbling with her backstroke. "Mr. Carson, what I'm going to tell you is hard to believe. Hell, it's taken me months to get my head around it." Regi went on to tell Carson everything, from who his father was to how he intended to get his hands on the DNA. He didn't hold back, and he hoped the truth would literally set him free. "So, sir, in summing up, to get you your money, I need to get to the body. To do that, I need money."

During the telling of the story, Carson had leaned forward, convincing Regi he was not only believing him, but he was hooked.

"You're trying to tell me that Milton Ashcroft is your father."

"Correct."

Carson burst out laughing. It was the first time Regi had ever seen him do this, and he had absolutely no idea what it meant.

After he'd finished his hysterics, he steepled his fingers. "I knew him."

The blood drained from Regi's face. Not in a million years had he considered this. Yet in hindsight, he should have. Milton had been an extremely wealthy Seattle businessman, as was Carson. "He was quite the player, you know. With the women."

"No, actually I don't know. As I said, I had no idea who my father was until five months ago."

Carson huffed. "From what I saw, I wouldn't be surprised if there were dozens of bastards just like you trying to stake a claim on that fortune."

"There's just me. For now." Regi's research told him that Milton had left his fortune to his son, his fiancée, and a pile of charities. Because his son died too, and because Milton's ex-wife got zip, it'd been tied up in the courts since the will was discovered. Thanks to Victoria fighting the payouts, Regi could make a claim to the estate. He was about to throw a giant wrench into Victoria's case, and he couldn't wait.

"Well, Mr. Tate, you're one of the luckiest sons of bitches I've ever met." Carson's smile was contagious and Regi grinned too.

"I know."

Carson eased back on his chair. His eyes were as sharp as ice picks. "How much do you need?"

Regi's heart was in his throat. On his way to Carson's he'd played with all sorts of numbers in his head. The last thing he needed was to fail because he was a couple of bucks short. Besides, if anyone could afford it, it was Carson. "I figure fifty grand will cover my costs."

"Fifty." Carson didn't show any emotion at the figure, giving Regi a glimmer of hope that he had the right number.

Regi stood his ground. "Yes, sir, that'll cover travel, accommodation, the helicopter, and the DNA tests. Then there'll be lawyer fees…" While Regi carried on listing every cost he'd thought of, the woman climbed out of the pool and strolled toward them. She plucked a towel from one of the deck chairs, and as she scrubbed her hair she joined Carson's side. She made absolutely no attempt to cover herself, and Regi couldn't get his brain or his mouth to work, so he stopped talking.

Carson seemed to have no trouble ignoring her. "Okay, you can have your fifty, but…"

Regi's already thumping heart hit a whole new level as he waited out Carson's irritating pause.

"Pope's going with you." Carson's sick grin was triumphant.

CHAPTER TWENTY-TWO

Ever since the night in the cabin when Amber had not only told Oliver the astonishing details of her past, but also her immediate plans for the future, the barriers she'd built that'd kept them apart had fallen away. For the first time since he'd opened Upper Limits, Oliver's business was taking a back seat while he and Amber spent every possible moment together. When they were apart, his heart ached like nothing he'd ever felt before.

Telling him the truth seemed to have set Amber free, and she'd truly come out of her shell. She laughed more freely, and he found a cheekiness about her that she'd been hiding. His only hope was that once she'd completed this crazy mission, whether she succeeded or not, she'd be able to put her past behind her for good.

As per her request, he'd kept her true identity a secret, and between the two of them they'd concocted a story to explain the burn scar on her face. So far, everyone believed that Amber had been in a terrible car crash, and thankfully they hadn't asked for specifics. His family loved her, which he knew they would.

Their twelve days together on the mountaineering course had been some of the most incredible days of his life. The course itself had been tough, but fun. And every minute he'd spent with Amber had been an eye opener. Her strength, both mental and physical, never ceased to amaze him. Especially now that he knew the extent of her injuries.

Her missing toes hadn't hampered her ability to climb a frozen waterfall. The waterfall had, however, beaten two other able-bodied men. She'd never mentioned her wounds to any of the other six mountaineers in the course. Oliver however, was so proud of her he'd wanted to shout it from the mountaintop.

When they'd finally boarded the plane for Canada, his emotions had swung from relief to trepidation, yet he couldn't deny the good dose of excitement he felt too. Their time had gone so quickly Oliver barely had time to comprehend what they were planning to do. Amber, however, seemed to grow more agitated with each passing hour.

After a little over seventeen hours in transit, they arrived at Kelowna International Airport in Canada. Once they disembarked the plane, Oliver reached for Amber's hand and led her through the glass sliding doors. They collected their luggage from the carousel and headed for the exit. Oliver spied a man in a green bomber jacket and army print peaked cap holding a sign with "Holly Parmenter" written on it. It was a timely reminder that until they returned to this airport, he was to call her Holly.

Holly stepped forward and offered her hand. "Hello."

"Afternoon, folks. I'm Chancy Holden." He shook Holly's hand and then turned to Oliver. "And you must be Oliver." While Chancy's grin seemed genuine, it was his steely eyes that gave him a no-nonsense military quality.

"That's me."

"Okay, let's get going." He plucked Holly's bag from her hand and lead them through the terminal and out a small exit marked for personnel only. The roar of an engine had Oliver turning in time to see a small plane taking off along the runway. They headed toward a giant aircraft hangar, but rather than go inside they skirted around it and, positioned on giant white crosses painted on the tarmac, three stationary helicopters came into view. The second they were in sight, Holly reached for his hand, and with each step they took toward them, her fingers squeezed tighter.

Oliver wanted to wrap his arms around her and tell her everything would be okay, but there was no time to pause. Chancy opened a utility basket positioned above the chopper's skid, tossed Holly's bag inside, and indicated for Oliver to shove his in too. Chancy opened the door to the chopper. "Ladies first."

Oliver saw the fear in her eyes and placed his hand on her arm. "It's okay, babe."

"You got a fear of flying?" Chancy didn't mince words.

She spun to him. "No, actually. A fear of crashing."

He did a little jerk of his head. "Well, that ain't happening. Not on my shift."

"I'm pleased to hear that, Mr. Holden." The look of determination that Oliver had come to recognize was back on Holly's face as she clamped her jaw and climbed into the cockpit to take her place in the back seat.

Oliver clapped Chancy on the back before hauling himself up beside Holly. She clutched his hand and he squeezed her fingers, trying to portray a sense of security.

Once he was in the pilot's seat, Chancy handed them both headsets. Oliver placed the padded disks over his ears and heard the crackle of the airways. Chancy explained how to buckle up, and once they were set, he pressed a few buttons to kick the rotors into gear. Within twenty minutes of landing at Kelowna, they were airborne again.

They flew from the airport and headed toward snowcapped mountains, and as much as Oliver tried to conceal his excitement, for Holly's sake, he couldn't. When Chancy tilted the chopper sideways to change course, Oliver whooped with exhilaration. When Holly turned to him, he saw a mixture of curiosity and fear in her eyes. He decided the best thing to do was show her how relaxed he was. For the next two hours, he pointed out one interesting aspect after another, and after a while her grip relaxed, and he was certain Holly's fear was dissipating.

Miracle Lodge was positioned high on Revelstoke Mountain and accessed only by helicopter, which meant only a select few people could afford to stay there. Holly had insisted on paying, and although he was very grateful, he felt guilty about it too.

The lodge was perched on the western side of the mountain and was built with red brick and red cedar. With snow capping the roof and smoke trailing from the stone chimneys, it was picture-perfect against the alpine backdrop.

Chancy landed the helicopter on the giant X and cut the engine. "Here we are."

They climbed out, and Chancy unclipped the latch on the utility basket to remove their bags. He handed one to Oliver. "Okay, I'll get you inside, then I'm heading back to the airport to get the rest of your party."

Holly shot a glance at Oliver, then to Chancy. "Who?"

"Oh, you're in luck. Since we last spoke, I had a call from a guy who needs to take pictures of that plane wreck up there for insurance. It's right near where you're going, so it worked out well." Chancy made no apology.

"We hired you as a private charter." Holly clamped her jaw.

"No. You hired me to guide you to that crevice. There was no mention of a private charter."

Oliver saw the anger brimming in her eyes.

"You should be happy, Ms. Parmenter." Maybe Chancy saw her fury too, because his eyes darkened when he glared at her. "It's not going to be easy hauling those bodies out of the crevice. The more hands we have, the better." Without waiting for a response, he clutched her bag and strode toward the building.

Holly looked up at Oliver. "Shit."

"It's okay, nothing has changed." Oliver frowned at her fury.

"A lot has changed. They better not slow us down."

He curled his arm over her shoulder and led her toward the building. "I'm sure they won't."

Chancy was waiting for them at the reception counter. If he was still ready for an argument, he showed no signs of it. His smile was back, and he indicated for them to come forward. "Okay, I'll leave you with Miranda for now, but can you please meet with me in the lounge at eight o'clock? I'll introduce you to the rest of your party and go over the final plans for tomorrow."

"Okay, thank you." Oliver spoke for the two of them.

Chancy strode back out the door and Oliver turned his attention to Miranda.

She led them from reception and showed them through the lodge, pointing out the sofa Chancy had mentioned, the restaurant, the day spa, the massage rooms, the fitness center and business center, and the private ski lockers. Oliver only saw seven other people along the way—a vast difference to every other ski resort he'd been to.

The private chalet was the stuff only the rich and famous usually experience. He ogled one magnificent aspect after the other. The floor to ceiling windows that took in the mountain ranges. The enormous bed. The cozy fire. And, to top it all off, their private hot tub had a fantastic view.

Miranda finished up the tour by presenting them with a box of what looked like handmade chocolates and a bottle of Armand De Brignac Brut champagne. The eye-catching bottle, with an ace of spades embossed into the glass, convinced him it was expensive. But with the amount Amber had probably paid for this accommodation, this welcome gift was justified.

Once Miranda said goodbye and shut the door, Oliver held the champagne toward Amber. "Hold this."

A second after she clasped it, he swept her into his arms and she giggled as he carried her to the bed. "Can you believe this place? I think I'm dreaming."

He placed her on the covers and took a moment to take in her smile. For the first time in his life, he was in love. Amber was the woman he wanted to spend the rest of his life with. A woman who deserved the world. From what he'd seen so far, she could afford the world too—he just hoped she had a place in it for him, permanently.

After a quick glance at the bedside clock, he met her gaze. "We have three hours to fill. I say we get nude, have a little play, then slip into the hot tub with the bubbles and chocolates."

She wrapped her hands around his neck and pulled his lips to hers. He took that as a yes, and within a minute they were naked. He cupped her breast and they resumed kissing, but this kiss wasn't constrained. It was filled with a greed for each other, heated and extraordinary. As their tongues dueled, he squeezed her breast, playing with the full weight of her bosom and tweaking her nipple until the bud hardened beneath his touch. She moaned, and when he moaned too, she drove her fingers through his hair and tugged a handful, pulling him down to her.

She tasted divine, and her delicate scent that he'd come to love drove him wild.

He fed his hand between her legs and drove his finger into her hot zone.

Amber gasped, and as she tilted her head back, he watched the expressions of carnal bliss dance across her face until he brought her to climax. It was an erotic show that had his manhood throbbing like a beast.

Amber opened her eyes, and the desire burning in them made his flesh sizzle and his body set to self-combust. She grabbed his shoulders, and he allowed her to roll him over. Amber straddled him, and as he cupped her breasts, she used her hand to guide him into her. Her heat swathed him like a clenched fist as she lowered herself onto him.

When she opened her eyes, her pupils where huge and the fire he saw in them took his already thumping libido to raging. She placed her hands on his chest, and with her eyes locked on his she rose up, taking him to the very edge, and then lowered again. The sensations were an exquisite overload.

She glided up and down, over and over, and a tidal wave of pleasure plundered him, building an orgasm of mammoth proportions. He didn't want to stop. He wanted this to last all night, every night, for ever and ever.

Her pace increased. Every muscle in his body stiffened. He gritted his teeth and tried to hold back as long as possible. With each plunge he went deep inside. Every thrust was hard and complete, and she rode each one to its full glory.

Amber cried out, and his awareness of her hot juices tipped him over the edge. Unable to hold back a moment more, he dug his fingers into her hips and released a primal groan as she rode out his final thrusts.

She fell forward, fashioning their sweat-slicked flesh together, and he closed his eyes and trailed his hands up and down her back, barely noticing the scar below her left shoulder blade.

When their breathing returned to normal, she pushed up from his chest. "Ready for the spa?"

"Sure am."

She slid off him, and he admired her sexy butt as she walked toward the bathroom. Before she'd revealed her secrets, she'd made every attempt to hide as much of her flesh as possible. But now, it was like she was making up for lost time. Maybe it was fabulous to be free again. He wasn't complaining—he'd be happy to look at her naked every moment of the day. Even with all the scars. They may have been brutal reminders of what she'd been through, but they were also proof of what a survivor she was, and that only made him love her more.

The spa was as divine as the champagne and chocolate, and it was with reluctance that he noted they were running out of time. It was seven thirty when they climbed from the hot tub and dressed again.

Holding hands, they made their way back to the main lodge and settled into a leather chesterfield sofa by the fireplace. They ordered drinks from the waitress, who greeted them the second they sat, and Chancy joined them five minutes later.

"Hey guys, you settled into your cabin okay?"

"Yes, thanks. Very nice," Oliver said.

"Great. Well, enjoy it; after tomorrow morning it won't be so luxurious. Ah, here they are." He stood to wave over a couple of men who'd entered the lounge. "Holly, Oliver, I'd like you to meet Regi and Pope."

Oliver hid his surprise over their appearances by offering to shake hands.

They did, and then Chancy indicated for the newcomers to sit. "How about you explain to each other what you want to achieve with this hike up the mountain? Regi, want to start?"

Regi cleared his throat and made no attempt to hide his attention on Holly. Oliver had seen people look at her scar before—usually they tried to be discreet. Not this guy; he was practically gawking at it. "I… we"—He indicated to Pope—"work for Heathcote Insurance, and the plane wreck they found up there has an outstanding claim. We need to take a few photos for the file."

Oliver had always prided himself on his ability to read people, and he had a niggling impression that the men opposite him weren't being truthful. Regi looked like he was about eighteen years old—way too young to be doing what he was doing. And Pope looked like he'd be just as comfortable if they'd said they were robbing a bank.

As Holly told them about their plans to retrieve the bodies of Milton and Kane, neither man showed any emotion. Regi continued to stare at Holly, but Oliver felt that it was no longer just inquisitiveness—it was something else. He couldn't quite pinpoint it, but for some reason, he had the impression Regi loathed her.

After the introductions were over, Chancy shifted in his seat. "Right, have a decent breakfast tomorrow, 'cause we're on packet meals after that. You've timed it well; we had a huge dump of snow last week, but the prediction for the next four days is perfect. You got all your equipment?"

Both Holly and Oliver nodded. "We think so."

"Crampons? Headlamps? How much rope?"

Oliver relayed what they'd brought, and Chancy confirmed with a curt nod.

"Right, you won't need your skis; we'll be walking the whole way." He turned to the other men. "And you two?"

Regi and Pope looked to each other. "We'll need to rent everything."

"Okay, you boys can come with me to the equipment room." He pointed at Oliver. "Meet me with your gear at reception at seven in the morning. Pack light, 'cause whatever you take, you'll be lugging for four days. We can put some gear on the body sled and take turns dragging it."

Pope grunted, and everybody turned to him.

"You got a comment, Pope?" Chancy looked ready to start a fight.

Pope squared off to Chancy, then clenched and unclenched his fists.

"No."

"Good." Chancy turned back to the group. "Anyone have any questions?"

When no one answered, they all stood simultaneously.

Oliver clutched Holly's hand. "See you all in the morning."

"Night," Regi said, but Pope remained mute.

Oliver and Holly returned to their room, and the second they were inside he turned to her. "It's not too late to pull out."

"I knew you were going to say that. I'm not quitting now."

He cocked his head. "I knew *you'd* say that."

"So why'd you ask?"

"Because I had to. Didn't those guys seem weird to you?"

"Yes. I don't believe that insurance story one bit. I think they're looking for the cash."

"Cash?"

"Yes. Remember Angelique's husband handed over half a million dollars' ransom money, and it's never been found."

"Oh, that's right. They must think it's in the plane."

"Maybe." Her lips formed a thin smile. "But it's not."

"It's not?"

"No. I bet it's in the suitcase that's with Angel and Fred in the crevice."

CHAPTER TWENTY-THREE

Holly and Oliver adhered to Chancy's suggestion and ordered breakfast in their cabin: scrambled eggs, mushrooms, and beans for her, and the same for Oliver, but with toast and bacon—lots of bacon. While they ate, she applied sunscreen to her face and double-checked the equipment she and Oliver planned to take.

The staff on the mountaineering course must've thought all their Christmases had come at once when she'd purchased all her gear from them at the start of the program. Despite Oliver's objections, she'd insisted on buying all his equipment too, and because she demanded the best and the lightest in weight, it wasn't cheap. But she didn't care. Even though it was still hard to believe, money wasn't something she had to worry about.

Their base clothing and insulated jackets and pants were the best money could buy too. She was pretty certain the quality of her clothing had been a major factor in saving her when she'd fallen into that crevice. Milton had insisted that she have the best, and it was a good thing he did or she probably would've frozen to death. Ironically, he'd bought her a heated blanket for the alpine picnic as a joke, and fortunately she'd placed it inside her jacket prior to takeoff. That blanket had been integral to her survival too.

Maybe she'd become superstitious, because she'd bought nearly exactly the same equipment this time and, like last time, she'd shoved a safety blanket inside her jacket and insisted that Oliver did too. To keep her pack's weight down, she intended to wear the same clothes for the entire trek; her underpants were the only change of clothing she needed.

She lifted her pack and guessed it to be just fifteen or so pounds.

"You good? I can take some—" Oliver reached for her pack.

"I'm fine, how about you?" She had absolutely no intention of shirking her responsibilities.

"I'm good to go."

As much as she'd been initially shocked at Oliver's insistence on going with her, she was now truly grateful that he was. Especially after seeing their travel partners. She hadn't wanted to mention it to Oliver, but there was something hauntingly familiar about Regi that unsettled her, and Pope, well he just looked like trouble.

On keeping with schedule, they kissed their luxurious lodgings goodbye and headed toward reception with twenty minutes to spare. Her Alpine clothing was too warm for the indoors and she couldn't wait to get into the freezing temperature outside.

Reception offered a view of the chopper landing pad, and Chancy was already there. In his hands was a body stretcher. It was an unnecessary piece of equipment, but she couldn't risk advising Chancy of her true plans yet. It was better to get to the crevice first and then declare her real intentions. Hopefully he wouldn't be livid.

Oliver opened the door for her, and she pulled her sunglasses into position and walked ahead of him. Halfway toward the chopper, a premonition of impending death hit her like an avalanche. Her knees nearly buckled at the severity of the thought. She turned to Oliver, and his giant grin brought her right back to her final moments with Milton. Moments when she was terrified and Milton was loving every minute. But unlike last time, she had no intention of hiding her ominous feelings.

She went to pull Oliver aside, but she was too late.

Chancy waved them over. "Good, you're early. Give me a hand." As she watched Chancy and Oliver manipulate the supplies and equipment into the chopper's small luggage hold and utility basket, layers of dread stacked in her mind.

At the sound of steps, she turned to see Regi and Pope walking toward them. Regi looked like an excited teenager, and she recalled the same boyish enthusiasm on Kane in his final hour too. Pope, on the other hand, had a scowl that drilled his eyebrows together and pulled his lips to a thin line. Holly contemplated that he looked to be there under duress, but then, as she watched his brutish stance and clenched fists, she'd couldn't fathom how anyone could have control over a man like him.

Before she had a chance to get in Oliver's ear she was asked to climb up and sit by the window in the back seat. Chancy seated them according to weight, and fortunately Oliver was positioned beside her. Pope was to Oliver's left, and Regi sat next to him at the other window. With all of them in their padded ski gear, it was incredibly tight. And hot. When sweat dribbled down her back, Holly was grateful she was wearing the best wicking underclothing money could buy.

Holly frowned when Chancy took the front passenger seat, until moments later Miranda climbed into the pilot's chair.

"What the hell're you doin'?" Pope's gruff voice boomed about the cramped space.

Chancy turned with a wry smile. "Miranda's our pilot."

"Thought *you* were the pilot."

"Can't be both pilot and guide. Someone's gotta fly the chopper back." Chancy's grin confirmed he was amused by Pope's discomfort.

Miranda didn't acknowledge Pope's comment; instead, she flicked a series of switches that triggered the rotors into motion. As they increased in speed, she pulled her headphones into position. "Can you all hear me?"

"Yes," Holly said, and a series of affirmations confirmed they were all in communication with each other.

Holly watched Miranda toggle the gear stick, and moments later they were airborne. Oliver reached for her hand, and when their fingers entwined, she squeezed so tight her knuckles hurt.

The higher they went, the more snow there was, and the less there was of anything else. Vegetation disappeared altogether, and only the odd rock marred the whiteout.

It was about thirty minutes before she spied the shark fin-shaped mountain in the distance. The sun glinted off the whiskey-colored rock as if winking at her. With each mile they flew closer, the fin grew wider and higher, casting a triangular shadow over the snowcapped western ridge.

Miranda guided the chopper over the looming shadow beneath the jagged peak, and when Holly heard a change in gear, she realized they were descending.

"Here we are." Miranda confirmed Holly's assumption.

But the angle of the terrain meant Miranda couldn't actually land; instead, she positioned the craft so the nose aimed into the slope and maintained the skids about two feet off the ground. Chancy jumped out and came around to the side to instruct them on disembarking one by one. The last thing Miranda needed was for the chopper's weight to shift too quickly.

Once they were all out, while Chancy and Oliver worked together to remove all the equipment, Holly fitted her helmet into place. Approximately three minutes after disembarking, Miranda lifted the chopper again and Holly shielded her eyes from the glare to watch its departure. When she turned back to the others, she spied the twin pillars she'd seen all those years ago in the distance. If her memory served her right, it meant they were much closer to the crevice than Chancy had indicated.

Under Chancy's instruction, they put their crampons on and each took their own pack. The remaining supplies of food and equipment, such as ropes and ice axes, were heaped onto the sled.

Chancy roped the group together, keeping a distance of about twenty feet between each of them: Holly at the front, then Oliver, Regi, and Pope at the end. He then strapped the sled to his waist, and without any fanfare Chancy set off toward the towering columns. Determined to keep as close to him as possible, Holly jumped in behind and kept pace.

The snow beneath her boots was about ten inches deep, much deeper than what they'd practiced in during their mountaineering course, and it was an effort to place every step. Surrounding silence hung thickly in the crisp still air, interrupted only by her breathing and the crunching of snow beneath her boots. The sky was as pure and blue as she'd ever seen, and the morning sun reflected like thousands of crystals in the frozen blanket around them. Without her sunglasses, the glare would have been excruciating. Not one cloud was visible, which was saying something, because Holly estimated she could see for hundreds of miles.

She lifted her eyes to the distance. Snow capped the ridges like the fluffiest meringue. Ahead of her, Chancy seemed to be aiming directly toward the double pillars. It was the same direction their helicopter had taken all those years ago, and, if her memory was correct, the moment they crossed that threshold they were in for a dramatic change of weather conditions.

"You okay, Holly?" She smiled at Oliver's continual use of her true name. It must be hard for him to remember to call her that.

"I'm fine. You?"

"Great. This's magnificent."

It was true. The vista was truly glorious. Mist swamped the valleys below, giving her the impression she was walking in heaven. Whiskey Mountain lived up to its name, shimmering like copper in the morning sun. As they approached the pillars, she spied tendrils of silvery mist trailing from the exposed rock. It confirmed her fear that once they crossed over they would experience a whole new side of the mountain, literally.

Chancy stopped ahead of her, and when Holly checked her watch, she was surprised that they'd been walking for an hour. Once they were bunched up again, Chancy instructed them to rest for ten minutes.

Oliver stepped in alongside Holly and placed his arm across her shoulder. "This's awesome."

She pointed toward the towering rocks. "It's nice now, but once we get through there it's going to be hell."

"What d'ya mean?" Pope glared at her.

"See the wind trail? It means the gusts whip up the other side. Once we pass through, it's going to get tough."

Pope grunted, and Holly noticed a slight smirk on Regi's face. So far, the two of them had had almost zero communication. If they were colleagues, as they claimed to be, then they must hate working together. By the pained looks on their faces, she had a feeling they'd done minimal preparation for this climb, if any. At the moment, the angle of the slope wasn't too difficult. Certainly not as bad as Holly's practice mountain had been. She was pretty sure that was about to change, though.

Holly found it hard to believe people climbed mountains without any serious training, and that governments allowed it to happen. She wouldn't be here without her training, that's for sure.

Chancy announced they were moving again. "Keep your distance, guys.

Don't bunch."

Holly waited until there was almost no slack on the rope between her and Chancy before she started walking again. The next two hours were a repeat of the first, and it was nearing one o'clock when they reached the threshold. When Chancy stopped again, Holly took the opportunity to pluck a power bar from her pack and eat it. The glares from both Regi and Pope indicated neither of them had packed their own food. *Fools.*

"If you have balaclavas, now'd be the time to put 'em on. It's going to be super windy beyond here." As if demonstrating, Chancy tugged his blue face mask over his nose and mouth.

Holly removed hers from her pack and Oliver did the same. Neither Regi nor Pope seemed to have them.

Once they were ready, they set off again, and Holly's fears were quick to be realized.

The second they stepped through the gateway, the wind speed increased tenfold. It whipped up the mountain, carrying snow and ice with it, and the wind chill factor skyrocketed.

They were heading downhill now, putting additional pressure on her knees, but she clenched her teeth and trudged on regardless. Exposed rocks dotted the snowy landscape like blackheads, and she had to take extra precaution with each step.

An hour into the downhill climb the wind intensified, unleashing its fury like they'd walked into hell. It blasted her so hard she had to lean forward just to remain upright. But the downward angle of the slope made that even more difficult, and the strain on her calf muscles had them burning.

Every time she thought Chancy would stop, he continued. She checked her watch and noted that he'd gone well beyond the one-hour stops he'd been making on the other side of the mountain. The ice-laden wind created a whiteout that made it impossible to see more than a few feet in front of her. Chancy was lost in the oblivion, but thankfully the rope snaking its way toward him gave her something to follow.

Nearly every muscle in her legs was aching when the rope between her and Chancy finally began to slacken. Twenty or so paces more and she spied Chancy through the haze, and when she looked up, she couldn't believe what she was seeing.

The plane wreck appeared out of nowhere. One side of the plane was completely obliterated by accumulated snow. But as the wind curled around the metal fuselage it lifted any snow that attempted to settle and carved it away. The result was that the side of the plane positioned toward the mountain peak was still visible.

She turned to see Oliver's reaction, and she was glad she did.

His eyes bulged, and the balaclava concealing the rest of his face made his expression even more dramatic. "Holy shit. Will you look at that?" He wrapped his arms around Holly and squeezed her in a bear hug.

Regi looked beyond exhausted when he arrived and barely showed any reaction.

When Pope appeared, Holly had to resist gasping at the sight of him. The flesh on his face looked red and raw. Clearly he hadn't worn sunscreen, and wind burn contributed to the rest of his suffering. When he lifted his dark eyes, it was anger she saw simmering in them. "Thank fucking Christ."

"Hey, watch your language, buddy." Chancy pointed a finger at Pope.

"Fuck you." Pope's eyes were evil daggers, and for several heartbeats the two men glared at each other.

Holly was relieved when Chancy unclenched his jaw and began untying the rope from his harness. She followed his lead and unhooked the rope from her belt too. Chancy plucked the shovel from the sled, stomped through the snow, ducked beneath the plane's wing, and bent over to scoop the remaining snow away from the bottom of the door. Oliver left her side to help Chancy.

She could feel the evil glare from Pope, and when she glanced over her shoulder at him, she was horrified at how red his face had become. Come tonight, he'd be in agony.

A tormented screech announced the plane door opening. Chancy peeled his face mask away. "Okay, put your belts and crampons on the sled, then get your asses inside."

Holly unclipped the crampons from her boots and tossed them onto the sled. She did the same with her equipment belt, and the hooks and ice axes jangled as she placed them atop everyone else's gear.

Oliver held his hand toward Holly and she tugged off her balaclava, stepped forward, and ducked her head as she entered the plane. Five seats were inside: three on the left-hand side and two on the right, with a central aisle. There was a small empty space behind the last two chairs. She chose the seat at the front, sat with her pack on her lap, turned toward the front, and gasped.

The pilot was still in the cockpit.

His head was slumped forward onto the controls, and she didn't need to look hard to see the damage to his skull. From where she sat, it looked like the steering column was embedded in his head. A couple of the glass instruments were shattered and looked to still have blood dripping down them.

She snapped her eyes away, and when her mind jumped to her earlier premonition, she hoped for everyone's sake that this was the death that'd instigated her omen.

Regi climbed into the seat behind her, and when Pope came in, he glanced toward the cockpit then went to the back. If he'd seen the pilot, he made no reaction. He scanned the space at the back, and the stony look on his face had her wondering if he was looking for the money. Pope tossed his pack in the back, and the cabin groaned when he plonked his weight onto the back seat.

Oliver chose the seat opposite Holly and reached out to touch her knee.

"Oh shit, is that the pilot?" Regi said.

"Was the pilot," she corrected.

"Jesus, why's he still here?"

Chancy climbed in and tugged the door shut. "It's not always possible to get bodies off mountains," he said. "Not everyone's as lucky as your guy. Retrieval costs money. A lot of money. And risk."

"That's so sad," Holly said.

"Yep. I've been working on mountains for twenty years, and this is only the third body retrieval I've done. There's bodies dotted all over the place." He remained standing but, unlike Holly, he had to hunch over.

"Thought you said the weather was good." Pope seemed to growl with his comment.

"Oh, this *is* good. You should see it on a bad day. It'll be much better in the morning."

Pope's clenched teeth squared his jaw, making him look even more evil. "Where's the bodies?" Pope snapped.

Holly cocked her head. Pope had obviously forgotten their scam about needing photos for an insurance caper.

"They're in the crevice." Chancy thumbed over his shoulder, indicating down the mountain.

"How far?" Pope hissed.

"'Bout a couple a hundred feet or so. But it's too late now. That's why this's our campsite for tonight." Chancy rubbed his hands together.

Pope stood with his head butting the roof. "What the fuck?"

Chancy's eyes shot to Pope. "I told you to—"

"Yeah, well, you're no longer in charge, asshole."

Holly gasped at the gun in Pope's hand.

CHAPTER TWENTY-FOUR

The sight of the gun shot panic through Regi's gut like a bullet, and the urge to bolt out of there was huge. But Pope had them trapped. Although Regi had never witnessed it firsthand, in the deepest depths of his soul he knew Pope was not only capable of murder, but that he'd done it before. Probably many times. The Pope he knew was a thug, all muscle, no brains, and did exactly what he was told without any second thoughts. The Pope he was looking at now was no longer taking orders.

He was in charge.

And that scared the crap out of Regi.

Many times in the past four years, Regi had wanted to die. Begged to die. Not now, though. Not when he was this close to his billions—this close to getting his life back. No... not his old life. Regi was ready to make a whole new life for himself. A life so flush with cash that he could tell assholes like Pope and Carson to fuck right off. And if they didn't, he'd make them.

Regi edged back and slinked behind the seat with his hands up. "Jesus, Pope, what the fuck're you doing?"

"Shut up." Pope smashed the gun into Regi's temple and he howled. Searing pain shot behind his eyes.

The metal floor crunched beneath Pope's boots as he strode between the seats toward the front. "*You*, get to the back." Regi forced the pain from his eyes, desperate to follow Pope's movements.

Pope's jaw was clenched, his red-raw face hideous, and his eyes bulged so wide it looked as if his eyelids had been burned away. Pope had slipped over the edge of sanity.

"Okay, calm down, nobody needs to get hurt," Oliver pleaded as he stood.

"Shut the fuck up." Pope shoved Oliver toward the back, and when he stumbled and fell Holly squealed.

Pope thrust the gun in her face, choking the scream from her throat, and when Regi saw the glint in Pope's eyes, he froze. Holly was about to die. Regi's breath trapped. His heart thumped. The seconds ticked as he watched

Pope fight his own demons.

Holly held her hands up and lowered her eyes.

Out of the corner of his eye, Regi saw Oliver scramble to the opposite chair and clutch the back of the seat in front until his knuckles bulged white. "Pope! No!"

Pope ignored Oliver and turned to Chancy. "Get to the back."

Chancy offered his palms to Pope and edged sideways down the aisle.

Maybe Holly's downcast eyes were saving her. Or maybe Pope wasn't completely psychotic. He needed Holly, and Oliver and Chancy, to find Milton. Without Milton, there was no billions.

Pope tapped the gun on Holly's shoulder. "You too."

She jumped up, and the sound of her boots tracked her dash for the tiny slot behind Oliver's seat. Oliver reached around behind her in a lame attempt at protection.

Pope jerked his gun from one person to the next like a raving madman. "Right." The gun tapped the roof of the cabin, emitting a hollow metallic sound, and Regi thought if he wasn't careful, he'd pull the fucking trigger. "Toss your packs up here."

Oliver carried his and Holly's bags to the front, and when he returned Regi tossed his pack on top of the others. He glanced at Pope, who for a moment seemed unsure of himself. "Pope…" Regi decided to play the only card he could think of. "Is this what Carson wanted?"

Pope snapped his eyes up and grunted. "You think you're so fucking smart, Regi?" Spittle landed on Pope's chin as he spat out Regi's name.

"What're you talking about? "Regi touched the lump at his temple and winced. "I didn't make you come here. Carson did."

"You're such a fucking fool. You think you're so immune to it, don't you? Stupid naïve shit." Pope aimed the gun at Regi's forehead. The black hole was like the eye of a demon.

But rather than be scared, Regi was pissed off. He'd had enough of being bullied. He clenched his fists and glared around the weapon into Pope's bloodshot eyes. "Go on. Kill me. Get it over with." Pope clenched his teeth so hard his body trembled. The gun quivered too. Yet despite his obvious fury, Regi was confident he wouldn't do it. There'd been dozens of times when Pope could've killed him, but hadn't. He prayed this was another. Not when he was this close to his money.

"You still haven't figured it out, have you?" Pope edged back.

"Figured what out?" Maybe Pope wanted to see Regi's reaction to whatever he was about to say, because he lowered the gun. If he pulled the trigger now it'd go right through Regi's chest.

"Why Carson's been keeping you alive."

Regi'd been asking himself the same question for years. "Tell me, 'cause I've got no fucking idea."

"He's grooming you. You're taking over."

He cocked his head. "You've lost your mind, Pope."

"I was like you once. Young. Stupid. Up to my eyeballs in debt. When Carson gets his claws in, he ain't lettin' go." Pope held his free hand out as if using it for balance. A millisecond later, his fingers trembled. "Parkinson's," Pope said. "Carson's ready to get rid of me. Hell, he's probably hoping I stay up on this mountain like him." Pope pointed the gun at the pilot.

The frigid air seemed to crackle with silence. But there was something more. Anticipation. Pope was waiting for his response. Regi rolled the cogs in his brain and a question clicked into place. He glared up at the madman. "So why'd you come then, dickhead?"

Pope lashed out and smashed the gun into Regi's forehead. Regi howled and forced the tears from his eyes. "Fuck. Fuck!" He sucked air through his teeth and clenched his fists, determined not to give Pope the satisfaction of seeing his agony.

"I had no choice," Pope spoke through clenched teeth. "Just like you. You think this money's settin' you free? You're a fucking idiot."

"What money? Will someone tell me what's going on?" Chancy's gruff voice seemed to surprise Pope, because he looked at him like he'd forgotten he was there.

"Yeah, Regi, why don't you tell 'em?"

Regi dragged his eyes from Pope and turned to Oliver, then Holly. Fear riddled her wide eyes, and her face was so pale her lips had turned blue. Regi wondered if that's what he looked like every time Pope had him cornered.

"They're after the ransom money," Oliver said, maybe trying to distract Regi's attention from Holly.

Regi shot him a glance. "What?"

"The ransom money Angel and Fred took."

Shaking his head, Regi glared at Oliver. "What're you talking about?"

Both Holly and Oliver blinked at him.

"What money are *you* talking about?" Holly said.

"My father's... Milton Ashcroft's money."

Her jaw dropped, and when she looked at him like he'd lost his mind he got angry. He was not the crazy one. Hell, he was probably the only sane person on this fucking mountain. It was time to prove it. Regi decided to tell her every sleazy detail about the "sperm donor." Everything from Milton's twenty-three-year affair with his mother to Carson's admission that Milton fucked any woman he could get his hands on.

"You're lying." Tears spilled from her eyes and down her cheeks.

"I wouldn't be here if I was."

"Why *are* you here?" Oliver frowned.

"I need proof." Regi went on to tell them about how Milton and his mother had kept their affair so secret there wasn't even one photo. When he mentioned the five grand in cash his mom got every month, in person, Holly released a sob. But when he saw her sadness and how she seemed to have shrunk in size, it wasn't anywhere near as satisfying as he'd thought it would be.

"So," he said, "Milton's DNA is the only thing between me and twelve billion bucks."

"Twelve billion," Pope and Chancy said at exactly the same time.

Regi turned to Pope, his jaw dropping. "You mean Carson didn't tell you?"

Pope lunged with the gun again, but this time Regi was ready. A second before impact he launched from his seat, deflected the gun with one hand, and punched Pope in the nose with his other.

At the same time blood burst from Pope's nose, the gun exploded.

CHAPTER TWENTY-FIVE

The explosion was so loud and so unexpected it took Oliver a couple of seconds to react. Holly was quicker; she fell to Chancy's side and didn't hesitate to place her gloved hand over the gaping wound in his neck.

Oliver joined her, his heart thumping, his eyes darting to Pope, then Regi, then and back to the bloody wound. "Jesus, you shot him!"

While Regi's expression proved his horror, Pope's fury had hit a whole new level. With blood spilling from his nose, down his chin, and onto his jacket, he raised the gun again and pressed the barrel to Regi's temple.

Pope had his teeth clamped so tight his jaw trembled. As did his hand. Rage smoldered in his eyes.

Oliver's breath trapped; he wanted to drag his eyes away, but couldn't.

But Pope didn't pull the trigger; he beat Regi with the gun instead.

Oliver snapped his eyes away, and as he tried to block out the agonized grunts and horrid thuds, he turned his attention to Chancy. The guide's lips were coated in his blood, and a bubble formed and burst from the wound in his neck.

"What do we do?" Holly's wide eyes were pleading, desperate for Oliver to have answers. But he didn't. Even if he did, one glance at Chancy was enough to know they would've been futile. Chancy sucked in a ragged breath, and when he let it out, long and slow, it was his last gasp at life leaving his body.

His head rolled to the side. His eyes stared at nothing.

Oliver removed his glove and put two fingers beneath Chancy's chin. He'd never done this before, and he shifted his fingers several times before he confirmed there was no pulse. He shook his head and Holly broke into sobs. Oliver wanted to wrap his arms around her, protect her from their new hell, and tell her it'd be okay. But he couldn't. Everything was so far from okay that his mind shattered into a dozen scenarios. None of them good.

Silence, as deathly as a funeral parlor, filled the cabin.

Oliver turned to Regi. His heart was in his throat as he stared at his bloody face and prayed the kid was alive. His left eye was already swollen shut and the cut to his lip was so bad he'd probably need stitches. Regi's good eye fluttered and Oliver let out the breath he'd been holding.

Regi reached up to touch his split lip. "You fucker." He spat blood at Pope's feet.

The thug didn't seem to notice. Pope's meaty hand was smeared in blood, and he stared at it like it was the first time he'd seen blood. Oliver was certain it wasn't. His other hand was slack, the gun aimed at the floor. When Pope raised his eyes and looked at Oliver, a sick grin formed on his burnt lips.

Oliver waited.

Waited for Pope to make the next move.

Waited for Regi to.

Waited to be assassinated.

The plane creaked as if overwhelmed with the horror it contained.

Regi groaned and Holly cried soft little whimpers that broke Oliver's heart.

When Pope slumped into the front seat and blinked around at the carnage, Oliver had a feeling that the man was emerging from some sort of evil state. His rage, like his brutish stature, appeared to diminish. His eyes, which had emitted pure hatred just moments ago, had a glimmer of lucidity.

"Right." Pope's voice was brittle, like his throat too had been scorched by the sun. "We better get ready for the night."

Holly's hand darted to her mouth; her eyes skipped from Oliver to Pope and back to Chancy's lifeless body. Oliver knew what she was thinking. That they should get out of there. Get back to safety.

But it wasn't going to happen.

Not now.

Maybe never.

Pope won't let them go. Not after what he'd just done. After what they'd witnessed. They were dead. Just like the pilot, they were destined to remain on Whiskey Mountain. Maybe forever.

Oliver forced his brain to focus. They were alive. Pope could've shot them all right there and then. But he hadn't. He'd spared them for a reason. The answer came quickly. Pope needed them. Without them, he wouldn't get to Milton's body. He needed Regi too. Without Regi there was no billion-dollar estate to settle.

Their only option was to follow Pope's orders, keep him pacified, and hope for a miracle.

That glimmer of hope was enough to get him moving.

He touched Holly's arm and begged for her to look at him. When her red-rimmed eyes met his, he nodded and tried to portray a look of strength and control that implied everything would work out.

Oliver turned back to Pope. "What do you need me to do?"

Pope squinted at Oliver as if he was assessing whether he was planning to double-cross him. "I'll get the food," Oliver prompted.

Pope nodded. "Yes, the food. And don't try anything stupid or I'll shoot her." He aimed the gun at Holly. But rather than crumble under the weight of the threat, she pushed up from her knees and stood with her bloodied gloves rolled into fists at her sides.

The determination in her eyes, in her stature, in everything about her, made Oliver's heart swell, and for the first time in his life, he was willing to put his life on the line to save someone.

No matter what happened, he'd do anything and everything to protect her.

Oliver stood with his hands raised and stepped to block Pope's aim. The thug eyeballed him. "The food's outside," Oliver said. "On the sled." As he walked between the rows of chairs, Pope backed up to stand between the pilot and co-pilot's seats, giving Oliver access to the door.

The exit creaked open, and when Oliver stepped into the frigid air, he realized just how warm it'd become inside the plane. It gave him hope that they wouldn't freeze to death in their sleep.

Without the crampons, his boots slipped in the snow, and using his hands as stabilizers he crossed the short distance to the sled. He tugged off his gloves, shoved them in his pockets, and, working quickly, untied the knots to release the webbing that held everything in place. The satchel containing the food was on top. He removed it and tossed it toward the plane door, along with the cooking equipment and small cooking stove.

His heart raced when their belts caught his attention. Hooked into everyone's belts were ice axes. The temptation to grab one and shove it down his jacket was so strong he could barely breathe. But Pope would be watching through the cabin windows, of that he was sure.

He spied the lanterns, and while making a show of releasing them from the webbing he covered an axe with a roll of rope. All sorts of other equipment on the sled could serve as weapons too: hooks, ice screws, the crampons—hell, even the belay devices could do some damage. All Oliver needed was the right moment.

Just before he pulled his gloves back on, he saw a first aid kit. He pulled it from the rigging and resisted opening it until he returned inside. Oliver's fingers were aching with the cold by the time he put his gloves back on.

Back at the door, he tugged it open, shoved everything inside, and, mindful of the escaping warmth, quickly jumped back in and slammed the door shut. He turned to Holly; she was in the back seat, and she nodded at him, confirming she was okay.

Oliver tipped the contents of the food bag onto the front seat. There were several different choices of hydrated meals. He turned to Pope. "What do you want?"

Pope indicated with the gun for Oliver to go to the back. He turned his back on Pope and strode to Holly. They wrapped their arms around each other and he kissed her forehead. When he pulled back, he squeezed her hand and met her glare. "We'll be okay."

Maybe she believed him, or maybe she was too petrified to talk. Either way, she remained silent. Oliver turned to Regi and touched his leg.

Regi flinched and opened his right eye.

"Hey, man, I found the first aid kit. I'll get you painkillers in a minute." He nodded. "Thanks."

"I'll have this one." Pope tossed one of the food packets onto a spare chair, and Oliver picked it up.

"Beef curry. Good choice." Oliver hoped his upbeat response would give him some leeway. "Mind if I grab that first aid kit?"

Pope gave a curt nod. "Don't do anything stupid."

"I won't." Oliver unclipped the clasps on the kit as he stepped back to Regi. Using the opposite chair, he rummaged through the contents and plucked out a packet of painkillers.

He turned to Holly. "Can you get some water?"

She nodded and reached for her water bottle.

Oliver touched the younger man's shoulder. "Regi."

Regi's right eye opened and he wriggled back on his seat. "Yeah."

"Here's some painkillers." He placed two pills into Regi's palm.

"Here you go." Holly handed him her water bottle.

Oliver couldn't imagine the pounding headache Regi must be experiencing. When he opened his mouth to take the pill, Oliver noticed blood all over his tongue. Blood covered Regi's chin, and the swelling over his closed eye was now a nasty shade of purple. But other than his hideous facial injuries, the rest of him looked fine.

Oliver had lived a fairly uneventful life. He'd never been in a fight, at least not a physical one, and the only bruises he'd ever had were from sports. He'd never even broken a bone, so he couldn't comprehend what Regi was going through.

Holly certainly could, though. He turned to her. "You look after him, I'll get the food ready."

"Okay." She paused, her mouth ajar, her eyes wide, and he knew she wanted to say more, but, like him, it was impossible to find the right words.

He placed his hand on her cheek, and with their eyes locked he gave a slight nod.

Oliver tried to ignore Pope's glare as he returned to the equipment on the wreck's floor and removed the propane gas burner from the kit. With everything he touched in the set-up process, he wondered how the item could be utilized as a weapon. The pot, forks, gas bottle. Weapons were everywhere, though none were as efficient as the one Pope hadn't let go of.

The gun.

Darkness fell so quickly Oliver had to fumble to find the camp lanterns and matches. He gave one light to Pope and positioned one lantern on the floor between Regi and Holly. The glow made Regi's already gruesome facial injuries look hideous.

Meal preparation was as easy as pouring boiling water into the individual food satchels, letting them sit for ten minutes, and stirring. Oliver had to resist his urge to pour the water over Pope when it hit boiling point. His worry was that the brute would not only survive the attack, but that it would enrage him even further.

He handed out each meal with a fork, and then sat beside Holly on the floor at the back of the cabin. At their feet was Chancy. His body occupied a significant portion of the floor space, and Oliver contemplated moving him to one of the seats. But the idea of manhandling his lifeless body was enough to put him off his food. And he couldn't afford that.

Despite his swollen lip, Regi managed to eat his meal, and Oliver was impressed when Holly ate hers too. She didn't balk at the absence of a vegetarian option. She didn't hesitate over eating beside a dead body. And she didn't recoil at Chancy's dried blood on her gloves. Instead, she was robotic in her movements, forcing down each mouthful until she'd finished her rehydrated cottage pie.

Holly's determination never ceased to amaze him.

After they'd eaten, Pope went through everyone's packs and began throwing anything he didn't want them to have outside. When he found Holly's first aid kit, he downed a couple of painkillers, and Oliver secretly enjoyed knowing he was in pain.

Pope plucked Holly's camera from her bag, assessed it for a moment or two, and when he went to throw it aside, she spoke her first words in hours. "We'll need that."

Pope blinked at her, camera in hand.

"If Regi's to prove where he got the DNA from, he'll need the camera."

Oliver was impressed with her quick thinking.

"She's right, Pope." Regi croaked his assertion.

Pope grunted and shoved the camera back in her case and removed Holly's headlamp. He adjusted the strap, fitted it onto his head, and turned it on.

In the end there weren't too many things that Pope had rejected, and he tossed their packs aside. He flopped into the passenger seat in the front row, placed the gun on his lap, and folded his arms across his chest. "Get some sleep." He turned to them. The torch beam made it impossible to see Pope's face. "And don't do anything stupid, or I'll put a bullet through yer brain."

With nothing more to do, Oliver turned to Holly, and she tugged something from her jacket. The thermal blanket. Thank god for her. He removed the one she'd insisted he take and, realizing Regi would need it more than him, he shook it out and draped it over the young man.

Regi croaked a thank you and adjusted the shiny fabric to fit his body. Pope's torch beam was like an alien's eye when he jumped up from his seat, strode down the aisle, and snatched the blanket off Regi.

Regi clutched at the fabric but it slipped through his fingers. "Fucking bastard."

Pope returned to the front and the rustling sound confirmed he was wrapping the blanket around himself. Oliver wondered if Pope had made the fatal mistake of wrapping the gun up inside with him, but quickly conceded he had no intention of finding out.

Holly shook out her blanket, and rather than wrap it around them she handed it to Regi. Oliver was two seconds off snatching it back when he realized that not only was it the right thing to do, but also that she wouldn't have accepted it back anyway.

He sat on the floor with his back up against the curved wall of the plane and opened his arms. Holly sat with her bottom between his thighs, her legs curled over his right leg and her side against his torso. When he wrapped his arms around her, he realized that this was the exact same position she'd described Angel and Frederick being in when they froze to death.

It was a horrifying thought, but then… if these were to be his final moments, he was happy to be sharing them with the woman he loved.

Sitting still for the first time since he got into the cabin, Oliver noticed the cold seeping into his skin, especially from the metal beneath his legs and back. His bones too began to ache, taking on the cold like ice was leaching in intravenously.

The wind outside howled like a demon, and the wreckage creaked and groaned as if protesting the ferocious onslaught. Pope's snoring added to the noises, and again Oliver wondered if this was his chance. But he quickly discarded the temptation. Here inside the cabin, there was no margin for error. Chancy's death was proof enough of that.

Thinking of Chancy gave him an idea, and as much as the thought was horrifying, it made sense too. Chancy no longer needed his jacket. He and Holly did.

"Hey, babe," he whispered.

"Yeah."

"Hop off me for a sec. I'm going to get Chancy's jacket." When she didn't move, he added, "I need it to sit on; the cold's getting to me."

She slid off his lap and crawled toward Chancy. Again she showed incredible mental strength, as the two of them worked together to remove their guide's jacket. Oliver tried to ignore the metallic tang of Chancy's blood as he folded the jacket and placed it so it'd shield as much of his legs and back as possible from the cold metal.

When he sat on it, a bulge beneath his right thigh caught his attention. Feeling with his hand, he realized it was something in Chancy's jacket. When he plucked it from the zippered pocket, he had to resist whooping for joy. It was a two-way radio.

He concealed it from Regi's potential line of sight, and once Holly was back in position between his legs, he showed her. Holly's reaction was to wrap her arms around him and plant a firm kiss on his lips.

Oliver wasn't sure if it was sheer exhaustion, the comfort of the communication device in his pocket, or the woman in his arms that had him relaxing. But it wasn't long before he closed his eyes and surrendered himself to sleep.

A loud crack had Oliver snapping his eyes open. It was a couple of frantic heartbeats before he remembered where he was. Holly was in his lap, and her wide blinking eyes showed her confusion too. He glanced toward the front of the plane, where Pope had been when he last saw him. But he wasn't there, and when Oliver turned to peer out the small glass window it was fogged up. Wiping a circle clean, he wished he hadn't, because Pope was right outside, peeing onto the snow.

The fact that it was already morning surprised him. He'd slept right through the night.

When Holly pushed off him and groaned, he tried to move too and understood her verbal discomfort. Oliver pushed up from the floor, and every part of his body was stiff and painful. He rolled to his feet and tried to stretch the resistance from his muscles.

Regi opened his good eye and shifted in his seat.

"Hey, you okay?" Oliver asked Regi.

"Been better." Regi reached up to touch his swollen eye and winced.

"Look, don't try anything silly, okay? We'll figure this out."

"I'm sorry about Chancy, I didn't—"

Holly touched his shoulder. "Don't worry. We know it wasn't you."

Regi nodded and despite his gruesome injuries, the relief on his face was visible.

Pope's return to the plane was announced by both the groaning wreckage and his grunts. He glared at Oliver as if he hadn't expected him to be awake, let alone standing.

Pope pointed the gun barrel at Oliver's belly. "Get your spikes on, you lot. We've got a job to do." He motioned for them to get outside and pointed at their crampons veiled in a thin layer of snow.

Oliver placed Chancy's jacket over his body and face, and made a silent promise that they'd return to him and take him home. His only hope was that he'd be able to keep that promise.

Once outside, he plucked his crampons from the pile and handed Holly her pair. He climbed up the incline slightly and sat down on the snow. As he clicked them into position, he scanned the area. The morning brought with it perfect conditions, and he could see right down the valley.

He saw something else too.

A couple hundred feet below, to their left, was a giant gash in the white tundra.

The crevice.

He looked toward Holly, but it was Pope's glare that caught his attention. He'd been watching Oliver, possibly ready for his reaction—which meant Pope had seen the crevice too.

His grin was evil, knowing, and Oliver knew without a shadow of a doubt that once Pope had what he was after, he no longer needed him or Holly. Oliver needed to take control, without making Pope realize he was doing it.

"Hey, Holly, come here."

She looked up from her feet, frowned, then clomped up to him. "Look." He pointed toward what looked like a giant wound in the mountain.

"Oh." She turned to him, maybe unsure of what she should say.

He gave a very small nod. "Is that it?"

"Yeah. That must be the crevice."

"It's closer than I thought. Okay. Pope, do you want me to stack the sled? We're going to need a bit of equipment."

Pope squinted, revealing his skepticism. But thankfully he nodded.

With Pope watching their every move, Oliver and Holly pulled unnecessary equipment from the sled and restacked it with what they needed.

Twenty minutes after waking, the four of them left the wreck. Oliver was in the front, pulling the sled. Pope was at the rear, and he'd deliberately put Holly in front of him. At Pope's insistence, they were roped together. Maybe he thought they were going to run off.

Not that they'd get far before a bullet hit their back.

Overnight snow blanketed the slope with fresh powder that was about two feet deep, and Oliver tested each footfall for hidden holes by pushing his ice axe into the snow until it touched something solid. It was slow going, but thankfully not too taxing on his already aching muscles.

They arrived at the edge of the crevice without incident a couple of hours later. Oliver took a moment to peer into the hole, expecting to see the helicopter wreck, but he saw nothing but blue-hued ice. He turned to the others, and a shiver ran up his spine.

Pope had the gun pointed at Holly's head. The menace in his eyes showed Oliver he had no intentions of messing around. Oliver held up his hands. "Don't, Pope. We'll do whatever you want."

"I know you will. Get in that hole. You." He indicated to Regi. "Help him."

Bile rose to Oliver's throat at the fear in Holly's eyes. But he shoved his own distress aside, undid the rope that connected him to the sled, and released the webbing to access everything else.

"Holly, can you get the ropes ready?"

Without waiting for Pope's approval, she stepped forward to take the three loops of rope from Oliver's outstretched hand. Working together, they set up a belay system that would lower Oliver into the crevice.

Pope stepped up to the chasm and peered down. The temptation to run at him full pelt was so strong Oliver could picture Pope's demise. But there were so many things that could go wrong that he managed to talk himself out of it.

Instead, Oliver stepped in close to Holly. "I have a plan," he whispered.

Her gaze shot from Oliver to Pope and back again. She shook her head. "No, Olly—"

He nodded. "It's okay, just be ready when I come back up."

She bit her lip, blinking, then after a long pause, she nodded. When her jaw clenched, he saw the look of determination he'd seen on her numerous times. She'd be ready. She gave him the camera and he zipped it into his jacket pocket. "Take heaps of photos of the bodies." She didn't need to clarify which bodies she was talking about... Oliver knew.

A couple of minutes later, it was time to take the giant leap.

With his rope attached to the belay device on Regi's waist, Oliver turned his back to the crevice and planted his feet on the edge. "Climber ready."

Holly was on her stomach, right on the edge of the hole, ready to follow his progress. A rope attached her to Pope, and as much as she'd been repulsed by it, Oliver had been able to convince her of this safety precaution. Should the crevice give way, especially with how far she was leaning out over it, Pope would stop her fall. She turned to glance over her shoulder at Regi. They'd cleared away the loose snow to reveal the compacted ice, and Regi was seated with the spikes of his crampons driven into the ice to act as a brace. "You ready?"

"Yes." His gloved hands clamped the rope in the downward position just as Holly had shown him. His left eye was swollen shut, but his good eye was clear and focused, and when he nodded, Oliver was confident Regi understood that their lives were in his hands.

Pope stood back, the gun slack at his side, but that was the only thing slack about him. His pupils were wired, and the two black eyes he sported after Regi's punch in his nose made him look even crazier. Oliver was under no illusion that Pope would let them get off the mountain alive. It was something Oliver planned to change. He just didn't know how yet.

Oliver inhaled a long deep breath, let it out in a huge gush, and then, with his eyes on Holly, he descended into the hole. Each step required effort to dig the toe spikes into the ice. The lower he went, the cooler it became, and the harder the ice was to penetrate. It was impossible not to look down, but he saw no signs of the helicopter, let alone frozen bodies.

About ten feet into the crevice, the wall curved inward. Over the years, since the helicopter opened the original chasm, snow had fallen and hardened with the seasons. The result was a growing overhang that would one day completely cover the crevice again.

Beneath the overhang the chasm became wider, and when Oliver looked down this time, not only did he see the ledge that he assumed Holly had fallen onto four years ago, but he also saw parts of the wreck a further hundred or so feet below.

Trouble with the overhang was that the more the wall curved inward, the harder it was to keep his feet on the wall. "Holly, I need to go free."

She would know what that meant, and after a second's pause, in which he assumed she instructed Regi, she called back to him, "Okay, ready."

He released his ice axes and when he wriggled his crampon spike free and swung from the edge, Regi's rope was the only thing stopping him from dropping into the void.

Regi gradually released the rope in a smooth motion that had Oliver spinning in slow circles as he lowered. A ledge was a further five feet down. If it was the same one Holly had fallen onto, it was a miracle she'd landed there at all. It was barely two feet wide. "Nearly there… a couple more feet… stop."

"Stop." Holly repeat his command.

"I'm going to swing onto the ledge."

"Okay." He heard her repeat his intention to Regi.

Using his legs, he gradually worked momentum into the rope so he swung like a pendulum. With each swing back and forth he gradually got closer to the wall. His feet touched the ledge but he missed.

"Give me an inch of slack."

He dropped a fraction, and this time when he reached the wall, he pushed off of it, fast and hard so he swung out to the middle of the chasm. When he swung back, he waited till the very last second before he rammed his crampons into the ice.

It worked. "I'm here. Give me some rope."

Once the rope slackened, Oliver eased away from the edge and glanced around. Within a second he knew he was on the same ledge Holly had fallen onto. Her blood was still there, permanently inked into the ice.

But he couldn't see the bodies.

For a couple of thumping heartbeats, he wondered if her story had indeed been a figment of her imagination. At that time, she'd been severely wounded, lost, alone, and most likely in shock. The mind does weird things to shield a person from their tortured reality.

Desperate to believe her, he inched along the ledge as it curved around what appeared to be a giant ice pillar. And there they were. Exactly as she'd described them.

A man and a woman, frozen forever in a loving embrace. Holly was right: these two were not kidnapper and victim, as they'd been portrayed in the news. They were lovers who'd gone to great lengths to escape something or someone. Oliver now understood Holly's determination to bring them and Frederick's mother justice.

He removed the camera and took a series of photos, paying particular attention to their faces, the heart-shaped gold locket in her fingers, and the suitcase at their feet. After stepping back as far as he dared, he snapped a few photos of their embrace and their position in the crevice. He photographed their icy grave, both up and down. Across the crevice was a giant piece of metal jutting out of the ice like a spike. It took Oliver a few moments to realize it'd been one of the helicopter's skids. The blast must've driven it into the ice with some serious force.

Thinking of the helicopter, he eased up to the edge, looked down, and, using the camera, zoomed in on the wreckage below and took a few photos. But when he spied a pair of legs protruding from beneath the charred wreck, he lowered the camera. Nobody needed to see that. He pocketed the camera again and reached for the suitcase.

Oliver needed to buy some time to think. "I need a shovel," he called up.

Holly relayed his instruction, and, aware that they couldn't see him, he knelt on the ledge, flipped the suitcase flat, and wrestled with the clasps to open it.

Years of frigid air made the locks a struggle to open. Using the point of his axe to pry the metal clip, he prayed he didn't damage the locks. One then the other popped up, and he opened the lid. His breath hitched.

Cash. Hundreds of thousands of dollars. All stacked up in neat bundles.

Out of the corner of his eye he saw the shovel being lowered by rope. He stood, and with his feet firmly planted on the ice he used his ice axe to try to reach it. "Hold it there." It stopped lowering, but it was still a good three feet beyond his grasp. "I can't reach it. Can you swing the rope?"

Gradually, the shovel swung back and forth. "That's it, keep going."

"Got it." He pulled the shovel over and unhooked it from the rope. He looked at the shovel as a weapon rather than a tool, and found it impossible to comprehend he was even thinking like this.

His mind raced, desperate to formulate a plan.

He turned back to the money, and that's when an idea hit him. Oliver shut and locked the suitcase, then he stepped up to Frederick's corpse, removed his hat, and, using a utility knife, he cut a frozen lock of hair from the body. He put it into his top zippered pocket and hooked the shovel onto his utility belt. After one final glance at the bodies, he looked upward. "Okay, I'm ready to come up."

The rope went taut. Oliver sat back in his harness, and seconds later he left the safety of the ledge. As he dangled over the chasm with the suitcase in his hand, he prayed his plan would work.

Because the second he showed Pope the lock of hair, they were all dead.

CHAPTER TWENTY-SIX

Holly was surprised when Oliver announced he was ready to come up. There was no way he'd reached the bottom of the crevice, which also meant there was no way he'd seen Milton, or cut a portion of his hair. Her knowledge of the crevice gave them the advantage.

Neither Pope nor Regi would know Oliver hadn't reached the bottom.

Oliver said he had a plan. Whatever it was, she was ready to be part of it. "About time!"

Holly turned to Pope's gruff voice with clenched teeth. Forcing back the abuse she wanted to spray at him, she channeled her fury into something useful. Something that she'd be willing to unleash at the perfect moment. The gun was still in his hand, and Pope had done nothing but pace back and forth since Oliver had disappeared into the crevice.

Regi, on the other hand, had done everything perfectly.

She glanced his way. The steely determination on Regi's face confirmed he was taking his role seriously. Then again, his life did depend on Oliver succeeding. There was something else about his expression that caught her off guard, though. His squared jaw, the determination in his uninjured eye… it made him look so much like Milton that it took her breath away. It also convinced her that he was telling the truth about Milton being his father, which also meant that everything else he'd said about Milton was probably true too.

The man she'd once loved had been a fraud.

While he'd serenaded her with his gentlemanly charm, he'd been having a long-running affair with another woman. Bile rose to her throat at how stupid she'd been. But the truth did something else too: it made her hate him. Until this moment, she'd been distraught over how Milton had died. But now, with this new knowledge, she considered his frozen grave the perfect place for a man whose heart was obviously cast in stone.

The sight of Oliver's yellow safety hat launched her from her troubling thoughts. "There he is."

He looked up, and when their eyes locked it was obvious he was trying to tell her something. If ever there was a time she wished she could read minds, this was it. He held a suitcase out sideways, showing her, and she realized it was the one Fred had had positioned at his feet. She blinked at it a few times, trying to interpret the significance. But she had nothing.

All she knew was that she needed to be ready.

Regi continued to raise Oliver, moving his hands over and over in a movement that belied his inexperience.

"A little more; he's nearly here," she said.

"Hey, guys," Oliver said once his head was above surface level. "Look what I found." He held up the suitcase and offered it to Holly. She reached for it, placed it onto the snow on the opposite side where Pope was standing, and eased back from the edge.

"Who cares about a fucking case?" Pope snapped. "Did you get the DNA?"

Oliver crawled over the edge and didn't answer until he was standing on solid ground. "Yeah, but you gotta check this out."

Using his eyes, Oliver indicated for Holly to get back from Pope. She did, and Oliver bent over to unclip the locks on the case. "Look at all this money." He flipped the lid and turned the case so Pope could see inside.

Pope stepped forward. His eyes widened at the contents. Oliver reached in, plucked a bundle from the case, and tossed it Pope's way. The second Pope reached for it, Oliver swung the shovel, fast and hard, at Pope's head.

The blade smashed into Pope's already shattered nose with a sickening thud. He howled, stumbled sideways, and an inhuman noise burst from his throat as he fell into the void. The rope curled at Holly's feet snaked into the hole. Icy terror shot through her as she realized she was still attached to Pope.

Her heart slammed in her chest. "Shit!"

Frantic, she tried to undo the knot. But blind panic rendered her gloved fingers useless. It was too late. There was no time. She turned to Oliver.

A single look said so much. Shock. Horror. Hell.

His eyes bulged wide. "No!" Screaming, he launched at her.

She reached for him, clawing through the distance.

The rope snapped like a whip and Holly shrieked as she plunged into the hole for a second time.

Tons of ice flashed before her eyes as she braced for the crunch she knew was coming. A jolt stopped her fall, whipping her backward and spinning her in crazy circles.

Oliver's cries above confirmed she wasn't dead. She couldn't believe it herself, and she struggled to comprehend what'd happened. They hadn't hit the bottom, and her rope was taut above her.

By some miracle, she'd snagged on a piece of metal in the ice wall. Pope had gone to one side and she'd gone to the other. Their weight had counterbalanced each other and then become entangled. Pope dangled about four feet below her.

"I'm okay," she called out.

"Oh Jesus, thank god." Oliver's voice was frantic.

She looked down. Pope was almost doubled over backwards. He swung around in lifeless circles, but other than that, he didn't move. She thought he must've broken his back, but when his head came around, she saw something she wished she hadn't. Half his face was missing. At first she thought Oliver's hit with the shovel had done the damage, but when a drop of blood fell from the spike that'd saved her, she realized Pope must've hit the metal on the way down.

The icy walls began to spin. A dark fog crept in. Her stomach churned in sickening somersaults. Holly squeezed her eyes shut, desperate to eradicate the hideous image, and willed the darkness to take her from this new horror.

"I'm coming down. Stay there."

Oliver's shrill voice snapped her from her mental murkiness. She looked up the icy walls and saw blue sky, and seconds later Oliver appeared as he backed down over the edge. His movements were frantic. Dangerous.

"Wait, Oliver, don't hurry, I'm fine."

He paused, tried to look down.

"I'm fine. Trust me. But I think Pope's dead."

"Thank Christ," Oliver said. Even from her distance below she could hear Regi cheer.

"I need my axes and a rope." She glanced down at the body and realized she needed one more thing. "I need a knife too."

Oliver climbed back up, and seconds later he edged into the crevice again. As she dangled there, held in position by a dead man, she stared across the chasm. The ledge—her ledge—was there. Barely visible, to the left of a giant ice pillar, she saw Frederick's shoe. She remembered the first time she'd seen it and how it'd scared the hell out of her.

But as sad as Angel and Fred's demise had been, Holly had no doubt their final moments hadn't been filled with grief. Their faces didn't indicate they were distraught—quite the opposite. Fred and Angel died in each other's arms, a blanket of love keeping them warm. They'd accepted their fate.

Was finding their bodies her fate?

If she'd hadn't been in that helicopter crash, or fallen onto that exact ledge, she would never have seen them. If people had believed her story, then she wouldn't be back here trying to prove it. And if she hadn't learnt to rock climb, she would never have met Oliver. She glanced up at him now and her heart swelled. Fred and Angel had brought Oliver to her, and for that she would be forever grateful. She owed it to the couple to give them a final chapter.

Oliver lowered to her side, and when they reached for each other he wrapped her in a bear hug. "Oh my god. I'm so sorry. I thought I'd lost you."

"It's okay, I'm okay. You know I'm indestructible."

"I'm beginning to think you are." He glanced down at Pope's hideous injuries. "Jesus. Did I do that?"

"No, I'm pretty sure he hit that."

Oliver glanced upward and shook his head. "I saw that before. It's the helicopter's landing skid. You're one lucky woman."

She huffed. She'd never considered herself lucky. In fact, she'd always thought she was the opposite. But despite everything life had thrown at her, she was still here, so maybe she *was* blessed somehow. When she looked into Oliver's concerned eyes, she realized just how lucky she was.

He glanced down at Pope and then up to their rope, looped over the spike. "If we cut him loose, you'll fall."

"I know. Fix me a new rope, then climb back up, and when I cut him free, you can pull me out. Okay?"

He nodded. Working together, they tied a new rope to Holly's harness. Then he handed over her ice axes and she hooked them over her wrists.

Oliver clutched her cheeks and drew their lips together. "Be careful."

"I will."

"See you at the top."

"Okay." He looked upward. "Regi, pull me up."

He inched upward, and a few minutes after he disappeared over the top, the slack on her new rope was taken up. "Okay, Holly, cut the rope."

With one hand on the new rope, she held the blade against the rope attaching her to Pope. "Ready?"

"Yes."

The instant she slashed the line, she jolted out to the middle of the crevice. Seconds later she heard a dull thud, confirming Pope's body had hit the bottom.

She glided upward, and using her axes and crampons she crawled up the overhang. At the top, she wrapped her arms around Oliver and he squeezed her tight.

After a long pause, he pulled back. "Okay, let's get off this bloody mountain."

But as much as she agreed, she didn't want to go until she had what she came for. "Did you see the bodies?"

"Yes. Yes, I did. I took lots of photos."

"Show me." Regi stepped toward them, his hand outstretched, and that's when Holly realized her mistake. When he saw the photos, Regi would know it wasn't Milton.

She glanced at Oliver, and his darting eyes confirmed he realized her mistake too.

"Let's look at them later," Oliver said. "When we get in the plane."

"No," Regi snapped. "I want to see them now. And the hair too."

"Regi," Oliver pleaded.

"Show me." His clenched teeth indicated he knew something wasn't right.

Oliver handed him the camera, and Holly shared her gaze between the two men and the camera display. Regi turned the camera on and flicked through the pictures.

"What is this?" A frowned corrugated Regi's forehead. "Who're they?"

"It's Fred and Angel. Remember the ransom money we—"

"Where's Milton?"

"He's too far down, I couldn't get to him."

"Bullshit, I need his hair." Regi's fury was swift. He balled his fists and clamped his jaw. But after a couple ragged breaths, he changed again. His chin dimpled. A tear trickled out his good eye and he flicked it away. He strode to his left, bent over, and when he turned to them he had a gun in his hand. Pope must've dropped it when Oliver struck him with the shovel. "I need that hair."

Holly froze. Pope's gun slotted into Regi's right hand, not quiet menacing, but effective enough. "What're you doing, Regi?"

"I need that DNA. Carson will never stop until I repay him."

"You can have this money." Holly pointed at the suitcase.

"It's not enough. And it's not just about the money. You don't get it. He's never gonna let me go, ever."

"We can tell the police."

"No!" Regi clamped his teeth and his jaw trembled. "Carson has the police in his pocket. Has everyone in his pocket."

"We can help you," Oliver pleaded.

Regi shook his head. He seemed torn between what was right and what he had to do.

"Tell us, Regi." Holly opened her hands, hoping to portray genuine concern. "Tell us everything and we'll help you. I promise."

He glanced from her to Oliver and seemed plagued with indecision. Regi plonked onto the snow, the gun still in his hand, rested on his right knee. He inhaled a long deep breath. "When I was twenty-two, I took my mother's boyfriend's car for a joyride." A slight grin curled on his lips. "It was a Firebird. You know. . . the car."

When Oliver nodded, Holly did too.

"Afterwards I stopped to get cigarettes, and when I reversed outta the shop, I smashed into a guy's car. A Corvette Stingray. Seven hundred-thousand-dollar car. Owned by Jeremiah Carson. You know him?"

Both Holly and Oliver shook their heads.

"You're lucky. He owns an oil well, and he's got more money than God. Anyway, ever since that day Carson's owned me. He beats me up whenever he feels like it. Not Carson, exactly—Pope and his gang of assholes do Carson's dirty work. He's made me do other stuff too. And he's messed up my mom's house. What Pope said back there, in the plane, about Carson getting his claws in? Well, he's right. I'm never going to be free. That's why I need this money. To pay Carson off, to get a new life for me and my mother."

The anguish in his voice convinced Holly that every word was true. He'd been living in hell for years. She could fully relate to that. "Let us help you," she pleaded.

"I am letting you help me. I need that DNA." He stood and aimed the gun at Holly, then at Oliver. Then, with his chin dimpling and a tear pooling in his good eye, he tossed it into the crevice. "If I don't get that DNA, I may as well stay right here. I'm fucked either way."

He was trapped. Holly knew exactly how that felt. She'd had her life taken out of her hands once before, when Victoria had forced her into a corner that she couldn't get out of.

Holly had lost control of her own destiny. It'd taken years and a complete change of life to flip it around.

The look of absolute failure on Regi's face had her coming to a decision. She turned to Oliver. "I'm going back into the crevice."

"Holly…" Oliver pleaded her name and she shook her head.

"You're not going to stop me, so you either belay for me, or I'll ask Regi to."

Oliver clenched his jaw and squeezed his eyes shut. But when he opened them again, he was in efficiency mode. He strode to the sled. "We'll need all the rope we've got. Regi, clear a new patch of snow for me." He tossed the shovel toward him.

"Thank you. Thank you both." Regi's eye was bright, lit up with hope and appreciation.

"Don't thank us yet. That body is a long way down."

"I know you can do it, Holly."

She turned to him, and the gratitude in his good eye convinced her she was doing the right thing. Within a few minutes, Oliver was ready with the belay rope and Holly had all the equipment she thought she'd need, including the camera. Oliver pulled her into a hug. "Don't do anything silly."

"Me? Never." She tried to make it a lighthearted moment, but Oliver didn't take the bait.

"Holly, please… I mean it."

She kissed him. "I won't, I promise."

"I'll lower you as fast as I can so you can get back up here as quickly as possible."

"Okay. Good."

The weight on her belt was heavy as she clomped to the edge of the crevice and turned with her back to hole. "Climber ready."

Oliver nodded at her, and with their eyes locked together he released the rope. She eased her weight onto the harness and walked backwards down the overhang. Oliver wasn't joking when he said he'd lower her quickly. Within a few seconds she passed her ledge. In another twenty or so the crevice opened into an enormous chamber, remarkably circular in shape. The crevice was shaped like half a giant hourglass, narrow at the top and bulbous at the bottom.

It grew darker and colder with each foot she lowered and, turning on her headlamp, she played the beam over ice walls so dense they permeated a blue tinge. The chasm was silent at first, eerie. But as she lowered further, she started to hear the ice creaking and cracking, and the wind seemed to whisper around the abyss. She had to push away thoughts of ghostly whispers. It didn't help that she was sharing the chasm with six bodies.

Down below, the middle of the cave was a giant mound that rose dozens of feet higher than the outer edges. The center was in direct line with the opening above, so the hill was the result of years of snow falling in one place. Just off center of the mound was Pope. He'd fallen face up, and had his arms and legs apart like he was in the process of making a snow angel. What was left of his face was worse than any Halloween mask a designer could dream up.

She snapped her eyes away and forced herself to scan the area for Milton.

Against one side of the chasm lay the helicopter carcass. The charred blemish, upside down and displaying its red underbelly and registration number, was a brutal contrast to its natural surroundings. She assumed it'd rolled down the mound to where it was now.

Fifteen feet before her feet touched solid ground, she stopped. Swinging in a lazy circle, she glanced up. "A bit more," she yelled.

"No more rope." Regi's voice drifted down to her.

"Shit."

She was so close. Too close to give up now. She turned her attention to the walls of the cave. They were pure ice. She'd climbed walls with greater difficulty before. Hell, she'd climbed a frozen waterfall. These looked easy in comparison.

Holly made a snap decision. She plucked her glove off with her teeth, and working quickly, before Oliver began pulling her back up, she released the clips holding her in place and fell the rest of the way. After free falling for a couple of heartbeats, several feet of snow cushioned her fall.

"Holly!" Oliver bellowed.

"I'm okay."

"Jesus, Holly, what the fuck're you doing?"

"I'm okay."

"Damn. You crazy woman."

He was furious. But she didn't care. Blocking out his angry torrent, which continued above her, she clambered down the snow hill toward the wreck. She shoved her glove into her jacket and removed the camera. A pair of legs protruding from beneath the chopper caught her eye, and as she made her way toward it, she prayed it wasn't Milton. Because if it was, she had no hope of getting a sample of his hair.

She'd nearly reached the legs when she spied another body. It was Milton. He'd been flung clear of the wreck. He was on his side, one arm stretched upward like he'd used it as a pillow. His legs were curled up, almost in a fetal position. The beanie on his head was down over half his face and his mirrored glasses were skewed. But other than that, he looked peaceful, and if she didn't know better, she'd be tempted to believe he was sleeping.

An overwhelming dose of sadness gripped her as she made her way toward him. But she forced it back. She'd been crying over his death for years. Enough was enough. She'd grieved more in her short life than most people had in their lifetime.

It was time to move on. Time to put this past behind her.

She knelt at his side and reached for the beanie but stopped. It'd been his favorite head warmer. The Seattle Seahawks logo was embroidered on the front, and around the edges he'd had the player's signatures inked into the fabric. It was one of a kind, and perfect to prove it was Milton's original beanie.

She stepped back and photographed him, taking care to zoom in on the beanie. Then, with the video on, she filmed her hand removing the beanie. It was frozen solid and cracked as she pulled it upward. She lifted his mirrored glasses off too.

Thankfully his eyes were closed, and other than a red graze to his right temple, he didn't appear wounded. She turned back to the camera and replayed the footage to confirm it was sufficient. Satisfied, she removed the knife from her pocket and cut one of the frozen curls from Milton's head. She put it in the beanie and put both in a zippered pocket in her jacket.

With that done, she raised her face toward the opening. "I'm coming up now."

"Thank Christ."

Holly took her time surveying the crevice walls, planning out the best route. She decided the one that led to her ledge was the best, if only because it'd provide her with a decent place to rest. Oliver could get a rope down to her from there and haul her up the rest of the way.

She put her glove back on, and with nothing left to do, she rammed her ice axe into the wall and took her first step upward. Holly ensured each spike with the axe sounded solid and complete, just like her mountaineering guide had taught her. Only once she was happy with the axe's position did she move. Every couple of minutes Oliver shouted encouragement down to her and she relayed her progress.

It was therapeutic: right axe, left axe, boot, boot. She repeated the move over and over and over. Her advancement was slow. Too slow, and she imagined Oliver pacing back and forth up top.

But she wouldn't rush. This took time, patience, concentration, and determination.

Whiskey Mountain had tried to kill her twice before. It hadn't succeeded then. Damned if she'd let it win this time. Not when the man of her dreams was waiting for her at the top.

The entire time she was climbing, she'd resisted the urge to look up or down, so it surprised her when she reached the ledge. "I'm at the ledge." After climbing up and over the side, she sat with her back against the wall and her feet splayed out before her to catch her breath.

Her dried blood was still in the ice to her left. Just a few spatters. Not enough, considering the hundreds of stitches the doctors needed to patch her up. She rolled away and crawled to Angel and Fred.

She stared at them for a long while, then, heaving a heavy sigh, she placed her hand on Fred's knee. "Rest in peace, my friends."

Holly lifted the locket from Angel's fingers and opened it. Inside were two pictures of the pair. They were both smiling in the photo on the left, their arms around each other. In the photo on the right, they were sharing a kiss.

This proved their love affair. Holly gradually wove the gold chain from Angel's frozen fingers and placed the prized possession in her top pocket.

"I'm so mad at you." She turned toward Oliver's voice. He was dangling from a rope in the crevice.

"Hi, honey."

"Don't 'hi honey' me. That was a stupid thing you did down there."

"But it's okay. I'm here now."

He tossed a rope toward her. "Yeah, well don't mess around anymore."

Holly clipped the rope to her harness. "Okay, boss."

"I'm not joking, Holly. A big storm is coming. We've gotta get back to that plane."

CHAPTER TWENTY-SEVEN

Regi was on his stomach, peering into the hole, waiting to see Holly finally show on the end of the rope. The weather had changed dramatically. Clouds had come out of nowhere, covered the sun completely, and made it even harder to see anything down the damn hole. The wind whipped up, spitting frozen pellets from the icy overhang into his face.

"There she is." He turned to Oliver, whose look of pure grit showed just how quickly he was trying to haul Holly up.

She smiled up at him. "I got it, Regi. Photos, hair, and his beanie."

Regi swallowed back the lump in his throat that made it difficult to breathe. "Thank you. Thank you so much."

Holly crawled up over the edge, and the second she was free he went to her and wrapped his arms around a woman he barely knew. She'd just saved his ass. "I can't believe you did that for me. Thank you."

She clapped him on the back. "Thank you."

He pulled back. "For what?"

"For telling me about Milton."

"Oh." He had no idea how that was a good thing.

"Holly! We need to get moving." Oliver jabbed a finger skyward.

Black clouds swirled like they'd been caught in a blender, and the wind howling up the mountain was both freezing and packing a punch.

Oliver took charge, roping them all together and making decisions on what they'd take and what they'd leave. Within fifteen minutes of Holly stepping out of the chasm, they started walking. Regi looked up the mountain, trying to see the wreck, but it was gone, hidden completely by years of snow. Thank god the two stone pillars gave them something to aim for.

They formed a line, Oliver in the front and him at the end. Holly was in the middle, and as he watched her progress through the increasing whiteout, he tried to comprehend why she'd done what she did. Holly had put her life on the line for him. No one had ever done that before. Not one person. He wasn't even sure his mother would do it.

Holly had said she'd help him. But the extent she'd gone to was crazy.

His thoughts turned to Carson, and he wondered how he'd react to the news of Pope's death. The answer came quickly: he wouldn't. Carson didn't care about anyone. Not Pope, not Regi, and not even the women he surrounded himself with.

Once he gave him his money, Regi had no intention of ever seeing that asshole again.

But then he thought of Pope's comment. Was it true? Would Carson still have his claws in, even after Regi payed him off?

The wind howled at him like a tormented beast, driving the anger growing inside him. With each step he took, he grew more certain that even once Carson had what he was owed, Regi would still be trapped.

His calf muscles were killing him, and his ears were aching so much from the cold he wondered if they were frozen solid. They seemed to be taking forever. It'd grown dark too, and he wished he had a headlamp like Holly. Thank god he was attached to her rope; it was the only thing showing which way to go.

The howling wind changed slightly. It seemed more high-pitched, and he looked to his left, trying to work out why. To his surprise, he saw the plane. Oliver and Holly had walked right past it. He planted his feet and pulled on the rope. Three short tugs.

The rope tried to pull him forward, but he pulled back. Again, he gave three short tugs.

There was a moment's pause, and then Holly signaled back to him by pulling on the rope. Soon the rope was loose, and he looped it over and over, taking up the slack, confirming they were walking back to him.

As soon as he saw Holly materialize out of the whiteout, he cupped his hands and yelled, "Plane!"

She looked in the direction he pointed and moments later gave him a thumbs-up signal. When she reached his side, she touched his shoulder. "Good work. I can't believe we missed it."

"Holy shit," Oliver said once he got to them. "That could've been bad."

Regi couldn't remember the last time he'd done something that filled him with such pride. Riding that wave, he led the way to the plane door, shoved the new layer of snow from the bottom of the entrance, and swung it open.

He stepped in and plonked into the middle seat. The other two didn't come in right away, and when he looked out and saw them untying their rope, he removed his gloves and did the same.

Holly came in and he handed her his end of the rope. She tossed it outside.

Oliver remained outside, sorting through stuff in the sled. Regi hoped he was planning on food, because he was starving. None of them had eaten since the night before.

Holly went to the back of the plane and sat looking down at Chancy's body.

"What're we going to do with him?"

She looked Regi's way and shrugged. "I don't think we should take him back ourselves. I'll arrange for someone to come get him, though, and the pilot."

Holly seemed really beat up about what happened to Chancy, though he was pretty certain they didn't know each other.

She turned to him, and when their eyes met, he was stunned by how blue they were. "Regi, you know we'll need to make up a story, don't you?"

He raised his eyebrows. "Like what?"

"Well, Oliver and I said we were coming up here to retrieve Milton's body, but we didn't succeed. You and Pope said you were here for an insurance claim. Now that people have died, we need to figure a few things out."

"I didn't kill anyone."

"We know. None of us did."

Regi was thinking that Oliver *had* sorta killed Pope. Then again, if Regi hadn't punched Pope, the gun wouldn't have gone off. So maybe he sorta killed Chancy too.

The door creaked open, luring Regi from his tumbling thoughts. "Who's hungry?" Oliver tossed a couple of packets of freeze-dried meals onto the front seat.

"Hell yeah."

As Oliver set about making their meals, Regi toyed with his earlier thought. If he wanted to, he could label Oliver as Pope's murderer—if he needed to, that was. If Holly and Oliver decided to throw him under the bus when they got back, he'd have his own backup plan.

Holly moved away from Chancy and sat opposite Regi. "Olly, I was just talking to Regi about our need to get our story straight."

Oliver looked up from the stove he was getting ready to light. "What story?"

She turned to Regi. "It seems that we both have secrets. You didn't want anyone to know you were looking for Milton's DNA, and we didn't want anyone to know we were looking for Angel and Fred's bodies. It's a crazy coincidence that put us all together."

"You got that fucking right. Why were you looking for those people anyway? Was it the money?"

A look of sadness crossed her eyes. "It's a long story."

He held his hands wide. "Got nothin' else to do."

She huffed and looked at Oliver as he ripped one of the packets open. "He's right."

Holly pulled her water bottle from her pack, and after taking a swig she turned to him. "Four years ago, I took a helicopter flight up here with Milton. We crashed, and well… your father and everyone else died."

The way she spoke, almost trance-like, made him wonder if this was something she needed to talk about. Regi decided not to tell her he'd read all about it in the paper. When she told him about Angel and Fred, though, he was glad he didn't stop her.

She was right about it being a long story, and they'd all eaten their meals by the time she finished. Regi had never met anyone like Holly. He thought she was amazing before, when she'd fetched that stuff for him, but her willingness to risk her life for people she'd never even met was the most unselfish thing he'd ever heard of.

It was there and then that he knew he'd never need that backup plan with Oliver. And when Holly had said she'd help him, he was certain she would.

"So," Holly said, "we need a favor. When we get back, I don't want anyone to know about Fred or Angel. At least not until I've had a chance to tell Fred's mother."

Regi nodded. "I can manage that. But I'm going to need your help."

"Sure." She didn't even hesitate.

"Well, I assume it's going to take time to get the DNA tested and stuff. Then there'll be more time settling the estate." He screwed up his nose. "I don't really know any of that stuff, but I need to get Carson off my ass as soon as I can." He cleared his throat. "Do you reckon I could have that money? In the case?" He pointed out the window. "I'll pay you back when my money comes through."

"There's no need to pay us back. It's not our money."

"Oh… um." He was stunned speechless by her response.

"Let's see how much it is." Oliver went outside to fetch the case, and between the three of them they began counting the money stacks. Regi had never seen so many hundred-dollar bills in his life. As he counted up the thousands, it began to hit him that he was about to be rich. Mega-fucking-rich. He could ditch his boring job, buy a new car, a new house. Get one for his mother too. He could buy fancy clothes and shiny leather shoes like he'd seen Carson wear. The thought of Carson brought the whole fantasy crashing back to reality.

None of it was worth a cent if Carson continued to own him.

"Holly, when you said you'd help me, did you mean it?"

"Of course."

He believed her. One hundred percent.

The next day, everything went to plan. The weather was back to perfect and they set off as soon as the sun lit the horizon. Once they crossed through the towering pillars, Oliver used Chancy's two-way radio to call for a rescue.

They were back at Miracle Lodge before lunch and the police were choppered in a few hours later. Holly, Oliver, and Regi were interviewed together. Regi made a point of keeping his mouth shut, and it worked exactly as planned because Holly answered most of the questions. No one seemed to question her story about Pope looking for the ransom money he'd thought was in the plane. They also didn't ask too many questions when she told them how Pope had gone crazy and shot Chancy when the money wasn't there.

"So, where'd he go?" the redheaded policeman asked Holly.

"We don't know." She shrugged. "After Pope shot Chancy, he just left the plane. Maybe he tried to come back down. We never saw him again."

Oliver and Regi both nodded, agreeing with Holly's story.

What the police didn't need to know, nor anybody else, was their visit to the crevice after Chancy had been shot. As far as the police knew, they spent over twenty-four hours hiding in the wreck, from both the storm and the madman outside.

When the interview was over and the police left, Holly arranged for them all to get a helicopter back to the airport. On the way back, she handed Regi a piece of paper. "Here's my cell number. Call me whenever you need."

As much as he hoped he wouldn't, he was also pretty certain he'd be needing her help again, and probably very soon.

They landed to a mob of reporters all shoving microphones in their faces. But it wasn't him they were after, it was Holly. And while Oliver tried to save her from the pushy bastards, Regi snuck away, and that was the last he saw of them.

When his plane landed in Seattle, the temptation to go home, shower, eat, and sleep was strong. But the need to get it over with with Carson was stronger. He looked like shit. His hair was a mess, and in addition to the split in his fat lip and his black swollen eye, his face was sunburnt. He stunk too.

But he didn't care.

Regi took a taxi from the airport straight to Carson's gate. He paid the driver and tugged his pack from the trunk. It was the same guard from last time, but it wouldn't matter and he knew it. He'd still have to go through the motions. Even though the pit bull had seen him walk up, he still waited until Regi knocked on the small glass panel.

"What?" he grunted.

"Reginald Tate, here to see Mr. Carson. Tell him I have his money."

The guard cocked his head as if Regi's comment jogged his memory. It should've, because it was what got him through the gate last time.

Once again Regi was ordered to sit on the bench nearby. As he waited, he wondered who Carson would send this time, now that Pope was dead.

Pope was dead.

He hadn't even had time to celebrate.

Regi waited out the minutes by trying to count how many times Pope had beaten him up. He was at number twelve when Carson's Rolls-Royce Wraith curved into the waiting zone.

The side gate popped open, and Regi grabbed his pack and aimed straight for the back seat. He climbed in and checked out the driver. He'd seen him before. The man had joined Pope in many of Regi's beatings, but Regi had no idea of his name.

He said nothing, so Regi didn't either.

Once again he was driven down to Carson's twelve-car garage, but this time, when the car stopped Regi got out and made his own way to the exit. He climbed the steps, and at the top he searched for Carson. The entire house was lit up, but nobody was around. Some kind of buttery pastry was cooking in the kitchen, and the smell had Regi's stomach growling.

Unsure of which way to turn, he waited for the driver to make his way up from the garage.

"Where is he?" Regi asked the second the man appeared on the stairs.

"In the bar." He pointed in the direction and Regi strode that way.

After a few strides on the polished white tiles he heard music, and then laughter. Women and men. And a loud crack that sounded like the start of a game of pool.

He entered through the open double doors and Carson was there, arms open as if ready to hug him. "Ah, there he is, the man of the hour."

Regi pulled to a stop and did a quick scan of the room. Other than Carson, he recognized only one other man, another one of Pope's goons. Centered in the room was a giant pool table. To the left was an enormous bar, and the brunette behind it was topless. The remaining women ranged from fully clothed to nothing but G-strings. All six men and seven women around the room turned to face him. Everyone had a glass in their hand.

"Can I talk to you, please, Mr. Carson?"

"Of course." Carson indicated to the bar.

"Alone." Regi pleaded.

"But we all want to hear your story. It's been headlining all day."

That was news to Regi, and he wondered just how much Carson knew. But as he squeezed the handle of his backpack, loaded to the brim with half a million dollars, he knew Holly wouldn't have said any more than she needed to.

"There's nothing to tell," he said. "Pope's dead. I've got your money. We've got a deal to settle."

"Oh, come on, don't be like that. Have a drink with us."

"I don't want a drink, Mr. Carson. I want you out of my fucking life. Forever."

Carson's eyes narrowed. Regi had stepped over a line, a line that would force Carson to show those in the room who was in charge. And without Pope around to do his dirty work, Regi was interested to see how he planned on doing it.

"You've got a lot of gall coming into my home and saying that."

Regi unzipped his pack and upended it, spilling bundles and bundles of money onto the plush carpet. "Here. Five hundred thousand dollars. That's how much you said I owed you."

Carson blinked at the stash. A murmur rumbled around the room.

"For the damage to the Stingray. *And* so I could walk away. That's the deal we had, right?" Regi clenched his jaw.

"Yes. That *was* the deal. Before you... how shall I say it... *lost* Pope. My best man. So that deal's no longer on the table. You're mine, Reginald Tate. No amount of money can release you." Carson had a way of making a threat real. Calm, calculating. Like wielding an axe loaded with menace.

"Yours? What d'ya mean I'm yours? I'm nothing like Pope. I can't go around beating people up, just 'cause you ask."

"Pope told me you're fast on your feet."

"That's because when he's around, I'm running for my life."

Carson sipped his drink, then chuckled. "You'll learn."

Regi kicked the bag, then picked up a wad of cash and threw it at Carson.

Carson ducked, but he didn't need to, because the money separated and fluttered to the floor. Once it settled, Carson pegged his glass at Regi. Regi could've ducked, but he'd learned that lesson years ago. The glass hit him square in the chin, showering him in ice and liquor. He howled at the sting to his split lip and the pain to his already thumping bruises.

There were as many gasps around the room as there were sniggers.

Regi glared at Carson with a hatred so deep it burned.

Carson laughed. Laughed and laughed. Then they all started laughing. Regi turned and ran, sprinting down the long corridor, out the enormous front doors, down the broad road with the fancy trees, and out the panel in the gate.

The whole time he was running he expected to be tackled to the ground.

But he wasn't.

Carson let him go.

But only because Carson could get him any time he wanted.

KENDALL TALBOT

CHAPTER TWENTY-EIGHT

After they'd come down from the mountain, and survived the media frenzy and endless police interviews, Holly and Oliver had parted ways. While he returned to Brambleton, back to his work and worried family, Holly had stayed in Seattle.

She had business to attend to. And she was determined not to return to Brambleton, *or* Oliver, until she was done. But after just seven days, she couldn't wait to get out of the place she'd once called home.

While the taxi ambled along in the bumper-to-bumper traffic, Holly looked out over the bay. The scene was picturesque, but it was no longer the thing of beauty that she'd once considered it. Holly reached for the gold locket in her purse, opened it again, and stared at the photos of Angel and Fred inside. Not that she needed to; their smiling faces would be permanently implanted in her mind.

Her heart was pounding out a frantic beat by the time the taxi pulled into the curb outside the four-story apartment complex. She paid the driver and stepped into the uncertain Seattle weather. It seemed that one minute the sun was blazing and the next minute black clouds plastered over it, threatening rain. When she'd lived here all those years ago, she hadn't really noticed its volatile weather patterns, but it'd certainly put on a show in the last few days. The weather perfectly matched how she was feeling, and as she walked up the uneven brick path, her nerves swung from dread to excitement.

No matter what happened, she was about to change an old woman's life.

Holly climbed the short stack of steps and walked along the narrow wrought iron-lined balcony. She stopped outside the door with a large number seven screwed into a middle panel.

When she couldn't procrastinate a moment more, she reached up and knocked.

Several heartbeats later, the door opened a couple of inches, until a chain stopped its progress. "Hello." The woman's quivering voice matched her age.

"Hello, Mrs. Pearce, my name is Holly Parmenter. I rang you yesterday about—"

"Yes, yes, just a moment." The door shut, and after a metallic shuffling sound it reopened again. Dorothy was short, and her dependence on a walking stick had her leaning over, reducing her height even further. "You say you have some information on my Frederick?"

"Yes, I do. Would you mind if I came in? I brought us a tea cake." Holly held up the white box containing the treat.

"Oh, that's very thoughtful of you, dear. Come in. Come in. I'll put the kettle on."

Holly stepped into a small lounge area dotted with trinkets, fake flowers, and a variety of photos. Several photo frames housed pictures of Frederick. Him in his police uniform, playing sports, and with his arms around a much younger version of his elderly mom.

As she followed Dorothy's slow progress into the apartment, Holly prayed the news she was about to give the elderly woman wouldn't ruin the image Dorothy had created for her son.

Dorothy made tea and indicated where Holly could find small plates and a knife to cut the tea cake. She may look frail, but Dorothy could assert herself just fine. Once they were ready, she led them back to the living room, and while the elderly woman sat in a small recliner, Holly sat on the two-seater sofa, close to Dorothy. She put her bag on the couch beside her and swallowed hard.

She'd rehearsed over and over how she'd convey what she knew, and the only way that'd made any sense was to start at the beginning. Holly placed her tea cup on the coffee table and turned to Dorothy. "Dorothy, what I have to tell you is a long story."

"I've got all afternoon, dear." She sipped her tea.

"You may need it. Okay, so four years ago, I traveled to Canada with my fiancé, Milton."

Dorothy was an excellent listener, she nodded and blinked and sipped her tea, but didn't utter a single sound until Holly said, "The helicopter explosion released a giant chunk of ice. That's when I saw... Frederick and Angelique. They were there, on the ledge with me."

Dorothy gasped. Frowned. Her hand went to the pearls around her neck and tears welled in her eyes as she put her tea cup down. But still she remained silent. Holly reached into her purse and removed the photo she'd chosen as the most moving, yet beautiful picture of the couple.

It was peaceful, loving.

Dorothy reached for the photo and her lips parted. For a long moment she stared at the photo with her trembling fingers, making it shiver. Finally, a small smile curled at her lips. "They make such a handsome couple."

Holly sighed. "Yes, they do."

She reached into her bag and removed all the photos she'd taken. Holly explained their position in the crevice, how far down they were, and how far they'd walked from the plane wreck. "It was a miracle they survived the crash."

"It must've been awful."

"They tried to walk out, but their shoes would've made it impossible… see?" Holly pointed to the close-up of Angel's feet.

"My Frederick was a real gentleman; he probably carried her."

Holly could see him doing that. Dorothy ran her finger over the photo of Angel's hand with the locket draped through her fingers and Holly removed the locket from her purse. "I think they would've wanted you to have this."

She placed the locket into the soft skin of Dorothy's palm, and when she opened the pendant a tear spilled from her pale blue eyes. "This's beautiful."

Holly carried on with her story, explaining why it'd taken her so long to tell anyone about Fred and Angel, why no one believed her, and how she'd seen the news report with the plane wreck that Carter Logan had found. She told Dorothy about seeing her on the news and how devastated she'd been that nobody had believed her story either.

"Nobody did. I knew Frederick would never hurt anyone." Her eyes grew wide. "Oh my. All this time, I've blamed David, but it wasn't him." Her hand went to her mouth, and it was obvious that her false accusations hurt.

That's when Holly removed the small leather-bound pocket book they'd found in the suitcase. "Fred wrote a note. I guess he hoped they'd one day be found."

Dorothy frowned, but then a smile crept across her lips. "He always kept a little notebook in his top pocket. All day long he'd be jotting things down in that silly book. That's why he was a good detective, you know. Frederick never missed anything."

Again, her hands trembled when Holly handed the notebook over. When she flipped up the cover, Holly reached for her cup of tea and sat back. Fred had meticulously detailed everything in the book. It read like a police report, and Holly had been surprised at how many of her assumptions were true. David had been an abusive husband to Angelique. Frederick had been the police officer who'd tried to convince her to lodge a complaint against David. But it was the ransom money that she'd completely misjudged. It wasn't ransom money at all.

The whole idea had been David's.

The conniving ratbag had *given* Fred the money. The sum was barely one-tenth of their combined wealth, of which Angel had earned the majority. In exchange for the money, Angel and Frederick were to run away, disappear, which suited them both just fine. But what they hadn't planned on was David accusing Fred of kidnapping Angel and stealing the ransom.

Once they were settled in Canada, they'd planned to expose David as the lying abusive husband he was and then invite Dorothy and her husband to come and live with them.

Holly waited for Dorothy to reach that detail in Frederick's notes. When she did, a sob released from her lips. "I knew he wouldn't have abandoned me."

"He didn't. He loved you."

"He loved me." The words whispered off her lips, convincing Holly that she'd finally brought justice to Angel and Fred, and brought closure to Dorothy.

When Dorothy reached the end of the book, she folded the cover closed, placed it in her lap, and curled her fingers over it. "Thank you."

Holly leaned forward and placed her hands over Dorothy's. "Let me know if you want to take this farther, and I'll help you all the way."

Dorothy frowned. "What do you mean?"

"Well, David has been living this lie for forty years. Maybe it's time for the world to know exactly what he did."

Dorothy blinked and blinked some more. Then her lips curled into a smile.

Holly reached into her purse. "Here's my phone number. Think about it, and let me know what you decide. Oh, and one more thing. We found the so-called ransom money with Fred and Angel in that suitcase that was at their feet. So, now that we know David gave the money to Fred, I guess the money is yours." Holly handed over a bank check for half a million dollars. Dorothy didn't need to know what really happened with the cash.

A twinkle danced in Dorothy's eyes when she saw the figure. "Oh my." When her fingers twirled the pearl necklace at her throat, the tremble she'd displayed several times was no longer there. "Thank you."

"You're welcome." Holly stood. "It was lovely to meet you. Please don't stand up, I can show myself out."

But Dorothy pushed forward on her chair and used her cane to stand. Once upright, she held her arms open. Holly stepped into the woman's embrace and they hugged each other for a very long time.

It was three in the afternoon when Holly returned to the city and crossed the lobby of the Columbia Center skyscraper in downtown Seattle. She stepped into the elevator and pressed the button for the sixty-second floor. Where she'd been apprehensive about meeting with Dorothy, this next meeting was one she was truly looking forward to.

Holly applied a touch of lipstick in the mirror, and rather than hide the scar on her face, she hooked her hair behind her ear. Her stomach did a little flip at her arrival at the floor, and she stepped onto the plush carpet. At the end of the hall was Princeton and Howard Law Firm, and although this was the first time she'd been there, it wasn't the first time she'd dealt with them.

Holly stepped through the smoky glass doors, and a stunning woman with a perfectly styled blond updo looked up from a dark mahogany desk and smiled. "Good afternoon, Miss Parmenter. We've been expecting you."

The woman stood and indicated they should walk together. "May I offer you something to drink? Tea, coffee, juice?"

"Some orange juice would be lovely."

The receptionist knocked once on a large wooden door and then pushed to enter. "Miss Parmenter has arrived."

"Thank you, Madonna." Madonna retreated and a man stepped forward to offer his hand. "Good afternoon, Miss Parmenter. My name is Evert Howard."

She shook his firm grip. "Please, call me Holly."

"As you wish. Please take a seat. I've prepared all the necessary documents. Your guest is waiting in the other room."

Holly smiled. "Excellent."

As Evert summarized what he'd prepared, Madonna returned with Holly's juice. "Mrs. Ashcroft has arrived. Would you like me to show her in?"

He turned to Holly. "Are you ready?"

She sat back, straightened her shoulders, and nodded. "I've never been more ready in my life."

He turned back to Madonna. "Please, show her in."

When the door reopened, Victoria Ashcroft stepped into the room. The smile she'd had plastered on her face vanished in a second. "What is this?"

Evert stood with his hand forward. "Hello, Mrs. Ashcroft. My name is Evert Howard, I represent Ms. Parmenter. Please take a seat."

Victoria glared at Holly, and for a few thumping heartbeats Holly feared she'd step back out the door. But she didn't. She squared her jaw, flicked her hair over her shoulders, and sat into the chair Evert was holding out for her.

"I assume you've been following the recent events in the news." Holly wasted no time getting to the point.

Victoria fiddled with the engagement ring on her finger as she nodded. The three-carat diamond had been from Milton, and Holly had always been surprised that Victoria continued to wear it.

"Then you're aware that I attempted to retrieve Milton's body from the crevice."

"I heard you failed." Her lips formed a thin smile.

"Not entirely."

"What does that mean?"

"Did you know Milton had an affair with Fiona Tate for over twenty years?"

Her eyes flared. "Rubbish!"

Holly ignored her outburst. "They had a son. Reginald Tate."

"Kane was Milton's only son. But you killed him."

"Milton had at least one other son, I can assure you."

"You need to prove it."

"We have every intention of proving it. But we have a proposition for you first."

She rolled her eyes.

"Because you've been fighting over Milton's will for four years, the fact that it's still not settled means Regi is now able to make a claim to the estate. It's come to my attention that in addition to Milton's long-running affair with Regi's mother, he also had sex with numerous women while you two were married *and* while he was engaged to me. Milton was the epitome of a lying cheating bastard. But you already knew that, didn't you?"

Victoria made a short gasp and her eyes darted from Evert to Holly.

"There's a chance there are more children, just like Reginald. So the sooner you settle the estate, the better."

"I'm not letting this… *liar* get one cent."

"I thought you'd say that." Holly turned to Evert. He nodded and pressed a button on a panel on the table. Moments later Regi walked into the room. Holly had purchased the clothes for him to wear and had instructed him to get a haircut. Even still, she wasn't prepared for his transformation. The purple business shirt was exactly the same shade as the one Milton had worn regularly. Yet, even with the slight bruising still around his eye, his resemblance to her late fiancé was spooky.

Victoria covered her mouth and her eyes bulged.

"Good afternoon." Regi stepped forward and offered to shake hands with Victoria. "You must be Victoria. You may not remember me, but we spoke on the phone a while ago."

Holly had to choke back the chuckle in her throat. It was obvious Regi had studied video footage of Milton too, because he perfectly replicated Milton's voice and mannerisms.

Regi tugged a chair from the table, and when he placed a suave leather briefcase onto the polished wood, Holly wondered whether Evert had provided it.

"During our phone call," Regi continued, "you said, and I quote"—He paused for effect—"'unless she comes up with something solid like DNA, she's got nothing.'" Regi flipped up the lid of the briefcase and extracted Milton's Seahawks beanie and a Ziplock bag with a lock of dark wavy hair. He slid the items across the table and Victoria jumped back as if they were spiders.

"Ask and you shall receive."

Holly couldn't resist chuckling at Regi's impersonation of one of Milton's favorite sayings.

Victoria spun to her. "You think this's funny?"

"Come on," Regi said. "It's a little bit funny. I bet you never thought we'd find my father's—Milton's DNA."

Victoria's eyes were wild. She folded her arms across her chest. Her nostrils flared and her lips pursed as she stared at the Ziplock bag. She did a little shake of her head, as if shaking some horrible image free. "What's this proposal?"

"I'm glad you asked," Evert said. "Holly and Reginald have come up with what we believe is a fair and equitable distribution of Mr. Milton Ashcroft's estate."

She rolled her eyes. "Oh, I bet they have."

"As per Mr. Milton Ashcroft's request, Holly Parmenter will receive four billion dollars."

Victoria huffed and gave Holly dagger eyes.

"Mr. Ashcroft then requested the bulk of his estate to go to his son, and the small change to be distributed amongst Mr. Ashcroft's chosen charities. Nothing was to be allocated to you." He paused to let that sink in. "We propose Regi receives Kane's intended inheritance of six billion dollars."

"Six billion!" she blurted.

Evert ignored her outburst. "That leaves two billion that we're prepared to give to you, Mrs. Ashcroft."

She slapped the table, jumped to her feet, and backed away from the chair. "No fucking way."

Evert removed a stack of papers from the folder in front of him. "If you don't agree, we intend to use Milton's DNA to prove that Reginald is entitled to the full eight billion dollars. But that'll mean years of litigation, and in the end, Reginald will get what he's entitled to and you will receive nothing." Evert flashed his pearly white teeth. "As per your late ex-husband's request."

She alternated her bulging eyes from Holly to the ziplock bag to the men in the room. "I need to call my lawyer."

"Call your lawyer," Holly said. "But if you don't sign the documents before five o'clock today, Madonna has been instructed to email the report I've written to Komo News."

"What report?"

"Oh, it's a fascinating story about Milton's secret two-decade affair, and how Reginald now has a legitimate claim to the estate."

"See, at the moment, nobody knows about me," Regi piped in, "and I'm happy to keep it that way. Provided you sign the documents." Regi ran his hand through his hair, just like Milton used to do. "Now," he added.

"So what's it going to be? Two billion dollars, or not one dime?" Holly asked.

Evert slid the paperwork across the table.

"This's blackmail."

"Yes. I believe you know exactly how that works." Holly kept her cool.

"Bitch." Victoria's eyes raged with fury.

"Take the two billion, Victoria, while you can." Holly glanced at the clock on the wall over her shoulder. "Three minutes before my report goes to

Komo News."

Regi reached for Milton's beanie and tugged it onto his head.

Victoria stormed over and snatched it from his head. "Give me that. Okay, yes, I accept the fucking offer."

"So, to clarify," Evert said, "you're agreeing to two billion dollars."

"Yes. Two billion," she snapped.

"That's a very wise decision." Evert pressed the call button. "Madonna, please hold that email for now."

"Yes, Mr. Howard."

Evert passed the paperwork forward with a gold pen. "Read through, take your time, and sign where indicated on each page."

She huffed as she plonked back into the chair, and as she flicked the pen on her chin, she read down the page. "What's this?" She pointed halfway down the page.

Holly had been expecting this question. "That's the small change Milton left for the charities."

"Small change! What the hell?"

"Oh, let's just say the estate has invested wisely while you've tied this up in the courts for all these years."

"Three point seven billion." She spun to Holly. "You lying fucking—"

Holly stood and slapped her palm on the table simultaneously. "No. You're the fucking liar. You've been blaming me for Milton's death since the crash. Not once did you stop to think of what I'd been through. You're the liar. You don't deserve one cent. Milton hated you. I know it and you know it." Holly jabbed a finger at her. "I'm sick of your conniving deceitful crap. Sign the fucking papers and get out of my goddamned face."

A blaze of red flushed Victoria's cheeks and she looked set to explode. She grabbed the pen and scribbled her signature on the first page. Evert guided her through the remaining pages, then she stood and snatched her fancy purse off the table.

Evert stopped her. "Just one more thing."

"What!"

"You've just signed a suppression order. Utter one word of this to anyone, and we'll sue you for your inheritance plus double that amount in damages."

"Fuck you." She pointed at Holly. "Fuck you, and fuck you too." She glared at Regi, and his grin was a perfect replica of how Milton used to smile.

Victoria stormed from the room so fast the wooden door banged back against the wall.

They didn't wait for her to be out of earshot before both Regi and Holly jumped up and cheered. Just like he'd done on the mountain, Regi wrapped his arms around her. "I don't know how I can ever thank you."

"You don't need to thank me," she said. "You were entitled to that money."

He tilted his head. "Well, I'd never have been able to prove it without you." He reached for the beanie and pulled it on again.

"You look exactly like him with that on."

"I must. She freaked out." He flopped into the chair. "So, what do we do now?"

Evert pushed the paperwork toward Regi. "You need to sign these."

Regi took the pen and signed where indicated, and Holly did the same.

Evert rechecked that all the paperwork was in order, slipped them into the folder, and then turned to Regi. "So, I believe we have another matter to look after?"

"Yes, we do." Regi rubbed his hands together.

"Have you decided on your new name?" Holly raised her eyebrows.

"Yep. What do you think of Levi Mason?" His eyes beamed

Holly was swept up in his excitement. "It's perfect."

"There's something else I need you to do for me, Evert," Regi said.

"Yes of course. What do you need?"

Regi extracted his iPhone from his pocket and pressed the play button.

"Ah, there he is, the man of the hour." The voice was loud and clear, and Regi seemed happy with the sound because he clicked it off.

"Have you ever heard of Jeremiah Carson?"

"Of course. We're both members of the Broadmoor Golf Club." Evert grinned.

"Interesting. Well, you may enjoy listening to our last meeting together."

CHAPTER TWENTY-NINE

Five months later.

Holly rubbed her eyes awake, rolled out of bed, and reached for her silk robe. She adjusted the knot at her waist, stepped over the glass floor that revealed the ocean below, and opened the plantation shutters. Squinting against the glare, she stepped from the bungalow onto their private balcony and strolled to the railing.

She inhaled the salty sea air long and deep. Ahead of her the ocean and the sky fused together as a palette of aqua and blue. The panorama was magical, but the most beautiful aspect of the scene was Oliver. He was floating on his stomach, wearing just yellow board shorts. The broad expanse of his back was tanned and muscular, and from her vantage point, she noticed he was following a school of tropical fish.

She hadn't heard him wake, which wasn't unusual. While she preferred to sleep in, he hated to waste even a moment of sunshine.

Her cell phone rang and she trotted back inside to pluck it off the table. She frowned at the strange number on the screen and tapped the green button. "Hello?"

"Holly, how are you?"

"Levi! I'm fantastic. Oliver and I are in Bora Bora for a vacation."

"Awesome."

Levi had been in regular contact with Holly since they last met in Evert's office, and she was pleased that he was. She knew exactly what it was like to leave a life behind and create a new identity. "What about you, how're things going?"

"Fantastic. Mom and I've moved to Hawaii. You should see where we live! My house is a mansion. We overlook the ocean. Got my own jetty. You should see my yacht. It's so cool."

She smiled at his excitement. "That is cool. How's your mother?"

"She's great. She's got a new boyfriend and he's alright. She's playing golf and tennis. Hey, I took up golf too. But I'm crap at it. Got some lessons

219

coming up, though."

Holly chuckled at his rambling enthusiasm. "That's great, Levi. Really great. Any hassles?"

"No. But have you heard the news?"

She and Oliver had deliberately avoided the outside world since they walked through the doors of their thatched bungalow two weeks ago. "No, what is it?"

"Carson's been arrested."

"Really? What for?"

"All sorts of charges… extortion, aggravated assault, bribery, harassment, tax evasion. You name it, he's got it. There was even mention of first-degree murder, and 'cause of me, they'll get him for insurance fraud too. They reckon he's going away for twenty years."

"Holy shit. That's fantastic."

"Yep. Made my day. Hell, it's made my life."

"Wonderful."

"Sure is. You guys should come visit; I'll take you out on my boat."

Holly laughed. "We'd love to, but you know we can't." One of the biggest downsides of changing an identity was severing ties with everyone. Regi had taken some convincing that Holly would be one of those people. Whenever he did call her, it had to be with a phone that he threw away after just one call. It also meant she could never call him, which was a shame too, because she often thought about him and wondered how he was coping.

Although… it sounded like he was coping just fine.

"I know. It's a shame; you'd like it here. Anyway, I've gotta go. They've got a luau on the beach tonight. Me and some friends are going."

He sounded just like any twenty-six-year-old man should, and she was over the moon for him. After the years of torture he'd been through, he deserved everything and more.

They said their goodbyes, and Holly strolled back out to the balcony. A small boat was coming into their dock, and Oliver stood on the landing and watched it arrive.

Just as it approached, a rope was tossed toward him and he grabbed it and looped it around a wooden pylon. "I'll be right back," she heard Oliver say to the man on the boat, then he turned around, looked up her, smiled, and waved. "There you are, sleepy head."

He bounded the steps two at a time. "Get your swimsuit and hat on, we're taking a boat ride."

"We are?"

"Yep, come on." He clutched her hand and led her inside. "Get changed, quick."

She plucked her bikini from the drawer and went to the bathroom to change.

"Want this hat?" He held up her floppy white hat.

"Sure."

Under Oliver's urgent insistence, she dressed and grabbed a few bits and pieces and he led her back outside. An olive-skinned young man wearing khaki chinos and an unbuttoned Hawaiian shirt helped Holly into the boat and she sat at the front. Oliver plonked at her side, wrapped his arm over her shoulder, and kissed her forehead.

"What're you up to, Mr. Nelson?"

"You'll see."

The boat eased away from the dock, and seconds later the engine roared to life. They skipped over the pristine azure waters, heading away from the resort bungalows and toward a series of small tropical islands in the distance.

Holly knew Oliver wouldn't let her in on the surprise, so she took the opportunity to tell him about Levi's call.

"Holy shit. Twenty years!" Oliver laughed. "I bet Levi was happy."

"To say the least." A small island came into view. Golden sand framed a healthy clump of lush vegetation centered in the middle. Coconut palms dotted the perimeter. They skirted around the right-hand side of the island, and for a moment she thought they were going to keep motoring past. But when the engine slowed and the boat angled toward the shore, Holly noticed a small table decorated in a white table cloth nestled amongst the palms.

She tugged her lip into her mouth and turned to Oliver.

"Your deserted island, madam."

"Oh, Olly, it's lovely." She wrapped her arms around his neck and planted a kiss on his lips.

Sand crunched beneath the boat's metal hull, indicating they'd arrived, and Oliver stood and jumped into the ankle-deep water. She took off her sandals and, holding them in her fingers, he helped her out of the boat. As she waded toward the shore, Oliver pushed the boat backwards, and within seconds of arriving, the boat roared away again.

Oliver reached for her hand, led her to the table, and pulled out a chair. "Breakfast is served." From a basket nestled between them, he plucked glass jars filled with yogurt, fruit and granola, small mushroom tarts, and croissants that were still warm.

"You've been busy."

"Not me, I've done nothing but snorkel all morning, waiting for you to get your sexy butt up."

"Ha ha. Sleeping is what vacations are about."

He poured coffee from the thermos, and their morning juice was served in a coconut with a slice of orange and an umbrella adorning the brim.

They ate their breakfast to the sound of waves crashing into the shore and seagulls squawking over the scraps they threw onto the sand.

"I could wake up to this every day." She sighed and leaned back in her chair.

He chuckled. "That's funny, because you probably can."

It was true. The four billion dollars had arrived in her bank account about a week after they'd signed the necessary papers. And with advice from one of Evert's friends, she was earning more money off her investments each month than she'd earned in her lifetime. The only capital expense she'd made so far was a new car. She planned to buy a new home too, once she found one in Brambleton that she loved. One that *they* loved. She'd started to dream of them having a home together. Her heart skipped a beat as she allowed that dream to form now. They'd have a brand-new home, a blank canvas to fill with their own inspirations.

It would be a haven, filled with peace and love.

Once they'd finished breakfast, Oliver stood and held his hand toward her. "Want to take a walk?"

As much as she'd like to sit there all day, she knew Oliver wouldn't sit still. "Sure."

"Take your sarong off, get some sun."

Oliver had helped her choose her new bikini at the resort shop when they'd first arrived at Bora Bora. Before she'd met him, she'd locked herself away in her home, too embarrassed to even walk out her door. Thanks to Oliver and Kelli, she'd learned how to live with her scars. They were no longer an affliction weighing her down. She was proud of them, as they were physical proof of how strong she was.

And she especially liked watching Oliver admire her body in her colorful, albeit scant, bikini, which he did often.

She'd learned that once people got over their initial shock, they no longer seemed to notice her disfigurements. People were now seeing her for who she really was … Holly Parmenter. And it was great to be back.

After placing her sarong over the back of the chair, she put on her hat and sunglasses, and hand in hand they strolled along the sand. The sun on her flesh was warm and welcoming, and her body seemed to drink in the sunshine.

He edged her away from the water and she saw where he was heading. Two hammocks had been strung between a pair of coconut palms, and the sun filtered through the foliage, offering just the right amount of light and heat. Oliver helped her into the hammock, then trotted off to the trees to relieve himself.

Holly decided to utilize his absence to do something she'd never done before. She removed her bikini top. It was so exhilarating her nipples started to peak immediately. Turning her head, she waited for the moment he saw her. And what a delight it was.

His eyes bulged and lit up. "Well, hello."

Oliver stepped right up to the hammock and bent over to suck her nipple.

But he shifted the weight too quickly, and before she knew it, she was on her back on the sand.

"Oh shit, babe, are you okay?"

Giggling, she pushed to a sitting position and dusted her hands. "I'm fine."

He knelt at her side and brushed the sand from her shoulders. "Knowing you, you'd say that anyway."

Holly chuckled. "Probably."

Oliver placed his hands on her cheeks and the intensity in his eyes took her breath away. Her heart skipped a beat at the love she saw in his gaze. Deep in her heart she knew she'd found something extraordinary.

Oliver was her holy grail, her one and only, the man she wanted to be with forever.

He wove his fingers through her hair and drew their lips together. His kiss was gentle, tender, yet it said so much more: *I want, I need, I love.*

When Oliver eased back, he looked right into her soul. They were connected in every sense. Every thought was tied to him. Every mental picture of her future had Oliver at her side. He was her captain and together they'd sail their own ship.

He reached into his pocket, and when he removed a small black box, her heart leapt to her throat and tears pooled her eyes.

Wriggling around to face her, he took her hand. "I've never met anyone like you, Holly. You make my heart do crazy things, and I can't breathe when you're not around. I want us to move in together, to share a home, to have lots of babies. I want to be with you until I take my last breath. I offer you my heart, and I hope you'll offer me yours." He opened the velvet box to reveal an elegant radiant-cut diamond. "Will you do me the honor of marrying me?"

Holly launched at him, rolling him onto his back so she could pin him beneath her. She could barely breathe, let alone talk, yet she managed the most important words of her life: "Yes. Yes, yes, yes." Her thumping heart swelled to capacity as tears spilled down her cheeks.

"I love you, Holly Parmenter." He reached up, thumbed a tear from her lip, then cupped her breast.

"I love you too, Mr. Nelson." She leaned in and kissed the man who'd made her broken mind and body glisten like diamonds.

THE END

Dear Fabulous Reader, thank you for following Holly and Oliver's incredible journey to redemption. Kendall Talbot hopes you loved it.

Are you ready for another action-packed adventure? Keep reading for details on some of Kendall's other books including the two other titles in the Maximum Exposure series.

Also, by Kendall Talbot

Deadly Twist
Extreme Limit
Zero Escape
Treasured Secrets
Treasured Lies
Treasured Dreams
Double Take
Lost in Kakadu
First Fate
Feral Fate
Final Fate

If you sign up to Kendall Talbot's newsletter you can follow her journey to publication where you can help with fun things like naming characters and giving characters quirky traits and interesting jobs. You'll also get her book, Breathless Encounters for free. Here's her newsletter signup link if you are interested: **http://www.kendalltalbot.com.au/newsletter.html**

DEADLY TWIST

An ancient Mayan Temple. A dark family secret. A desperate fight for survival.

When a mysterious ancient Mayan temple is discovered by a team of explorers deep in the Yucatan jungle, the world is entranced. But Liliana Bennett is shocked by the images sweeping the headlines. She's seen the temple before, drawn in detail, in her late father's secret journal.

Now, the explorers at Agulinta aren't the only ones digging up secrets. Liliana is consumed by the mysteries surrounding her father's sketches and, refusing to believe she's out of her depth, she heads to Mexico, determined to see the temple for herself.

To reach the heart of the jungle, she'll have to join forces with Carter Logan, a nature photographer with a restless heart and secrets of his own. But a journey to Agulinta means battling crocodiles, lethal drug runners, and an unforgiving Mother Nature.

Lost and alone, they stumble upon something they should never have seen. Liliana's quest for answers becomes a desperate race to stay alive. Will Agulinta be the key to their survival? Or will Carter and Liliana become victims to the cruel relentless jungle and the evil men lurking within?

Deadly Twist *is a gripping action-adventure novel with a dash of romance, set deep in Mexico's Yucatan Jungle. It's a full-length, stand-alone* Maximum Exposure *novel.*

ZERO ESCAPE

To survive, Charlene must accept that her whole life was a lie.

For twenty years, Charlene Bailey has been living by the same mantra: pay in cash, keep only what you can carry, trust no one and always be ready to run. That is until her father is brutally murdered in New Orleans by a woman screaming a language Charlene doesn't understand. When police reveal the man she'd known all her life was not her biological father, Charlene is swept up in a riptide of dark secrets and deadly crimes.

The key to her true identity lies in a dangerous Cuban compound run by a lethal kingpin, but Charlene can't reach it alone. After a life of relying on herself, she'll have to trust Marshall Crow, a tough-as-nails ex-Navy man, to smuggle her into Havana.

The answers to Charlene's past are as dark as the waters she and Marshall must navigate, but a killer in the shadows will stop at nothing to drown the truth.

Zero Escape *is a heart-pounding action-adventure novel with a dash of romance that crosses from New Orleans to the back streets of Havana, Cuba. It's a full-length, stand-alone* Maximum Exposure *novel.*

LOST IN KAKADU

Surviving the plane crash was lucky.

Getting out alive, would be a miracle.

Crashing into an ancient Australian wilderness is pretentious socialite, Abigail Mulholland's worst nightmare. She survives the accident with two complete strangers; however, things go from bad to downright hellish when rescuers never come. As she battles to live in an environment that's as brutal as it is beautiful, Abigail finds herself also fighting her unlikely attraction to Mackenzie, a much younger man.

Mackenzie Steel is devastated by his partner's death in the crash, the only person with whom he shared his painful past. Now, as he confronts his own demons, he finds he has a new battle on his hands: his growing feelings for Abigail, a woman who's as frustratingly naïve as she is funny.

Fate brought them together, but they'll need more than luck to escape Kakadu alive. Could the letters of a dead man hold the key to their survival?

Lost In Kakadu is a gripping action-adventure novel set deep in Australia's rugged Kakadu National Park. Winner of the Romantic Book of the Year in 2014, this full-length, stand-alone novel is an extraordinary story of endurance, grief, survival and undying love.

TREASURED SECRETS

His secrets are tearing them apart.
But the truth may get them killed.

When Rosalina left Italy to pursue her culinary dreams, she didn't expect heartbreak to be on the menu. Archer Mahoney is the man of her dreams—handsome, wealthy, and filled with adventure—except for the recurring nightmares he refuses to talk about.

Archer has spent a lifetime hunting for lost treasure, but his own buried past now threatens to destroy his future. Each night he relives the horrific dive that claimed his father's life twenty years ago. But the events of that day, and the truth surrounding the golden medallion he found on the dive, are mysteries he can't solve alone.

When Rosalina shockingly connects the medallion to the stained-glass window of an ancient Italian church, she believes it may be the key to mending the ocean between them. But some treasures are buried in blood, and a deadly priest will stop at nothing to keep a nefarious secret contained…

***Treasured Secrets** is a thrilling action-adventure novel with a dash of romance. If you love your romance, high on the suspense, this is for you.*

"Treasured Secrets is a cross between an Indiana Jones movie and National Treasure. I was hooked from the first sentence to the last." - ★★★★★ AusRom Today.

DOUBLE TAKE

A crime of love. The chance of a lifetime.

Jackson Rich is at risk of losing the love of his life, and he'll do anything to save her. Even if it means robbing a bank. So it's time to call in a few favors from his old gang because they owe him. Big time.

Gemma's spent her entire life doing the right thing. Now doing the wrong thing could be the best decision she's ever made, if she's brave enough.

When Detective Steel gets a tip-off of a planned heist, he doesn't know where the robbery will be. Only that it's going to take place during the famous horse race that stops a nation—the Melbourne Cup. And when it goes down, he'll be ready.

Except what happens next, only one of them sees coming. And for the others, it's suddenly no longer about the money. It's about retribution.

A fast-paced, stand-alone crime thriller that will keep you guessing until the final page, from award-winning, bestselling author of thrill-seeking fiction, Kendall Talbot.

What readers are saying about DOUBLE TAKE:

"This story is so well planned and well written, it was as if it had actually happened! I was riveted to my chair while reading the twists and turns. If I could give it 6 stars, I would." ★★★★★ *Multi-Mystery fan.*

KENDALL TALBOT

ABOUT THE AUTHOR

Kendall Talbot is a thrill seeker, hopeless romantic, virtual killer, and award-winning author of stories that'll have your heart thumping from action-packed suspense and steamy bedroom scenes.

Kendall has sought thrills in all 42 countries she's visited. She's abseiled down freezing waterfalls, catapulted out of a white-water raft, jumped off a mountain with a man who spoke little English, and got way too close to a sixteen-foot shark. When she isn't writing heart-thumping suspense in exotic locations, enjoying wine and cheese with her crazy friends, and planning her next thrilling international escape.

She lives in Brisbane, Australia with her very own hero and a fluffy little dog who specializes in hijacking her writing time. Meanwhile, Kendall's two sons are off making their own adventures – look out world.

Kendall's book, *Lost in Kakadu* won the acclaimed title of Romantic Book of the Year 2014, and her books have also been finalists for Best Romantic Suspense, Best Crime Novel, Best Continuing Series, and Best New Author.

Drop into Kendall's website sometime: www.kendalltalbot.com

Check out her crazy life on her facebook page:
https://www.facebook.com/KendallTalbotBooks

KENDALL TALBOT